Stuart McLean is one of Canada's best-selling authors. His CBC radio show 'The Vinyl Cafe' attracts over 700,000 listeners every weekend. He has twice won the Stephen Leacock Memorial Medal for Humour. Stuart McLean lives in Toronto.

HOME
From the
VINYL CAFE
A YEAR OF STORIES

Stuart McLean

Granta Books

London

Granta Publications, 2/3 Hanover Yard, Noel Road, London N1 8BE

First published in Great Britain by Granta Books, 2005
This edition published by Granta Books, 2006
First published in the US by Simon & Schuster, 2005

The stories in this collection were previously published
by Penguin Canada in either *Stories from the Vinyl Cafe*
copyright © 1995 by Stuart McLean or *Home from the
Vinyl Cafe* copyright © 1998 by Stuart McLean.

A CIP catalogue record for this book is available from
the British Library.

1 3 5 7 9 10 8 6 4 2

ISBN-13: 978-1-86207-856-7
ISBN-10: 1-86207-856-4

Printed and bound in Great Britain by
Bookmarque Ltd, Croydon, Surrey

To John Sheard

non magnum sed parvi

Contents

We may not be big,

but we're small.

Framed motto hanging by the cash register
at the Vinyl Cafe

Winter

Dave Cooks the Turkey

When Carl Lowbeer bought his wife, Gerta, *The Complete Christmas Planner,* he did not understand what he was doing. If Carl had known how much Gerta was going to enjoy the book, he would not have given it to her. He bought it on the afternoon of December 23. A glorious day. Carl left work at lunch and spent the afternoon drifting around downtown—window-shopping and listening to carollers and falling into conversation with complete strangers. When he stopped for coffee, he was shocked to see it was five-thirty. Shocked because the only things he had bought were a book by Len Deighton and some shaving cream in a tube—both things he planned to wrap and give himself. That was when the Joy of Christmas, who had sat down with him and bought him a double-chocolate croissant, said, I think I'll stay here and have another coffee while you finish your shopping. The next thing Carl knew, he was ripping through the mall like a prison escapee.

On Christmas Eve, Carl found himself staring at a bagful of stuff he couldn't remember buying. He wondered if he might have picked up someone else's bag by mistake, but then he found a receipt with his signature on it. Why would he have paid twenty-three dollars for a slab of metal to defrost meat when they already owned a microwave oven that would do it in half the time? What could he possibly have been thinking when he bought the Ab Master?

Carl did remember buying *The Complete Christmas Planner.* The picture on the cover had drawn him to the book— a woman striding across a front lawn with a wreath of chili peppers tucked under her arm. She looked like she was in a hurry, and that made him think of Gerta, so he bought the book—never imagining that it was something his wife had been waiting for all her life. Carl had been as surprised as anyone last May when Gerta began the neighbourhood Christmas group. Although not, perhaps, as surprised as Dave was when his wife, Morley, joined it.

"It's not about Christmas, Dave," said Morley. "It's about getting together."

The members of Gerta's group, all women, met every second Tuesday night at a different house. They drank tea or beer, and the host baked something, and they worked on stuff. Usually until about eleven.

"But that's not the point," said Morley. "The *point* is getting together. It's about neighbourhood—not about what we're actually doing."

But there was no denying that they were doing stuff.

Christmas stuff.

"It's wrapping paper," said Morley.

"You're *making* paper?" said Dave.

"Decorating paper," said Morley. "This is hand-printed paper. Do you know how much this would cost?"

That was in July.

In August they dipped oak leaves in gold paint and hung them in bunches from their kitchen ceilings to dry.

Then there was the stencilling weekend. The weekend Dave thought if he didn't keep moving, Morley would stencil him.

In September, Dave couldn't find an eraser anywhere in the house. Morley said, "That's because I took them all with me. We're making rubber stamps."

"You are *making* rubber stamps?" said Dave.

"Out of erasers," said Morley.

"People don't even *buy* rubber stamps anymore," said Dave.

"This one is going to be an angel," said Morley, reaching into her bag. "I need a metallic ink-stamp pad. Do you think you could buy me a metallic ink-stamp pad and some more gold paint? And we need some of those snap things that go into Christmas crackers."

"The what things?" said Dave.

"The exploding things you pull," said Morley. "We're going to make Christmas crackers. Where do you think we could get the exploding things?"

There were oranges drying in the basement on the clothes rack and blocks of wax for candles stacked on the Ping-Pong table.

One day in October, Morley said, "Do you know there are only sixty-seven shopping days until Christmas?"

Dave did not know this. In fact, he had not completely unpacked from their summer vacation. Without thinking, he said, "What are you talking about?"

Morley said, "If we want to get all our shopping done by the week before Christmas, we only have . . ." She shut her eyes. ". . . sixty-two days left."

Dave and Morley usually *started* their shopping the week before Christmas.

And there they were with only sixty-seven shopping days left, standing in their bedroom staring at each other, incomprehension hanging between them.

It hung there for a good ten seconds.

Then Dave said something he had been careful not to say for weeks. He said, "I thought this thing wasn't about Christmas."

Which he immediately regretted, because Morley said, "Don't make fun of me, Dave." And left the room. And then came back. Like a locomotive.

Uh-oh, thought Dave.

"What," said Morley.

"I didn't say that," said Dave.

"You said 'uh-oh,' " said Morley.

"I thought 'uh-oh,' " said Dave. "I didn't *say* 'uh-oh.' Thinking 'uh-oh' isn't like saying 'uh-oh.' They don't send you to jail for *thinking* you want to strangle someone."

"What?" said Morley.

Morley slept downstairs. She didn't say a word when Dave came down and tried to talk her out of it. Didn't say a word the next morning until Sam and Stephanie had left for school. Then she said, "Do you know what my life is like, Dave?"

Dave suspected—correctly—that she wasn't looking for an answer.

"My life is a train," she said. "I am a train. Dragging everyone from one place to another. To school and to dance class and to now-it's-time-to-get-up and now-it's-time-to-go-to-bed. I'm a train full of people who complain when you try to get them into a bed and fight when you try to get them out of one. That's my job. And I'm not only the train, I'm the porter and the conductor and the cook and the engineer and the maintenance man. And I print the tickets and stack the luggage and clean the dishes. And if they still had cabooses, I'd be the caboose."

Dave didn't want to ask where the train was heading. He had the sinking feeling that somewhere up ahead, someone had pulled up a section of the track.

"And you know where the train is going, Dave?" said Morley.

Yup, he thought. Off the tracks. Any moment now.

"What?" said Morley.

"No," said Dave. "I don't know where the train's going."

Morley leaned forward over the table. "The train starts at a town called First Day at School, Dave, and it goes to a village called Halloween, and then through the township of Class Project, and down the spur line called Your Sister Is Visiting. And you know what's at the end of the track? You know where my train is heading?"

Dave looked around nervously. He didn't want to get this wrong. He would have been happy to say where the train was going if he knew he could get it right. Was his wife going to leave him? Maybe the train was going to D-I-V-O-R-C-E.

"Not at Christmas," he mumbled.

"Exactly," said Morley. "To the last stop on the line—Christmas dinner. And this is supposed to be something I look forward to, Dave. This is supposed to be a heartwarming family occasion."

"Christmas dinner," said Dave tentatively. It seemed a reasonably safe thing to say. Morley nodded. Feeling encouraged, Dave added, "With a turkey and stuffing and everything."

But Morley wasn't listening. "And when we finally get through that week between Christmas and New Year's, you know what they do with the train?"

Dave shook his head.

"They back it up during the night when I'm asleep so they can run it through all the stations again."

Dave nodded earnestly.

"And you know who you are, Dave?"

Dave shook his head again. No. No, he didn't know who

he was. He was thinking maybe he was the engineer. Maybe
he was up in the locomotive. Busy with men's work.

Morley squinted at her husband. "You're the guy in the bar
car, Dave, pushing the button to ask for another drink."

From the way Morley said that, Dave could tell that she
still loved him. She could have told him, for instance, that he
had to get out of the bar car. Or, for that matter, off the train.
She hadn't. Dave realized it had been close, and if he was
going to stay aboard, he would have to join the crew.

The next weekend he said, "Why don't I do some of the
Christmas shopping? Why don't you give me a list, and I'll
get things for everyone in Cape Breton?"

Dave had never gone Christmas shopping in October. He
was unloading bags onto the kitchen table when he said,
"That wasn't so bad."

Morley walked across the kitchen and picked up a book
that had fallen on the floor. "I'm sorry," she said. "It's just that
I like Christmas so much. I *used* to like Christmas so much. I
was thinking that if I got everything done early, maybe I
could enjoy it again. I'm trying to get control of it, Dave. I'm
trying to make it fun again. That's what this is all about."

Dave said, "What else can I do?"

Morley reached out and touched his elbow and said, "On
Christmas Day, after we've opened the presents, I want to
take the kids to work at the Food Bank. I want you to look
after the turkey."

"I can do that," said Dave.

———

Dave didn't understand the full meaning of what he had
agreed to do until Christmas Eve, when the presents were
wrapped and under the tree and he was snuggled, warm and
safe, in bed. It was one of his favourite moments of the year.
He nudged his wife's feet. She gasped.

"Did you take the turkey out of the freezer?" she said.

Dave groaned. He pulled himself out of bed and went downstairs. He couldn't find a turkey in the freezer—in either freezer—and he was about to call for help when the truth landed on him like an anvil. Looking after the turkey, something he had promised to do, meant *buying* it as well as putting it in the oven.

Dave unloaded both freezers to be sure. Then he paced around the kitchen trying to decide what to do. When he went upstairs, Morley was asleep. He considered waking her. Instead, he lay down and imagined, in painful detail, the chronology of the Christmas Day waiting for him. Imagined everything from the first squeal of morning to that moment when his family came home from the Food Bank expecting a turkey dinner. He could see the dark look that would cloud his wife's face when he carried a bowl of pasta across the kitchen and placed it on the table she would have set with the homemade crackers and the gilded oak leaves.

He was still awake at two A.M., but at least he had a plan. He would wait until they left for the Food Bank. Then he would take off to Bolivia and live under an assumed name. At Sam's graduation one of his friends would ask, "Why isn't your father here?" and Sam would explain that "One Christmas he forgot to buy the turkey and he had to leave."

At three A.M., after rolling around for an hour, Dave got out of bed, dressed, and slipped quietly out the back door. He was looking for a twenty-four-hour grocery store. It was either that or wait for the Food Bank to open, and though he couldn't think of anyone in the city more in need of a turkey, the idea that his family might spot him in line made the Food Bank unthinkable.

At four A.M., with the help of a taxi driver named Mohammed, Dave found an open store. He bought the last turkey there: twelve pounds, frozen as hard as a cannonball, grade B—whatever that meant. He was home by four-thirty and by six-thirty had the turkey more or less thawed. He used an electric blanket and a hair dryer on the turkey and a bottle of Scotch on himself.

As the turkey defrosted, it became clear what grade B meant. The skin on its right drumstick was ripped. Dave's turkey looked like it had made a break from the slaughterhouse and dragged itself a block or two before it was captured and beaten to death. Dave poured another Scotch and began to refer to his bird as Butch. He turned Butch over and found another slash in the carcass. Perhaps, he thought, Butch had died in a knife fight.

Dave would have been happy if disfiguration had been the worst thing about his turkey. Would have considered himself blessed. Would have been able to look back on this Christmas with equanimity. Might eventually have been able to laugh about it. The worst thing came later. After lunch. After Morley and the kids left for the Food Bank.

Before they left, Morley dropped pine oil on some of the living room lamps. "When the bulbs heat the oil," she said, "the house will smell like a forest." Then she said, "Mother's coming. I'm trusting you with this. You have to have the turkey in the oven—"

Dave finished her sentence for her. "By one-thirty," he said. "Don't worry. I know what I'm doing."

The worst thing began when Dave tried to turn on the oven. Morley had never had cause to explain to him about the automatic timer, and Dave had never had cause to ask about it. The oven had been set the day before to go on at five-thirty. Morley had been baking a squash casserole for Christmas dinner—she always did the vegetables the day before—and until the oven timer was unset, nothing anybody did was going to turn it on.

At two P.M. Dave retrieved the bottle of Scotch from the basement and poured himself a drink. He knew he was in trouble. He had to find an oven that could cook the bird quickly. But every oven he could think of already had a turkey in it. For ten years Dave had been technical director to some of the craziest acts on the rock-and-roll circuit. He wasn't going to fall to pieces over a raw turkey.

Inventors are often unable to explain where their best ideas come from. Dave is not sure where he got his. Maybe he had spent too many years in too many hotel rooms. At two-thirty P.M. he topped up his Scotch and phoned the Plaza Hotel. He was given the front desk.

"Do you cook . . . special menus for people with special dietary needs?" he asked.

"We're a first-class hotel in a world-class city, sir. We can look after any dietary needs."

"If someone brings their own food—because of a special diet—would you cook it for them?"

"Of course, sir."

Dave looked at the turkey. It was propped on a kitchen chair like a naked baby. "Come on, Butch," he said, stuffing it into a plastic bag. "We're going out."

Morley had the car. Dave called a taxi. He shoved the bottle of Scotch into the pocket of his parka on his way out the door.

"The Plaza," he said to the driver. "It's an emergency." He took a slug from the bottle.

The man at the front desk asked if Dave needed help with his suitcases.

"No suitcases," said Dave, patting the turkey, which he had

dropped on the counter and which was now dripping juice on the hotel floor. Dave turned breezily to the man behind him in line and said, slurring only slightly, "Just checking in for the afternoon with my chick."

The clerk winced. Dave wobbled. He spun around and grinned at the clerk and then around again and squinted at the man in line behind him. He was looking for approval. He found, instead, his neighbour. Jim Scoffield was standing beside an elderly woman Dave assumed must be Jim's visiting mother.

Jim didn't say anything, tried in fact to look away. But he was too late. Their eyes had met.

Dave straightened and said, "Turkey and the kids are at the Food Bank. I brought Morley here so they could cook her for me."

"Oh," said Jim.

"I mean the turkey," said Dave.

"Uh-huh," said Jim.

"I bring it here *every* year. I'm alone."

Dave held his arms out as if inviting Jim to frisk him.

The man at the desk said, "Excuse me, sir," and handed Dave his key. Dave smiled. At the man behind the counter. At Jim. At Jim's mom. He walked toward the elevators, one careful foot in front of the other. When he got to the polished brass elevator doors, he heard Jim calling him.

"You forgot your . . . chick," said Jim, pointing to the turkey Dave had left behind on the counter.

———

The man on the phone from room service said, "We have turkey on the *menu,* sir."

Dave said, "This is . . . uh . . . a *special* turkey. I was hoping you could cook *my* turkey."

The man from room service told Dave the manager would call. Dave looked at his watch.

When the phone rang, Dave knew this was his last chance. His only chance. The manager would either agree to cook the turkey, or Dave would book the ticket to Bolivia.

"Excuse me, sir?" said the manager.

"I said I need to eat this *particular* turkey," said Dave.

"That *particular* turkey, sir." the manager was noncommittal.

"Do you know," said Dave, "what they feed turkeys today?"

"No, sir?" said the manager. He said it like a question.

"They feed them . . ."

Dave wasn't at all sure himself. Wasn't so sure where he was going with this. He just knew that he had to keep talking.

"They feed them chemicals," he said, "and antibiotics and steroids, and . . . lard to make them juicier . . . and starch to make them crispy. I'm allergic to . . . steroids. If I eat that stuff, I'll have a heart attack or at least a seizure. In the lobby of your hotel. Do you want that to happen?"

The man on the phone didn't say anything. Dave kept going.

"I have my own turkey here. I raised this turkey myself. I butchered it myself. This morning. The only thing it has eaten . . ." Dave looked frantically around the room. What did he feed the turkey?

"Tofu," he said triumphantly.

"Tofu, sir?" said the manager.

"And yogurt," said Dave.

It was all or nothing.

The bellboy took the turkey and the twenty-dollar bill Dave handed him without blinking an eye.

Dave said, "You have those big convection ovens. I have to have it back before five-thirty P.M."

"You must be very hungry, sir" was all the bellboy said.

Dave collapsed onto the bed. He didn't move until the phone rang half an hour later. It was the hotel manager. He said the turkey was in the oven. Then he said, "You raised the bird yourself?"

Dave said yes.

There was a pause. The manager said, "The chef says the turkey looks like it was abused."

Dave said, "Ask the chef if he has ever killed a turkey. Tell him the bird was a fighter. Tell him to stitch it up."

———

The bellboy wheeled the turkey into Dave's room at a quarter to six. They had it on a dolly covered with a silver dome. Dave removed the dome and gasped.

It didn't look like any bird he could have cooked. There were frilly paper armbands on both drumsticks, a glazed partridge made of red peppers on the breast, and a small silver gravy boat with steam wafting from it.

Dave looked at his watch and ripped the paper armbands off and scooped the red-pepper partridge into his mouth. He realized the bellboy was watching him, and then he saw the security guard standing in the corridor. The security guard was holding a carving knife. They obviously weren't about to trust Dave with a weapon.

"Would you like us to carve it, sir?"

"Just get me a taxi," said Dave.

"What?" said the guard.

"I . . . can't eat this here," said Dave. "I have to eat it . . ." Dave couldn't imagine where he had to eat it. "Outside," he said. "I have to eat it outside."

He gave the bellboy another twenty-dollar bill and said, "I

am going downstairs to check out. Bring the bird and call me a taxi." He walked by the security guard without looking at him. "Careful with that knife," he said.

Dave got home at six. He put Butch on the table. The family was due back any minute. He poured himself a drink and sat down in the living room. The house looked beautiful—smelled beautiful—like a pine forest.

"My forest," said Dave. Then he said, "Uh-oh," and jumped up. He got a ladle of the turkey gravy, and he ran around the house smearing it on lightbulbs. There, he thought. He went outside and stood on the stoop and counted to twenty-five. Then he went back in and breathed deeply. The house smelled like . . . Christmas.

He poured himself another Scotch and looked out the window. Morley was coming up the walk . . . with Jim Scoffield and his mother.

"We met them outside. I invited them in for a drink."

"Oh. Great," said Dave. "I'll get the drinks."

Dave went to the kitchen, then came back to see Jim sitting on the couch under the tall swinging lamp, a drop of gravy glistening on his balding forehead. Dave watched another drop fall. Saw the puzzled look cross Jim's face as he reached up, wiped his forehead, and brought his fingers to his nose. Morley and Jim's mother had not noticed anything yet. Dave saw another drop about to fall. Thought, Any moment now the Humane Society is going to knock on the door. Sent by the hotel.

He took a long swig of Scotch and placed his glass by the paper napkins that Morley had painted.

"Morley, could you come here," he said softly. "There's something I have to tell you."

Holland

When you strap skis to your feet, winter skies are always blue and the temperature always crisp. When you strap a dog to your arm late on a winter night, crisp changes to cold, frosted becomes frozen, and walking up and down neighbourhood streets, you can imagine yourself struggling across the Russian Steppes with a pack of wolves on your tail. There were nights in January when there wasn't much Dave wouldn't have done to get out of walking Arthur. Dave is not, by inclination, a winter person.

January, however, has always been Morley's favourite month, and she has tried to teach Dave how to enjoy it. Every January they spend a weekend away together, usually in the outdoors. They have been skiing in Vermont and snowshoeing in Algonquin Park and once to an inn north of Montreal. One of the best weekends ever was the one when they went to Ottawa. They stayed in a little bed-and-breakfast in the Glebe, and they skated on the canal—up to Dow's Lake to look at the ice sculptures and all the way back to the Château Laurier. That night they ate in a restaurant in the market and skated home.

They were planning to go back to Ottawa this year, but there was a big storm, the airport was closed, and they couldn't drive. Even the trains weren't running.

Morley said, "Too much ice for skating. Frozen out of the rink. Go figure."

Dave couldn't leave his record store the next weekend; he had been advertising a January sale for weeks. Before they knew it, the month was over, and they hadn't gone away for the first time in ten years.

———

When Morley was a child, her father, Roy, used to make a skating rink in their backyard—just for her. It wasn't always the easiest thing to do when you lived in Toronto. Some winters Roy had to take Morley's wagon out late at night and steal snow from yards around the neighbourhood in order to have enough for the base of her rink. He was happy to do it, because Morley loved to skate. She used to lie in bed at night while her father was out in the backyard—peeling his frozen hands off the hose—and she would imagine her ceiling was an ice-covered lake. She would fall asleep dreaming that she could skate on her ceiling forever.

Her all-time favourite book was *Hans Brinker.* Her all-time favourite dress was the pink chiffon costume that her mother made for her to wear in the Christmas Pageant on Ice. She was a sugarplum fairy. The pink dress had sequins. The years before, she had always had plain white dresses. She loved the pink dress because of the sequins and because the year she wore it was the only year that the Christmas pageant wasn't a total disaster. The worst year was the yellow dress. That was when she was twelve.

For your solo number, you had to provide your own music, but those were the days before cassette tapes. So every girl would go to Mitchell's music store and cut her own record. Each record had two sides, and because side B was a throwaway, Morley had them put "The Stripper" on side B—just for fun.

The man who was playing the records that year was the
father of one of the other competitors. When it was Morley's
turn, he put on the wrong side of her record—"The Stripper"
instead of Doris Day singing "Que Sera Sera." Morley began
her program as if nothing were wrong. But then everyone
started clapping along to "The Stripper." When somebody
yelled, *"Take it off,"* she started to cry, and then she fell and
didn't get up. She lay along the blue line until her father came
and picked her up and helped her off. He said it wasn't her
fault, but it didn't make her feel any better. She never skated
in the pageant again. And she never again owned a yellow
dress.

In fact, she didn't even put on a pair of skates for ten years,
not once during her adolescence, not once. Not until the
summer she left home.

She had a job working in summer stock, in a theatre in
Providence, Rhode Island—eight plays, two months. She was
a seamstress.

There was a three-thousand-seat arena not far from the
theatre. It offered a free skate from eight to ten every Monday night. That was the only night the theatre was dark. Morley kept meaning to go skating. She finally did—at the end of
August. It was the night she met Dave.

Dave was in town with a Dick Clark *Caravan of Stars* production—eight acts in two hours, including ? and the Mysterians, the Archies, and Bobby Goldsboro. It was a hateful
tour. The musicians hated the music they were playing, and
they loathed the venues they were playing in. A sourness descended on the whole enterprise before the end of the first
week. Dave, who began the tour as the technical director,
soon realized he was presiding over the rock-and-roll equiva-
lent of a Ford Pinto. He could count on something going
wrong every day. He kept waiting for the explosion. The only

salvation was the most hated moment of all—the last number of every show—when Bobby Goldsboro sang "Honey."

About two weeks into the tour, one of the Mysterians bought a battery-operated megaphone, and every night a group of musicians would huddle offstage, trying to distract Bobby Goldsboro by singing alternate lyrics during his song. They would sing just loud enough so he could hear them and the audience couldn't. In Saratoga Springs they rigged up a microphone behind the stage. The plan was to feed their version of "Honey" through Goldsboro's monitor. Somehow the feed got rerouted—it was never clear how—and their lyrics, which involved Honey doing unspeakable things with a shaved, greased goat, got routed through the arena PA.

To the audience, this unbelievable rewrite appeared to be coming out of Goldsboro's mouth. Goldsboro, who was dimly aware that something was horribly wrong, gamely finished the song while the crowd watched in disbelief. When the tune came to an end, there was a moment of pure silence. Then Goldsboro looked around in confusion as the audience rose as one and gave him the only standing ovation he got on the tour. After the show, he kicked up such a fuss that the Mysterians had to stop their evening antics. Instead, every night when it was time for "Honey," they would slip into the audience, where Goldsboro could see them, and put on oversize construction ear protectors, waving, smiling, and making rude gestures at him while he sang.

Things got so bad that Dave left the tour and began to advance the show. This meant arriving in each town a few days ahead of everyone to prepare the arena and then, thankfully, leaving before anyone else got there. He spent the entire summer arguing with arena managers about concession rights and electrical boards. And that was how he came to meet Morley in those last days of summer.

———

When he first saw her, Dave was leaning on the arena boards, waiting for the free skate to end so his crew could start laying a temporary floor over the ice. The lights were dim, and there were waltzes playing over the arena PA. Everyone was paired up, holding hands as they skated around and around. Dave suddenly felt alone. He bought a coffee in a cardboard cup and watched the skaters, and as he watched, he was transported back to the arena in his hometown of Cape Breton— to the annual Valentine Weekend Ice Waltz. They used to put lights in the arena ceiling. The lights would twinkle like stars. There was the big face of a moon, which would wink its eye every so often, and a live orchestra suspended on a plywood platform over centre ice. At the beginning of the night, the musicians would have to climb up a ladder with their instruments. Dave's mother made him promise he wouldn't skate under the platform during the polkas, because when the orchestra played polkas, the platform swung back and forth. Whenever that happened, Margaret would stand by the boards, light a Sweet Caporal, and say she didn't mind if the cigarettes got her, but she was damned if she was going to become an item on the TV news because she was the only woman in the history of Cape Breton to be squashed to death by a polka band.

———

That was what Dave was thinking about when Morley skated into his life. She had long chestnut hair with bangs that were at least an inch below her eyebrows. She was wearing a hand-woven poncho over a blue army-surplus turtleneck sweater, and bell-bottom jeans with embroidered cuffs. And granny glasses. Dave was bewitched.

She was the only person on the ice who could really skate—around and around all by herself—one leg crossing

er the other in the corners. Every so often she would glide
o centre ice and do a spin. Dave thought, She must be Canadian. He had to meet her.

He rented a pair of skates. But when he got onto the ice, he
couldn't catch up to her. So he slowed down to see if she
would catch up to him. She did. But she just kept going.

Dave was getting frantic as he watched the clock at the far
end of the arena. Then she was standing right in front of him
at the blue line. But Dave was going so fast that he was going
to shoot right by her. Without thinking, he reached out and
grabbed her. She screamed, and then they were suspended in
midair, clutching at each other and, for a horrible frozen moment, face-to-face. In that moment of eternity, as they hovered horizontally over the ice, Dave said, "Hi."

And Morley said, "Hi?" Like a question.

They landed in a heap.

Dave insisted on driving her to the hospital. She had three
stitches just below her chin. Afterward, he took her out to dinner. And then he drove her back to the arena, where she had
left her car. He invited her to the concert the next night. It was
only as she was driving away that Dave remembered which
concert it was. But by then it was too late. The next evening
she was sitting beside him fidgeting, he noticed glumly, as
Bobby Goldsboro stepped onstage.

They didn't see each other again for six years, but they
kept in touch by mail. Just occasional letters, and Dave's
never said much. But he sent her quirky things. The week
after they met, Dave sent her a package of Silly Putty. When
she opened it, Morley knew he was the man for her.

Another time he sent her glow-in-the-dark skate laces, and
once, a newspaper from Thunder Bay. Morley, who was back
in Toronto by then, read every page of the Thunder Bay

paper obsessively, looking for the significant article. W.
had he sent it? She finally decided it was her horoscope
which said: "Your love life is on thin ice. Time to make a decision. Don't let distance cloud your judgment."

"No. No," said Dave years later. "There was nothing special. I just thought you'd like to see it."

When they started to see each other, Dave was sick of life
on the road. He wanted to come in from the cold, and Morley seemed so normal.

When he told her these things, Morley was overcome with
the irony. She was tired of being polite. She didn't want to be
normal. She wanted to lose control. But she loved him. And
she had hope.

They got married before the summer was over and moved
into an apartment near a large park. On their very first night
together, when they were getting ready for bed, Dave said,
"Do you want a little snack?"

Morley said, "You go ahead."

He came back from the kitchen with four pieces of bread
slathered in mayonnaise. There were four slabs of cooking
onion. And there was a glass of buttermilk. Morley stared at
him, and he said, "It's okay. I haven't brushed my teeth yet."

A week later, when he had a sore throat, Morley said, "You
should gargle with salt."

Dave said, "No. No. Just throw me one of those socks."

Morley said, "What?"

Dave said, "One of those white athletic socks—the wool
ones."

Morley stared in confusion at the heap of unsorted laundry
in the basket at the foot of their bed. "What are you going to
do with a sock?" she asked.

Dave was pulling the covers up to around his chin like a

ιall child. It seemed perfectly obvious to him. "You soak it
ιn water and fasten it around your neck with a safety pin," he
said.

Morley stared at him.

Dave said, "You wring it out first."

What Morley was thinking was, What am I doing here?
But she wasn't about to quit.

She was so young. She believed what they were doing was
important.

On Saturday mornings Dave got up first and made them
scrambled eggs. Ever since he was a child, Dave had loved
scrambled eggs. Sometimes, when he was a boy, he could
hardly wait to get to sleep on Friday night because he knew
he was going to get scrambled eggs the next morning.

One Friday night as she was washing the dishes, Morley
said, "I make the best scrambled eggs you've ever had."

The next morning she squeezed fresh juice and got out
their matching coffee mugs. Carefully folding their one pair
of linen napkins, laying them out side by side, she whisked up
six eggs and brought them to the table. Dave stared at them.
There were little green flecks all through his scrambled eggs.
Pieces of chives Morley had snipped from the back garden.
In Cape Breton you don't add anything to scrambled eggs.
Except maybe ketchup. But this was his bride, and she had
made these eggs. Dave picked up his fork. When he had finished, he said, "I love your scrambled eggs."

The next weekend the eggs came with chopped-up mush-
rooms. The weekend after that, it was tomatoes and onions.
Then spinach. On the fifth weekend it was cheese.

Dave had begun to hate Saturday mornings. He would lie
in bed listening to the sound of a knife hitting a chopping
board. How did I get mixed up with this person? he wondered.

By the middle of that first winter, they were both think
This marriage is a big mistake. Here it was, January of .
things, and Morley was gloomy. Under a year married, and
she felt like she had been sentenced to life with a stranger.

One night on television there was a news story about the
canals in Holland. The reporter squinted awkwardly at the
camera as he interviewed an old man smoking a meer-
schaum pipe at an outdoor cafe. The old man said it was the
first time in ten years that the canals in the Netherlands had
frozen. The newscast cut from the old man to pictures of a
Dutch boy lacing up his skates on a canal bank and from him
to three girls in folk costume skating hand in hand through an
unidentified village.

Morley watched the entire report with her chin cupped in
her hand. Then she turned to Dave and said, "I've always
dreamed of doing that."

Dave, who had been only half paying attention, said, "Really? That was your dream?"

Morley said, "Yes."

Dave stood up and walked into the kitchen. When he
came back, he was carrying a beer. He looked at his wife and
said, "We should go."

Morley said, "To Holland? Don't be silly."

Dave said, "Maybe this is our only chance. Maybe the
next time it happens, we'll have kids and a mortgage and we
won't be able to go."

Dave had never said anything about kids before.

He smiled at her. And he went back into the kitchen and
picked up the telephone. When he hung up, Morley was
standing beside him. Watching. Nothing like this had ever
happened to her.

"We leave tomorrow. We'll be back on Monday," said
Dave. He was looking right at her.

ne next morning they bought Dave a pair of hockey
ates. At lunch Morley held out a present she had wrapped
n newspaper. She said, "It's almost finished. I was going to
give it to you for your birthday. I can finish it on the plane."
It was a heavy blue wool sweater.

"This is a beautiful sweater," said Dave. "I love this
sweater."

———————

When the plane landed in Amsterdam, Morley had her face
pressed to the window. She wanted to see everything. She
wanted to make sure the canals were still frozen.

They went skating right away.

But the canals in Amsterdam were wide and windy and
open, and the ice was soft and bumpy and treacherous. It
wasn't like Morley had imagined it at all. It was like skating
on a freeway.

The man at the hotel said, "You have to go to Friesland."

So on Saturday they rented a car and drove into the country. They parked at the end of a road and left their boots and
coats under a long row of willows that stood bare and wispy
along the banks of the canal. When Morley climbed down
onto the ice, it was like her dream—the canal was framed by
the high protective banks. She felt like she was a little girl
again and had stepped onto her ceiling. She was standing on
a narrow swath of ice that kept going as far as she could see.
She could start skating and go on forever.

It was the greatest skate of her life. They sailed past farm-
houses with roofs so low that they looked to be wearing great
wool hats pulled almost to their eyes; past huge creaking
windmills that Morley said reminded her of herons trying to
take off. For an hour they saw no one, and then they went
right through a village and saw an old man leading a donkey
with panniers, and a dog pulling a cart, and a family pushing

a baby carriage on wooden runners. Once in the middle nowhere, an old man passed them going the other way. F was sitting on a contraption that looked like a wagon on blades, and he was rowing it along the canal with what Dave swore were cross-country ski poles with toilet plungers fastened to the end. There were footbridges to duck under and frozen intersections, where smaller canals branched off toward villages and towns. At each of these icy intersections was a sign nailed to a tree—a white arrow pointing into the grey distance—with something like LEYDEN 50KM painted on it in neat black letters. There were no automobiles. No Ski-doos. It was like being in the nineteenth century.

They ate lunch on the ice, at a cafe on a boat that was frozen under a leafless elm. No one could speak English, so they ordered by gesturing with their red fingers at meals on other tables.

Instead of getting what they thought they were pointing at, they each got a large meatball covered in gravy, a mug of thick hot chocolate, and a huge square of gingerbread. The waiter smiled at them as they ate. It was delicious. Dave could have sat there for the rest of the afternoon.

But Morley wanted to keep moving. She was thinking, Now I understand why people like to dance. Dave, who had been having trouble keeping up with her, laced up his skates wondering how to say "cardiac arrest" in Dutch.

An hour after lunch, Morley stopped for a rest. Dave was out of breath. "My feet hurt," he panted. He flopped on the bank.

Morley said, "Stand up."

Dave struggled up. Morley made him cross his arms over his chest. She skated behind him. "Lean back," she whispered. He tipped his head back.

"All of you," she said. "Trust me. I'm here."

Dave leaned back into her arms, and she caught him and pushed him along the canal as if he were a statue. It started to snow. It was like skating through a painting. The snow was on their hats, their mittens, their sweaters. Everything was white, above and below them, the white sky and the white ice. Dave leaning back. Morley pushing, pushing.

They had waffles and hot cheese for supper, and bought a wooden toy that would move in the wind on their balcony.

————

On the plane, Dave carried the toy in his lap. He was being so careful not to knock it as he stood up to leave that he snagged the sweater Morley had knitted him on the side of his seat. He had taken four or five steps before he realized what had happened. The sweater had begun to unravel behind him. There was a strand of blue wool hanging from his waist that almost reached the floor. When he caught up to Morley, he was clutching the wooden toy and the line of wool was dangling behind him like a tail. He didn't know what to say, so he didn't say anything. He thrust the toy into her arms and turned around. They both stood in the middle of the walkway staring at the sweater. The man behind them said, "Excuse me," and people started to push past them.

Morley reached down and gathered up the line of wool. They started to walk through the airport, Dave a step ahead of Morley like a kid on a line. They walked that way to the luggage carousel and out to the taxis. And they still walk like that today—attached, drifting apart sometimes, but never so far apart that one can't reel the other one back.

Valentine's Day

There is something," said Dave, "about standing at the bottom of the stairs and yelling at your kids to come eat dinner that I find upsetting."

Morley was moving around the kitchen, straining potatoes, stirring beans, moving too fast for philosophy.

"Just get them," she said, dropping a frying pan in the sink.

Stephanie was the first down, her hair tied half-up, a horrifyingly yellow potion setting on her face. She was wearing a pair of Dave's boxer shorts and an oversize T-shirt that matched her face. She looked at the table, which Dave was in the process of setting, and said, "Why did you call me? It's not ready yet." Then she disappeared back upstairs.

An hour after dinner, she was still at the table, chewing on a stick of celery and painting her nails, balancing the brush on the table, picking up the celery, holding her fingers out in front of her, waving them in the air. Sam was sitting across from her, in another universe, chewing on a pencil and frowning at the maths book in front of him. When the phone rang, no one moved. They all looked at Stephanie.

"Why are you looking at me?" she said.

Before Morley went to bed, she knocked on Stephanie's bedroom door.

Stephanie was lying on her unmade bed, books spread

29

...d her and spilling off the bed, where they merged with ...ile of dirty clothes that stretched to the empty laundry ...amper in the corner. Stephanie was talking on the phone, listening to music, and apparently, working on homework.

"It's time to say goodbye," said Morley.

Five minutes later, she knocked again.

"Hang up," she said, sticking her head in the room. And then, spotting her hairbrush on the bedside table, Morley walked in and picked it up.

"I've got to go," said Stephanie into the phone. She lunged for the brush but was too late. "I need that," she said to her mother.

Her hand was out, and they were both looking at the hairbrush, which Morley was holding close to her chest. Morley said, "It belongs in the bathroom."

As she turned to go, Stephanie said, "There's a Valentine's dance on Saturday. I'm going with Paul Chalmers."

"On a date?" said Morley, stopping at the door.

Stephanie was sixteen. Ever since she became a teenager, she had moved around the city—to movies, to parties, on shopping trips, even to the library, with a pack of friends. As far as Morley knew, she had never been on a date.

Morley looked at her daughter and smiled. "That's wonderful, darling," she said.

Morley had begun dating when she was twelve. She was pleased when Stephanie hadn't shown any interest in boys during her early teenage years. But lately, she had begun to wonder when it was going to start. It was, she had thought, time.

Stephanie said, "It's no big deal."

Morley said, "Is he a nice boy? Do you like him?" What a stupid thing to say, she thought. She put the hairbrush down where she had found it, and she smiled. "Put it back when

you're finished, okay?" Then she said, "Well, it's nice.
he'd ask you."

Stephanie shrugged. "He didn't ask me. I asked him."

"Oh," said Morley, her fingers fiddling absentmindedly
with her lips. "Great."

———

Morley was a child of the sixties. She believes in equality of
the sexes. She thinks of herself as a feminist. Part of her was
delighted her daughter was living in a world where she could
do this. This powerful thing. Yet somewhere Morley felt an
uneasy rumble of anxiety. *The boys ask the girls.* That was the
rule she'd grown up with. Did her daughter have any idea
how much the rules had changed? And *had* they? Was everybody else doing this? What would the boys think? Morley
knew she shouldn't feel this way. She knew this could make
her a traitor to her generation, to her feminism, to her very
sex. But she couldn't help it. She didn't want anyone getting
the wrong idea about her daughter.

"Why am I feeling like this?" she asked Dave.

"Because it makes her vulnerable," said Dave. "You don't
want her to be hurt."

———

It was not as if the *boys ask the girls* rule had served Morley particularly well. As a girl, she had been subjected to an as-
tounding number of doleful dates. Evenings she had spent
with boys for whom the strongest emotion she felt was pity.

There was Colin, who, for weeks before he screwed up the
courage to ask her out, rode his bicycle endlessly up and
down the sidewalk in front of her house. This was when they
were sixteen years old. When so many of them had their
driver's licences that it wasn't cool to ride a bike any more.
What made it worse was that Colin used to pretend he was
driving a bus: When he thought no one was looking, he

d ring his bell and slam on his brakes, opening the bus
ors to pick up passengers. He could make all the bus
ounds with his mouth. And once the passengers were on, he
would hiss and ride down the street. Until the bell rang and
he had to let someone off again.

When Colin asked Morley out, she said yes. She was tired
of being the only one who didn't go out on weekends. She
thought, Surely Colin will be better than no one. She was
wrong.

They went to a movie—*Carry On Doctor*. The feature had
hardly begun when Morley became aware of Colin's hand
inching toward her, creeping across the armrest in the darkness.

Colin was looking straight ahead as if he had no idea what
his hand was doing, so Morley was able to watch its approach. She watched in dumbfounded fascination as his hand
left the armrest and headed out into space—it was inching
toward *her* hand, which was gripping her knee.

She watched Colin's hand get closer and closer, and then,
as it closed in, she held out her drink, watching as Colin's
hand sank into her Coke—up to the wrist—as if it were
thirsty. Colin didn't even flinch. Just as slowly as he had sunk
his hand into her cup, he pulled it out, easing it inch by inch
back into his lap, his gaze never leaving the screen. A few
minutes later, Morley watched him wiping his fingers carefully between his knees.

Colin wasn't even close to being the worst date in her life.
There was the night she found herself sharing the sofa in
Miriam Decker's basement with Michael Casabon. To be *that
close* to a face with *that look* is something that you never forget.
She was sitting on the couch talking to Michael when she no-
ticed his glasses had begun to fog up—for no apparent rea-

son—and he seemed to be out of breath. Which struck peculiar, because he wasn't moving. He was just sitting t with his arm around her shoulders. She wasn't sure how it g there. Then she realized his face, with that faraway look, wa. moving closer and closer, and she knew what was happening and she knew that it had nothing whatsoever to do with her. It could have been any girl sitting there beside Michael. She just happened to be in the wrong place at the wrong time—it was like a traffic accident. She didn't dare move, not a muscle, even though the arm of the couch was digging uncomfortably into her back. She was afraid if she even shifted, Michael might take it as a sign of passion. And things could get worse.

Maybe the worst date in Morley's life was with a boy called Bucky who moved in next door in the summer of 1968. Bucky was two years younger than Morley. He was fourteen years old when he asked if she wanted to go roller-skating. He said a whole gang was going. Morley had never roller-skated in her life, but Bucky said it didn't matter. Everyone she knew was out of town, and Morley thought, Why not? I can iceskate. I'll be fine.

She didn't understand that she was Bucky's date until she was squeezed beside him in the front seat of his family's Buick. The "whole gang" turned out to be Bucky's ten-year-old brother and *his* two friends. Bucky's older brother, Chucky, eighteen, the boy Morley *should* have been dating, was dropping them off at the roller rink.

It was one of those hot summer nights. Morley was wearing shorts, and she could feel the backs of her legs sticking to the vinyl of the front seat. Everyone was teasing Bucky because he had a date, cracking jokes as if Morley weren't in the car. All the way there, she kept lifting one leg and then the

...rying to keep them free of the seat. By the time they
..o the rink, she was feeling sick.

When they had their skates on, Bucky said they should
...old hands, and Morley, who was surprised to find how un-
steady she was, had no choice. So around and around they
went—Morley, against all her instincts, clutching on to this
boy who was four inches shorter than she was—praying that
no one she knew would see her. The music stopped, and the
man on the PA announced a couples-only contest. Bucky
wanted to enter.

There were only four other couples standing on the concrete oval waiting for the music to begin. The girls were all
wearing short skating skirts. The boys all looked as if they
could toss their dates between their legs.

This didn't seem to faze Bucky, but Morley drew the line
and said she wasn't going out. When Bucky couldn't change
her mind—and Lord knows, he tried—he disappeared, aban-
doning Morley, who had never been downtown in her life, in
the noisy roller rink.

After trying valiantly to skate around a few times alone,
Morley fell, and another girl landed on her and winded
her. When she got her breath back, she started to cry. She
couldn't phone her father—he'd have a heart attack. Instead,
she glommed on to Bucky's baby brother and spent the rest
of the evening with the ten-year-olds. She didn't see Bucky
again until eleven o'clock, when he mysteriously reappeared,
just as his father arrived to drive them home.

———

Stephanie had heard all these stories before. More than once.
It infuriated her that her mother seemed to believe that she
was destined for a similar string of disasters. Stephanie didn't
intend to have the same experiences as her mother. Stephanie's goal in life was to end-run all the disasters.

But you don't learn about love from someone else. L experiential. You have to make your own mistakes.

If Morley knew some of the mistakes that her daught had already made, some of the lessons she had learned, if she had any inkling of what a great act of courage it had been for Stephanie to ask Paul Chalmers to the Valentine's dance, and then to suggest that he *actually pick her up at home,* it would have broken her heart. And she wouldn't have felt so uptight about it.

Paul Chalmers was not the first man in Stephanie's life. Love first came to Stephanie the summer she was fourteen. It came in the form of a tall, long-haired, strong-faced, thirty-eight-year-old television producer. His name was Cameron Flemming, and he lived with his wife and two children on the same street as Stephanie. That summer Stephanie would take the newspaper onto their front lawn before supper and sit on the stoop, pretending to read, so she could be outside when Cameron Flemming walked by her house on his way home from work.

One afternoon when Sam had set up a lemonade stand, Cameron Flemming stopped and bought a glass of lemonade. As he put his glass down on the card table, he smiled at Stephanie. She felt herself flush. She was in love with him. The world was perfect because he was in it.

One evening he stopped and asked if she could babysit. Stephanie felt the bottom drop out of her stomach. It was his birthday, and his wife wanted to take him out to dinner. Stephanie said, "I took the babysitting course at school. I have a certificate." She was trying to sound sophisticated.

She arrived at his house with that month's *Reader's Digest.* "I'm going to read when the kids are in bed," she said. She thought this would impress Cameron. She was wearing her

rite pair of jeans and a sweater that was too large for
—she liked the way the arms hung over her hands and
vered her fingers.

His wife was upstairs. Cameron was sitting in the kitchen
with his youngest boy in his arms. He threw the boy in the air
and caught him over his head.

He reached out and touched her arm. "Nice sweater. It's a
sweater for walking along a beach in the wind."

She said, "I love the wind."

When the kids were in bed, she ignored the *Reader's Digest*
and wandered around the house imagining what it would be
like to live there with him. There was a picture in his bedroom of him standing beside his wife. They were on a beach.
The wind was in her hair. Stephanie opened the frame and
slid the picture out. With her heart pounding, she found a
pair of nail scissors in his wife's bureau. She took out her bus
pass and cut her picture out and taped it over his wife's face,
putting the altered photo back in the frame. Then she lay on
the bed, his bed, and closed her eyes, pretending she was
asleep. When she opened her eyes, she saw herself in the
frame, standing beside him, the wind in *her* hair.

The phone rang. She ran to get it, and then one of the children called. Stephanie forgot about the picture until it was
too late—until after the Flemmings got home and were standing in the living room. Stephanie was putting her sweater
back on, and Cameron Flemming was saying, "I'll walk you
home."

She didn't know what to do. She couldn't think of any reason to go up into their bedroom to retrieve her picture. So
she didn't do anything. When she got home, she thought of
killing herself. Instead, she stopped sitting on the lawn in the
evenings. No one ever said anything about the picture. But
the Flemmings never asked her to babysit again.

———

Grade ten was Doug. Stephanie kept a Doug book in her bedroom. She wrote poems to Doug and kept a list in the back of the book of all the things that made Doug cool: his sneakers, his backpack, the way he carried his backpack, the things that he probably carried in his backpack, his ski jacket, his earring, his ears, how he opened his locker, the things he probably had in his locker, his hair.

When Doug had a science project and was going to the library after school, Stephanie made up a project so she would have a reason to go to the library, too—but she didn't give him her work the way Jessica Aims did. Jessica gave Doug her maths homework every lunchtime. Stephanie thought this was contemptible. Though she wished he would ask her.

One day at lunch, Doug said Oasis was contemptible, and Stephanie panicked and prayed that no one would tell him that she used to like Oasis. Had liked them in fact until that day. It never occurred to her to defend her taste.

The Doug period of her life ended abruptly in the spring when Stephanie left her backpack in the gym and someone found her Doug book. Whoever it was tore out the back page and taped it to her locker. It was up for two periods before she found out about it. There were eighty-four entries of Doug coolness for everyone to read.

———

Paul had arrived this September. He sat directly in front of Stephanie in history. They were doing Canada. Again. By Halloween they were at Louis Riel. Again. And Stephanie knew everything there was to know about Paul's neck.

She had memorized his neck. She would know his neck anywhere. As Riel rode toward oblivion, she thought, For the rest of my life, I will know this neck.

She joined the debating team. So did Paul. She didn't even

ɔw she liked him until November, when he was away one
ɩonday and stayed away for the rest of the week. The next
Monday, when he still wasn't back, she began to worry. She
was worried that he would never come back.

She couldn't ask anyone about him, or they would figure
out she liked him. All she could do was worry. In history she
stared at the empty space in front of her where his neck
should have been. She wrote his name on a piece of paper
and then wrote her name below his and crossed out the letters that they had in common. She got an E and an A in their
first names. When she added their last names, she got an S,
an N, a T, an H, and an M.

She counted off the letters left over. "Love, hate, friendship, marriage. Love, hate, friendship, marriage." She got
"friendship." In maths, she worked out that if she cheated
and used his nickname and her middle name, she got "love."
She was startled by how pleased that made her. She wrote
over his name, again and again, "Love, hate, friendship, marriage," until it was a blue smudge. She didn't want anyone to
be able to read what she had been doing.

That night she phoned his house and hung up before anyone answered. She phoned again an hour later, and this time
got his mother on the second ring. She hung up again.

Then Becky Toma had a Christmas party. Paul and Stephanie danced together all night.

On Wednesday after supper, Sam and Stephanie had a huge
fight.

Dave and Morley were in the kitchen. As the screaming
escalated into slamming doors, Dave made a move toward
the stairs.

"No," said Morley. "Don't. If the audience doesn't show

up, the actors go home." She was making coffee. "They lo~
each other. These are battles for affection."

Half an hour later, when things were quiet, she went upstairs. Both the children's doors were shut. She knocked on
Sam's first.

"Hi," she said. "Do you want a cookie?" He was lying on
the floor moving trucks around.

In the room next door Stephanie was on her bed, reading
a magazine.

Morley said, "Do you want to go shopping? Tomorrow
after supper?"

Stephanie said, "Sam has my toothpaste."

Morley said, "Oh." She bent over and picked up a white
blouse off the floor and hung it on the back of a chair. She was
thinking maybe they could go somewhere and get a pair of
chinos and a blouse for Stephanie.

Stephanie said, "I don't want to go shopping."

Morley sat on the edge of the bed and reached out to touch
her daughter's hair. "I was thinking," she said, "that you
might like something for Saturday night. For the dance."

Stephanie pulled away from her mother. She rolled over.
"I'm going to wear one of Dad's white shirts and my black
jeans."

Morley said, "But your black jeans are ripped."

Stephanie said, "I'm going to have *long underwear* on."

It was a look that Morley hadn't considered.

———

When Morley was sixteen, her mother had a dress made for
her for a school dance. It was made by Elsie Steppich, a
seamstress who was married to the caretaker of their church.
The dress was sleeveless. It had layers of mauve chiffon over
purple silk. Her mother said it was a wonderful dress. It prob-

ly was—for a forty-five-year-old woman. When Morley
put it on, she felt like she was playing dress-up. The material
at the front was all gathered, puckering together to a centre
point so it looked like she had a massive target on her chest,
with a bull's-eye engulfing her breasts.

Morley was so horrified that she could barely speak all
night. She found the darkest corner in the gym and stayed
put, sitting on a bench with Elenore Pepper, who had a huge
nose. Morley went to the girls' room once and stared at herself in the mirror, but when she heard other girls coming
down the hall, she locked herself in a stall and waited there,
her feet lifted off the floor, until they had left and she could
slip out without anyone seeing her. When Mickey Billingsley
asked her to dance, she was so confused she said, "No, thank
you," not understanding that she was the only person he had
asked, that it had taken him all night and several trips to the
boys' bathroom before he managed to summon the courage
to approach her.

——————

When Paul arrived to pick up Stephanie, he was holding
flowers, a bouquet of twelve turquoise and green carnations.

"What a lovely thing," said Morley, warmly.

Paul looked at her defensively. "It's Valentine's Day," he
said.

Morley had spent the night before helping Sam address
forty-five *Jurassic Park* Valentines. Somehow she had disasso-
ciated that event from the actual holiday. She had forgotten it
completely. So had Dave.

Dave looked at the flowers this boy had bought for his
daughter and he winced.

Stephanie was still upstairs. Morley was struggling to make
Paul feel at home while Dave glared at him.

Paul was wearing a pair of tight black jeans, a white dress

shirt, a tie, and a dark sport coat. The tie was too thin, t. shirt rumpled, and the black shoes made his feet look enor mous—but he was trying. Awkward, thought Morley, but sweet.

Dave was thinking, This boy doesn't look a bit like me. He was muscled. His hair black. His face round. Dave felt a wave of relief. He had read that if a girl didn't feel love from her father, she would look for someone just like her father to love her. He felt liberated. He was trying hard to act naturally. He was about to ask what Paul's parents did for a living when he caught Morley sending him daggers. Paul couldn't have cared less. Because at that moment, Stephanie came bouncing down the stairs, and whatever it was Morley had been saying was left hanging. Paul turned away from Morley and looked at Stephanie and smiled and said, "Hi."

They went into the living room. Sam appeared, smirking, with a photo album and said to Paul, "Do you want to see a picture of Stephanie in a bunny costume at her ballet class?"

Stephanie glared at her brother. But five minutes later, she and Paul were hunched over the album.

"This is me at Halloween," she said.

Sam sighed with disappointment and headed upstairs.

Stephanie and Paul were so involved with each other that the rest of the family might as well have disappeared. Paul didn't even say goodbye to Morley, who was standing at the door as they left. He turned his back to her when Stephanie said something and walked by her as if she were invisible.

Morley found this reassuring. It made her completely happy.

"Love's young dream," she said. "What could be sweeter? That was wonderful."

Dave said, "I don't know. I don't know. I thought he was *too* sincere."

Out on the street, Paul had opened the door of his father's car, and Stephanie was climbing in.

Morley was watching them through the window in the front door.

"What do you call it?" she said. "That funny feeling when something nice makes you sad?"

Stephanie was sitting beside her date now. As the car pulled away from the curb, she was feeling anything but sad. Excited, nervous, sophisticated, and, to her great surprise—comfortable. She felt comfortable beside this boy. It was a night she would always remember.

Morley lingered by the door and blessed her daughter quietly. When she turned, Dave was looking at the bouquet of carnations. Morley looked at him and laughed.

Everyone was so caught up in the moment that no one noticed Sam, who had run upstairs and was in his room. The lights were on, the window open, and Sam's naked bum was sticking out into the cold night air. One last shot at his sister.

It was good enough to be alive.

But to be young and alive was very heaven.

Sourdough

Dave spent a frustrating week at the beginning of March trying to find someone who could sell him a box of the plastic disks that snap into the centre of 45 rpm records.

He had bought a lifetime supply of the disks in the early eighties from a manufacturer in Sarnia who was going out of business.

"Just send them all," said Dave after they had haggled for a while. "I'll pay seventy-five dollars, plus the shipping."

He nearly croaked when the trucker met him in the alley behind his record store, spat, and pointed to the crate in the back of the van. The crate was as big as a refrigerator.

"Are you sure?" asked Dave.

"Sign here," said the trucker.

Dave needed the help of three friends to wrestle the box up to his second-floor storage room. This is stupid, he thought as they humped the case up the stairs. But when he opened it, he felt pleased. The plastic disks were beautiful. Half of them were bright primary colors: reds, yellows, and brilliant blues. The rest were muted tones of pink and brown with swirling tortoiseshell highlights. There were thousands. Dave dug his hands into the box and let them fall through his fingers. He felt rich.

He bought a goldfish bowl at a yard sale and filled it to the brim with the disks and kept it on the counter by the cash register. He let anyone who asked dip in and take as many as they wanted, for free—even people who hadn't bought a record. He figured he would never get rid of them all.

He wasn't figuring on Brian.

Brian is a kid from Saskatchewan who came to Toronto to study film. He collects Hawaiian guitar music, and when he stumbled on the Vinyl Cafe, he started hanging around, always on the lookout for Dick Dale albums. Eventually, Dave hired Brian. It was Brian who invented the game they called Ringo. The goal of Ringo was to take one of the disks out of the fishbowl and flip it across the counter so it landed on the spinning turntable. One afternoon, after that had become too easy, Brian arrived with a catapult he had made out of a mousetrap. They took turns shooting the disks at the turntable from the far side of the store. The ultimate goal, never achieved—though not for want of trying—was to drop one onto the six-inch spindle.

The mousetrap ate up a prodigious number of the disks, and one day in early March, Dave went upstairs and realized he was about to run out. He phoned all over town, but no one had any, and no one knew where he could get them. Dave finally found eight of them at one of the big warehouse record stores for $1.50 apiece. He was going to buy all eight until the salesman said, "When these go, there won't be any more coming in," so Dave left four behind for whoever came looking after him. It was another nail in the coffin of vinyl, and it depressed him.

The same week, Dave got a phone call from a woman who worked at Sotheby's auction house in London. She called twice a year to ask if Dave would consider selling some of his collection of rock memorabilia. He didn't want to sell anything, but after she told him some of the prices that things had brought at recent sales, Dave said he'd think about it.

"Phone in a few weeks," he said.

In the late sixties and through the seventies, Dave was a technical director for a lot of big groups. Although a lot of them weren't big when he worked with them, some of the people he travelled with became famous. In the storeroom above his record store, where Dave had his now nearly empty crate of disks, is one of the largest collections of rock-and-roll memorabilia in North America.

The day the lady from Sotheby's phoned, Dave went upstairs with Brian after lunch. The storage room was dark. It smelled like a summer porch that had been closed for the winter. Dave flicked on a light switch and bent to pick up a shirt lying on the storeroom floor. It was purple.

"Did I ever tell you how Jimi Hendrix got kicked out of Little Richard's band?" he said as he held up the shirt in front of him. "He wore this onstage one night." Dave folded the shirt absentmindedly. *"No one* wore purple onstage except Little Richard."

He was looking around for a place to hang the shirt. He dropped it on a pile of boxes.

"Little Richard made his comeback right here in Toronto, at that rock-and-roll festival where Lennon played." Little Richard wanted to look sharp for that show, so he had a mirrored vest made. "I have it somewhere."

Dave was standing directly under the bare lightbulb that hung from the ceiling in the middle of his storeroom.

"That's Dylan's set list from the 1965 Newport Folk Festival," he said. He was pointing to a piece of paper with a handwritten scrawl thumbtacked to a pillar. He reached for it and knocked over a stack of cartons. "I don't know why I keep all this stuff. I should sell it."

"Whose guitar?" asked Brian.

"Which one?" said Dave.

"The Saturn," said Brian.

"Hound Dog Taylor's," said Dave.

Brian had the guitar around his neck. "Did he really have six fingers?" he asked.

Dave had picked up an envelope off the floor. "You know what this is?" he said.

Brian shook his head.

"This is the film—no, not the film. These are the negatives from Margaret Trudeau's camera from that weekend with the Rolling Stones."

"What weekend with the Rolling Stones?" said Brian.

"Look at this," said Dave. He was holding a negative up to the light. "This one will never get published."

Brian was fiddling with a cigarette case.

"That belonged to Leonard Cohen," said Dave, slipping the negative back in the envelope.

Brian opened the case. *"Love from M,"* he read. "Who is M?"

"Marianne. Do you like it? You can take it if you want." Dave wanted to get out of there. He was standing by the door, his hand on the light switch.

————

That night Carl Lowbeer called and asked if Dave could do him a favour. Carl and Gerta lived down the street. They were going to Florida for a month. Would Dave look after their sourdough starter while they were gone?

"It needs to be fed," said Carl. "A tablespoon of wheat flour. Once a week. It will only take you a minute or two—no more."

If anyone else in the neighbourhood had phoned with a request like that, Dave would have assumed they were joking, but Carl Lowbeer didn't joke. And Dave knew enough about Carl to know that if he had unexpectedly developed a sense of humour, it wasn't going to be about his sourdough.

Dave got the story at Polly Anderson's annual Christmas party. Carl had brought a loaf of his bread to the party, and Dave—who had missed lunch and breakfast—was stuffing it, and everything else he could lay his hands on, down his throat. Carl materialized out of the crowd and said, "I see you like my bread," and Dave replied, "What? Oh. Yes." And stood there, nodding politely, while Carl told him how he got the sourdough starter from his aunt Ola in Germany—how *she* got the starter from her mother, Carl's great-aunt; it had been in the family for over thirty-two years. "My mother used it, too," said Carl.

"It's very good," said Dave. And it was, although to be truthful, Dave had been thinking of the bread more as a utensil to convey great mounds of smoked salmon into his mouth. Until Carl mentioned his bread, Dave hadn't really noticed it.

"I have a genealogy," said Carl. "I could show you if you come over. My great-aunt made the first batch in Schaffhausen."

"You have a genealogy?" said Dave, swallowing a mouthful of salmon.

"Of the starter," said Carl. "Like a family tree. I have it in a frame in the den."

"Really?" mumbled Dave, reaching for the eggplant dip with another piece of the bread.

When Carl and Gerta appeared at his house this past Christmas with a loaf of bread, Dave wondered if Carl hadn't misinterpreted his enthusiasm. Dave and Morley hardly knew the Lowbeers. There was a moment of awkwardness when Dave opened the door and saw them standing there. Soon Carl and Gerta were in the kitchen slicing the bread so Morley could try it.

"Umm," said Morley, her mouth full. She was staring at Dave. Is this your fault? Dave shrugged.

The Lowbeers left as abruptly as they had arrived, declining to eat anything themselves.

"That was weird," said Morley after they had gone, cutting herself another piece of bread. "It's sort of sour—I don't think I like it."

"It's okay," said Dave without great enthusiasm. Then he added, "It's better with smoked salmon."

———

The night before he left for Florida, Carl phoned Dave with his instructions.

"Usually," he said, "we take it with us."

"The starter?" said Dave. "On vacation?"

"We took it to Germany last March," said Carl.

"To Germany?" said Dave.

"Gerta carried it in her suitcase. She was going to take it in her purse, but she didn't want it to go through the X-ray machine. She was afraid the X rays might kill the enzymes."

"You took the starter to Germany?" said Dave.

"Last summer we took it to the cottage, but it didn't do well. We had to feed it commercial flour, and when we brought it back, it was pale . . . out of sorts."

"You took it to the cottage?" said Dave.

"It has done three interprovincial trips and two international ones," said Carl. "Plus a change of planes in Holland."

Carl explained why he didn't want to take the starter to Florida. "What if there's a hurricane?" he said. "What if the power fails? I don't want to be worrying all the time. It's supposed to be a vacation."

Then he told Dave what he wanted him to do. "The starter is in the fridge. In a Mason jar. There's a bag of wheat flour on the counter beside the fridge. Once a week you put a tablespoon of the flour into the Mason jar. Okay?"

"Okay," said Dave.

———

After supper Dave said, "What is starter, anyway?"

Morley looked at her husband and shook her head. She said, "Why did he choose you, of all people? Doesn't he understand what he is dealing with? The idiot."

Dave didn't press the point.

The next day he went to Wong's Scottish Meat Pies for lunch.

Kenny Wong said, "Making sourdough bread is like making yogurt. You need something to get it going. When you're making sourdough, you use fermented dough from your last batch of bread. That's the starter. In the pioneer days, when you couldn't run to the corner store for a packet of yeast, sharing a starter was a true act of friendship. You should be honoured."

"He didn't give it to me," said Dave. "He asked me to look after it."

"Still," said Kenny. "If you don't feed it, it will . . . you know . . ."

"No," said Dave. "What?"

"It's a living thing. I don't know. If you don't feed it, who knows. It might die or something."

———

Dave's first visit to Carl's house was on Friday. When he got there, he couldn't find the keys, and he panicked. Had he lost them? He phoned Morley.

"You never had them," she said. "Remember? Carl was going to leave them under the garbage can."

Dave let himself into Carl's house and found the Mason jar of starter in the fridge. He pried the jar open and peered in. The starter looked like moist oatmeal. The pleasing sour aroma of fermenting yeast wafted up out of the jar and made Dave smile. He looked around for the bag of flour. The kitchen was full of ceramic knickknacks. The walls were covered with framed sayings, scrolls, tea towels from Germany and Arizona. The room had the feel of a souvenir shop. There was a set of ceramic containers shaped like dogs on the counter. They were lined up in descending order of size, each dog with a tag around its neck: SUGAR, COOKIES, TEA, COFFEE. The flour wasn't on the counter where Carl had promised. There was a brown paper bag by the telephone. It was full of white powder. Dave dumped a spoonful into the starter and put the starter back in the fridge. Then he spent half an hour snooping around the Lowbeers' house.

When Dave got home, Morley was in bed reading. He stood at the end of the bed and got undressed. "All his shirts are ordered by colour," he said as he pulled his sweater over his head. "All the blue ones together, all the white ones." Dave rolled up the sweater and tossed it toward his bureau like a basketball. It landed in the garbage can. He sighed.

Morley said, "You went through his closet?" She kept reading, but she sounded shocked.

"Of course I did," said Dave. "He has two pairs of lederhosen. Can you imagine Carl in leather shorts?"

He was using his feet to push his clothes into the pile at the bottom of Morley's closet that served as a laundry hamper.

"I can't believe you did that," said Morley. She was looking at him over the book. "Two pairs? Really?"

"You know what I found in the bathroom?" said Dave.

Morley put her book down on the bed. She was sitting up. Looking at him.

The next Friday, when Dave went to feed the starter, he thought maybe it didn't smell quite the same as it had the week before, but it was hard to tell. He didn't want to touch it with his fingers, so he got a fork and poked at it. He decided it was just his imagination. He put another spoonful of the flour into the jar like before and went into the den to look at Carl's books.

The third Friday he went directly to Carl's on his way home from work. He was feeling good—happy because on Saturday he was leaving with Morley and the kids for Montreal. They were going to St.-Sauveur in the Laurentian Mountains for a long weekend ski trip. He was going to feed the starter and go home and pack. He fished the jar out of the fridge and gasped when he opened it.

He ran to the phone.

Morley answered on the third ring.

"The starter," said Dave. "The starter."

"Who is this?" said Morley.

"It's me," said Dave. "I'm at Carl's. Something is wrong with the starter."

Something was terribly wrong with the starter. Instead of resembling a bowl of moist oatmeal, it looked hard and dry.

"And white," said Dave. "It's all dried up. I think it's dead."

"You sound like you're reporting a murder."

"I am," said Dave. "It's dead. It smells."

"It's supposed to smell," said Morley.

"Not like this," said Dave. "It smells horrible. Like chemicals. Like a jar of solid smog. It smells like death. What am I supposed to do?"

When Morley arrived, it took her under a minute to figure out what had gone wrong.

"This is what you've been feeding it?" she said, holding up the brown paper bag Dave had found by the phone.

"Yes," said Dave.

"Polyfilla," said Morley.

"Polyfilla?" said Dave.

"That's what it says here on the bag," said Morley.

It was written neatly in Gerta's handwriting.

Dave sat down and stared out the kitchen window.

The Lowbeers were due home Sunday evening. "What am I going to do?" said Dave.

"I don't know, but it's going to be interesting," said Morley. She was standing by the counter opening the dog containers. "She has brown sugar in the Coffee dog."

———

Later that night Morley was standing in her bedroom trying to stuff an extra ski sweater into one of the kids' suitcases.

"You're leaving," said Dave. "No matter what—right?"

"Right," she said.

"Right," said Dave.

He went downstairs and stared at the phone. Ten minutes later, he called Kenny Wong.

"I think I have a recipe for sourdough starter," said Kenny.

"I'm coming over," said Dave.

When Dave got to Kenny's restaurant, Kenny was waiting for him with a book, a bottle of buttermilk, a hair dryer, and a bottle of Scotch.

"We've got to get going," Kenny said. "It takes three days to make sourdough starter."

"We've only got two," said Dave.

"That's what the hair dryer is for," said Kenny.

When they got to Carl's, Kenny rubbed his hands together and said, "First things first." He started opening cupboards until he found the glasses. He poured two big tumblers of Scotch and propped his cookbook open on the kitchen counter. It was called *Cooking Wizardry for Kids: Learn About Food . . . While Making Tasty Things to Eat!*

Kenny smiled and held up his Scotch. "I get all my best stuff from this book," he said.

"You can't be serious," said Dave.

There was a moment of silence. Kenny and Dave stared deep into each other's eyes.

By three in the morning Dave and Kenny were anything but serious. They were still at step one of the recipe—waiting for a cup of buttermilk to warm and collect bacteria from the kitchen air, as the recipe called for, in the natural old-fashioned way. Kenny had the hair dryer set up to blow over the buttermilk.

"Like forcing a tulip," he said.

The bottle of Scotch was half-killed. Dave had discovered the Lowbeers' polka records. Kenny was wearing one of Gerta Lowbeer's aprons. There was a mop lying on the kitchen counter.

"Tired, my dear?" said Kenny to the mop. "It must be time to add the flour," he said. "I figure six hours under a hair dryer is the same as three days in a warm place. What do you think?" He was still talking to the mop.

Dave was sitting on the floor. His head was in his hands. He was staring into the distance. He was remembering the disdain in Carl Lowbeer's voice when he had told Dave about the Rutenbergs. "We gave them some of the starter because they said they wanted to bake bread, too. They killed it within six months. They're fools."

"I'm dead," said Dave.

They finished at ten on Sunday morning. Kenny had slept in the Lowbeers' bed, Dave on the living room couch.

When they left, the sourdough was bubbling like a pot of oatmeal.

"It looks sort of the same. It smells right. But it didn't bubble like that," said Dave.

"It'll slow down in the fridge," said Kenny.

"And there's more than there used to be—there was only half that much," said Dave.

Kenny picked up the Mason jar and scooped half of the new sourdough into the garbage. "How's that?" he said. "Does that look about right?"

The Lowbeers arrived home on Sunday, as planned. Dave flew to Montreal before they arrived and joined his family in St.-Sauveur. When they got home on Tuesday night, there was a loaf of bread and a note from Carl on the back porch.

> *You certainly looked after the starter.*
> *Thanks for everything.*

"He knows," said Dave. "He must."

"That's just Carl," said Morley.

———

Dave wasn't so sure. He gave Carl a wide berth for the next few weeks. They didn't rub shoulders again until the first neighbourhood barbecue, on the long weekend in May.

Dave was at the condiment table looking at the buns when Jim Scoffield leaned against him and whispered conspiratorially, "Aren't you going to have one of Carl's sourdough buns?"

"What do you mean?" said Dave nervously. Did everyone know?

Jim rolled his eyes. "Carl just gave me his bread lecture. Do you know he has a framed genealogy in his den?"

Dave felt relief wash through him. "Did he tell you about his aunt in Germany?" he asked.

Jim nodded.

Dave smiled. "He's a bit much," he said, "but I like his bread."

Dave picked out one of Carl's buns from the bowl on the picnic table. He wandered over to the grill, got a hamburger, and then looked around the yard. Carl was standing near the fence, a hot dog in his hand. He was alone.

Dave waved and headed over.

Music Lessons

The problem of Sam's piano lessons began with his Christmas report card. The music teacher, Mrs. Crouch, wrote: *Sam has an unself-conscious sense of rhythm. It appears to come from inside him.*

"What does that mean?" said Dave. He was sitting in the kitchen reading the report. " 'It appears to come from inside him.' Where else would it come from?"

"I think she means it's a gift," said Morley.

In February, at parent-teacher night, Mrs. Crouch sought *them* out. "Do you know he has perfect pitch?" she asked.

Morley smiled. It wasn't so much what Mrs. Crouch was telling her—just to have a teacher say nice things about her child was good enough. Morley didn't want her to stop.

"The other day in choir," said Mrs. Crouch, "he started to sing the descant quietly to himself. I just happened to catch it as I walked by. Most of the grade sixes can't do that."

Morley nodded earnestly.

By the time they got home, however, her joy had been sideswiped by a spasm of guilt. Sam was eight years old, and they hadn't done a thing to encourage this musical talent. When Stephanie was eight, she'd been taking piano *and* dance lessons. What if Sam did have a gift? Morley felt as if she'd been asleep at the switch.

She knew from her years in the theatre that every time you

see a great artist stand up onstage and perform, there is another person standing alongside. Usually, it's a teacher or a
parent. All great artists need a support system. Someone who
believes in what they have to offer.

She had done absolutely nothing for Sam.

———

That night Morley dreamed she was in the audience at a symphony concert. In the middle of her dream, the conductor
abruptly snapped his baton in two and hurled it on the stage.
The hall fell deadly quiet, and the conductor swivelled
around and looked at Morley. *Someone,* he boomed, glancing
back angrily at the orchestra, *has to leave the stage.*

Morley noticed for the first time that the musicians were
playing vegetables. Then she saw Sam push his way through
the middle of the leafy greens. He was waving a large eggplant over his head. "How do you expect me to play the eggplant," he said, "when I've only ever been given potatoes?"
Then he left the stage, passing the cucumbers with his head
hanging. As he went, Morley noticed that the entire root section was having dental work done as they played.

———

When she woke up, Morley turned to Dave and said, "I am
going to get Sam a potato—I mean piano—teacher."

She knew what had gone wrong. Stephanie had kicked up
such a fuss about her piano lessons that she had worn Morley
down. It wasn't fair. Sam deserved his own chance.

He started lessons at the beginning of March with the only
piano teacher in the neighbourhood who had space to take
him. The teacher's name was Ray Spinella, and he had only
one arm. He wasn't the teacher Morley wanted, but she
wanted to get Sam going. Everyone said the best teacher
around was Laurence Merriman. But Laurence Merriman

wouldn't take Sam until September, and only if Sam got his grade one first. Brian suggested a month at a music camp. "Camp Dutoit is good," he said.

The problem was that Sam didn't want to go to Camp Dutoit to get his grade-one piano. Sam wanted to go to the Lazy M Ranch and learn to ride a horse.

Dave said Sam should go to the horse camp. "Summers are for fun," he said. But Morley found herself uncharacteristically muddled. She was sure Sam would have fun at Camp Dutoit once he got there. But she didn't want to send him against his will. Morley thought perhaps if she gave him some time, a few weeks of lessons, maybe he would change his mind. The danger was, if she gave him too much time, there wouldn't be a spot left for Sam at either camp. So she sent a deposit to both. She thought things would be clear by the time the bulk of the fees were due.

Well, the bulk of the fees were now due, and things were no clearer. The forms from both camps were sitting on Morley's desk. And if she didn't choose one and get the check in the mail soon, Sam wouldn't be going away at all. Morley thought of sending money to both camps to give her a few more weeks. But she knew that was crazy. And if she did that, one day she would have to tell Dave. As much as you'd want to keep that sort of behaviour to yourself, it would be difficult—eventually, you'd just blurt it out.

———

On Thursday, Dave's sister, Annie, phoned from the airport. She said, "I just got into town. I'm recording some sort of, I don't know, thing. Tonight. I'm flying back tomorrow morning early. Are you free for lunch?"

Annie lived in Halifax. She played in the string section of Symphony Nova Scotia.

Morley said, "I'd love to have lunch."

They met in a large formal dining room, on the top floor of a downtown department store.

———

Music had always been a big part of Dave's and his sister's lives. It was no accident that Annie played in the symphony and that Dave owned a record store and had spent all those years working in rock and roll.

Dave and Annie's father, Charlie, loved music. There was no money for music lessons when Charlie was a kid, but as an adult, he taught himself to play the piano and, during the dark Cape Breton winter nights, the double bass. When Dave and Annie were growing up, they were constantly surrounded by music. Nearly every morning, when it was time to get the kids out of bed, Charlie would sing them awake. He would make up lyrics about the day ahead, the things they were going to do. He used tunes that drove them crazy, like "Hello, Dolly":

Hello, maths test
This is Dave, maths test
It's so nice to have a test
On Tuesday morn—

"Come on, Davey. Up and at 'em!"
Or "Big Spender":

The minute you walked in the room
I could tell you were a real cool fraction
Math-a-maction!
Numerator hangs out over the line
How'd you like to come and be reduced sometime?

What Charlie loved most were the nights when friends came over to the house and made music with him. He used to send away to a store in New York City for sheet music. He would hand out the music a week before his get-togethers so people could practice. Anyone was welcome as long as he or she could play something, which made for weird combinations of instruments: for example, a trio made up of recorder, double bass, and trumpet. Charlie was inevitably the worst player in these bands because, although he loved music, he had absolutely no sense of rhythm and a very unusual sense of pitch. So the guy on the recorder and the guy on the trumpet would be playing away, and Charlie would lumber along on his bass about twenty yards behind them. Charlie was often still playing when the others got to the end of the piece. When Charlie finally played his last note, his friend Fred, who regularly showed up to play the piano, would say, "Well, we won that one, Charlie." They had a great time.

———

Both Dave and Annie began piano lessons the autumn they began school. They studied with the only piano teacher in Big Narrows, Sister Emilienne, at the convent of the Sisters of St. Seriah.

Sister Emilienne came from Pointe-Verte on the south shore of the Baie des Chaleur. She was French, but she could speak English, and Annie thought she was the nicest, kindest woman in the world.

Sister Emilienne's studio, with the wainscoting and the two pianos, was the closest to religion that Annie and Dave ever got. The room was so ordered and quiet that it lent a sense of mystery and sanctity to music.

Sister Emilienne had names for all the notes on the piano.

Mrs. Treble Clef with her tightly folded skirt; Mr. Bass Clef with two buttons on his shirt. When Dave was having trouble with B-flat, Sister Emilienne drew little bumblebees wherever Dave was supposed to play the note. "Press hard," she said. "Make the bee flat." In one lesson, the B became Dave's best note. He became very attached to the B.

Sister Emilienne would sit on the piano bench as they played, and as she listened, her head would tilt to the right. She would smile and nod and tilt over, just like the nuns in *The Sound of Music*.

Annie adored her. One spring she went on a school trip to Quebec City and brought Sister Emilienne a little plastic snowglobe from Ste. Anne de Beaupré. It was the size of a baseball, with a miniature model of the shrine inside.

"Oh, look," said Sister Emilienne when she opened her present. "When I shake it, look how the angels fly around the shrine." She put it on a shelf in her studio.

Every lesson Annie would head off determined to find out if Sister Emilienne had any hair under her wimple, or if, as Dave had earnestly told her, she was as bald as a bowling ball. Annie was forever touching Sister Emilienne's long graceful robes. There seemed to be so many mysterious layers. Sometimes Annie would reach out and touch one of the crosses that hung around the nun's neck.

Sometimes when she came home from her lessons, Annie would dress up in her mother's skirts and put on some of her old jewellery. Margaret would sit patiently at the piano, and Annie would give her mother a piano lesson. "Put your thumb on the C," she would say, and Margaret would put her thumb on the D beside middle C and say, "This one?"

Piano seemed to come naturally to Annie. She was playing Bach in the first year. And maybe Sister Emilienne was right.

Maybe she could play better than any six-year-old in the country.

Indeed, the summer after she began her lessons, Annie was chosen to play for Queen Elizabeth when she came to Halifax.

The recital was on the lawn of the citadel. They set up a stage and a yellow and white awning for shade. Annie was sitting two rows behind the queen, and she saw her yawn while the choir was singing "Farewell to Nova Scotia." To this day Annie can remember watching the queen yawn and deciding that playing Bach was not a good idea. Thinking that the queen had probably already heard Bach, Annie decided it would be better if she made something up. When they called her name, she walked onto the stage in her new smocked dress, her white socks, and her black shoes. She sat at the piano, and when she began to play, she was making the notes up out of her head. If someone hadn't come and dragged her off the stage, she would have sat there forever, entertaining the queen, completely confident that her improvisation was far superior to Bach.

———

One day when Annie was seven, Charlie invited a fiddler to the house to play with him, and when Annie saw his violin, she fell in love with it. She had never been so close to a violin before. She loved the way it looked, and the smell of the rosin and the rich colours of the wood, and she adored the sound. When they finished playing, she asked her father if she could touch the violin.

———

The day Annie began her violin lessons was the most exciting day of her life. She came home from her first class and ripped open her violin case. She made the whole family listen to what she could do. She could play all four open strings: E, A, D, and G. She had her mother call out the notes, and she would play them. She couldn't believe how easy it was.

The next week her teacher taught her to put down her first finger, and she could play A and B on one string. That was a very big deal.

She wanted to learn how to read notes.

"Just show me where they are," she said. Pretty soon she was able to play small pieces with the teacher playing along. She was a violinist. It was brilliant.

It made Charlie extraordinarily happy to watch his daughter. But Annie didn't notice. Because the music made her happier.

———

Eventually, she got to a whole different level, and playing the violin became work. She did what lots of kids do: She pretended to practise. She would shut the door to her room and set up a novel on her music stand. She would play random notes and read the book as she played—she raced through *Anne of Green Gables* this way—and when her mother called from the kitchen, "That doesn't sound like practising to me," Annie would call back to say she was sight-reading.

But she kept at it. And if you keep at anything long enough, the work adds up. She went to McGill University and studied music. When she graduated, she got a job with the Montreal String Quartet. It was a wonderful honour for a young musician—playing with three great musicians, all of them at least a decade older—but she felt incomplete. She wasn't having fun. Everyone was so intense. And earnest. Annie had thought that when she got out of school, playing music would be fun again.

One day a friend who knew the famous Israeli violinist

Avi Stovman said, "He takes students, you know. If you want to write to him, you can mention my name." So Annie wrote. And to her great shock, Avi Stovman called her back. She came home from a rehearsal one afternoon, and her room-mate said, "You are not going to believe who called today."

When Annie called him back, he said, "Send me a tape." So she made a tape and sent it to him. But he didn't respond. She waited for a month and never heard a word. She thought, The tape was horrible. She decided he was laughing so hard, he couldn't make it to the telephone. Her friends said, "Phone him back." And one night after a big spaghetti dinner, when they had drunk two bottles of Mateus, her boyfriend, Owen, dragged her to the telephone and dialled Avi Stovman's number. He handed her the phone and held her to the wall to make her talk to the great violinist.

When Stovman answered, he said, "I've been going to the post office every day. Where is your tape?"

It had been lost in the mail.

He said, "There is nothing I can do. I only take seven students. My class is already full."

Annie decided he had listened to the tape and it was dreadful and he was just being polite. But her friends didn't let her quit. They said, "Go to New York and phone him when you get there. Play for him."

In April, Owen forced her into a car, and they set off for New York City. They drove until after midnight, following Highway 9 along the valley of the Hudson River. The next morning when they stopped for breakfast in Hastings-on-Hudson, Pete Seeger walked by them on their way to the cafe. Owen said, "It's an omen." They were in Manhattan just after noon. The idea was Annie would make a casual phone call and then go and play for Avi Stovman.

She called him from outside a bookstore on the corner of Fifty-second and Seventh.

He said, "Where are you? You sound like you're around the corner."

Annie said, "I am around the corner." She was standing on one foot and then the other, not looking at Owen, who was watching from inside the bookstore.

Stovman said, "Come on over. I'm leaving tomorrow morning at eight o'clock. But you can come tonight and play for me."

"That's okay," Annie replied. "I don't think it's a very good time." Then she said goodbye and hung up. Her music career was over. She didn't have what it took. She broke up with Owen on the way home at a gas station in Pough-keepsie.

———

Three months later, Annie told the whole story to the viola player in the Montreal String Quartet. It turned out that this woman knew Stovman's assistant. They had studied together.

"You're crazy," the woman said. "I'm going to phone Ruth. You are going to play for Stovman when he comes to Montreal."

———

Stovman remembered the girl who hadn't sent the tape and hadn't come to play. He was interested enough to see if she would show up on her third chance. He said, "All right. When I'm in Montreal, if she wants, she can come and she can play and I will listen."

Annie went to the Ritz-Carlton Hotel and knocked on his door nervously. He was playing with the Montreal Sym-phony that night. It was four in the afternoon, and he was sit-ting in his room watching *M*A*S*H* on television.

Annie warmed up in the bathroom. She thought she

sounded okay. But when she came out to play for him, a strange thing happened. She put her bow on the strings, and she couldn't hear anything.

She stopped, and Stovman looked at her and said, "What's wrong? Keep playing." So she started again, but she still couldn't hear the music. When she finished, she didn't have a clue what she had done. It could have been the same random notes she played for the queen.

Stovman said, "Is that a favourite piece?"

Annie just stared at him, horrified at what had happened. In the middle of this long silence, Annie realized Stovman was looking for a nice way to get rid of her. She said, "Maybe it's not a good idea that I come to New York." She was trying to help him out.

"What?" he snapped. "Do you think you won't learn anything? You think you have nothing to learn? Of course you have to come to New York. I'm just trying to think how we're going to get you started."

And that was that.

————

To help pay for the lessons in New York, Annie got a job playing at Radio City Music Hall. She did the Liza Minnelli show. She had to wear a sequinned gown even though the orchestra was in the pit, because at every show, there was a moment when the pit was raised. The orchestra would play a number as they hovered in the air, and then they would drop out of sight again.

Some of the people had been in the pit for over a decade. They hated what they were doing, but they didn't leave, because it was a good job and steady. One night Annie watched the trombone player filling out his income-tax form during the show—putting down his pen and picking up his trombone without missing a cue.

Stovman had an apartment on Riverside Drive, in the same building as Pinchas Zukerman and Itzhak Perlman. Perlman lived on the top floor in the apartment where Babe Ruth used to live.

Once, while Annie was warming up, she played a reel, and Stovman screamed at her. "Don't play like that in here," he said. The accompanist told Annie that Stovman was harder on her than any of his other pupils. That made her happy. She stayed two years.

When she left, she was offered a job with the Boston Symphony. She got married six months later. She thought she had everything she ever wanted.

But life with the orchestra didn't suit Annie. She found the programme repetitive, and when the conductor did choose new pieces to perform, they were seldom things Annie wanted to play. After rehearsals and performances, the younger members would sometimes gather at one another's apartments for a glass of wine, but invariably, the talk would return to the same tired complaints—the lousy salaries, the long hours, the lack of opportunity. Annie had the job she'd always wanted, but she couldn't find any joy in it.

Then the first violinist left the orchestra, and the undercurrent of rivalry that Annie had always suspected was there burst into the open. The woman in the chair beside Annie suddenly stopped talking to her, and it didn't take long for Annie to learn that the woman had tried to undercut her— had actually complained to the conductor that she was tired of carrying Annie, that Annie always played off tempo.

When her marriage began to fall apart, Annie decided she'd had enough. She quit the orchestra and moved back to Nova Scotia with her daughter, Margot.

Stovman was furious. He wrote her a blistering three-page letter. "What are you trying to do to me?" he wrote. To him?

thought Annie. What am I doing to *him*? Oddly, the letter made her feel better about her decision. She took a contract with Symphony Nova Scotia. She also joined a Celtic group. Suddenly, music was fun again.

———

Morley knew much of this, but she hadn't heard all of it before, not all at once. They were eating dessert when she told Annie about Sam's piano lessons and what his teacher, Mrs. Crouch, had said about him. She explained her plan to send Sam to music camp so he could study with Laurence Merriman.

Annie said, "Laurence Merriman is a prissy snob. I thought Sam already had a music teacher. You said he was having fun with the guy."

———

On Thursday, when Morley took Sam to his piano lesson she asked if she could stay and watch. Ray Spinella, the one-armed teacher, looked surprised but delighted. "You could sit over there," he said.

Morley did her best to disappear. She needn't have bothered. Ray and Sam were soon utterly absorbed by the music. Morley noticed that Ray obviously wasn't following a method. And he wasn't teaching the grade-one syllabus.

At the end of the lesson, Ray had Sam make up a tune. Then Ray took a trumpet off the top of the piano, stood beside her son, and played along. Sam smiled at his teacher, Ray nodded, and they both kept going.

———

On the way home, Morley said, "When you're at camp, do you think they'll give you your own horse, or do you have to share it?"

Sam said, "I think you have to share. But I'm going to save up and buy my own horse. I'm going to call him Bach. Ray is going to teach me some of the cowboy songs that Bach wrote. Can I do piano next year?"

"We'll see," said Morley.

Sam had his face pressed to the car window. He was whistling the tune that he had just made up. The tune he and Ray had been playing together.

Morley smiled.

Spring

"Be-Bop-A-Lula"

It was study break. And, as if on cue, spring was in the air. "Maybe a record high for this time of year," said the weatherman. Dave wore his spring jacket and sneakers to work. Walking out the front door, he felt . . . light. The sun warm on his face for the first time in months.

———

Morley had taken the kids to Florida.

"It's great," she said on the phone. "I wish you could have come. God, I needed this."

Dave was home alone.

"It's okay," he said. "I'm okay."

But he wasn't okay. Something strange was going on. It began after he drove his family to the airport. It began as a funny whirling feeling in his stomach. It wasn't like he was sick. It was a pleasant sort of feeling. Like being excited. Or nervous. But Dave wasn't feeling excited or nervous about anything. He was feeling . . . goofy.

At first he thought he was tired. He had stayed up late helping his wife pack. At midnight he had taken the car to the all-night gas station. His family was leaving at seven in the morning. They were at the airport at five-thirty. I must be tired, he thought.

He went to bed early on Wednesday and slept soundly,

but when he woke up in the morning, the feeling was still there. Except more so.

He felt . . . giddy.

It was another beautiful day.

"You wouldn't believe the weather," he said to Morley on the phone. "Everyone is outside. It's like someone pulled a switch."

On his way home, he bought a bottle of red wine and picked up a video. This is great, he thought. I never get to do this. He cooked pasta and mixed it with garlic and broccoli and drank half the bottle of wine. While he ate, he listened to Paganini's *Violin Concerto, Number One,* occasionally directing the CD with his fork. After he finished, he put on coffee and did the dishes. He was looking forward to watching his movie, but as he was putting away the Paganini, he spotted an old Beatles album, and the whirling in his stomach intensified. It was the sound track from *A Hard Day's Night.* He hadn't listened to the record in years. The summer he was sixteen, he had gone to England with his parents and had brought the album back with him. It was possible that he had been the first person in the country to own it. He pulled the record out of its jacket and spun it between his palms.

That first dissonant chord filled the kitchen like an old friend. Aficionados still argue whether it is an F-major or G-major 7th. In his book *A Day in the Life,* Mark Hertsgaard writes that the swelling opening chord of the album sounds like a hijacked church bell announcing the party of the year. Dave smiled, turned up the volume, sat down at the table, and poured himself another glass of wine. After all these years. The music washed over and through him. He played the album twice and then got down on his hands and knees and pawed about and finally found *Abbey Road.*

He killed the bottle of wine, sitting on the floor, listening to the second side of the album. The side with the incomplete song fragments. He had forgotten how much he loved the way the uncompleted songs had been mixed into one glorious movement. Woven together like that because McCartney and Lennon hadn't had the stomach to work as a team anymore and couldn't finish writing the individual numbers.

Dave staggered to bed after midnight. He never watched his movie.

On Friday, when he woke up, he didn't want to listen to CBC radio. He reached over and sleepily changed the station to CHUM—hits of the fifties and sixties, the music of his life. He brushed his teeth to Paul Simon's "Kodachrome." When he was eating breakfast, they played the title song from the musical *Hair.* He ran his hand over his head.

He felt . . . buoyant.

All day at work, old pop tunes kept bouncing into his imagination. He didn't know what the hell was going on, but he liked the way he was feeling. He usually played jazz in the store. On Friday he played rock and roll all day long.

Rock and roll had once been a big part of Dave's life. But lately, his tastes had shifted. He had become more aligned with the likes of Gershwin and Billie Holiday. Louis Armstrong and Gene Ammons.

Slowly, he had left rock and roll behind him.

———

As a teenager, he had spent hours gazing into Renee Atwater's eyes, strumming a guitar and singing Beatles tunes.

Actually, the guitar was imaginary. Actually, he was staring into his bedroom mirror, not Renee's eyes, but it was almost as good.

In his adulthood, these private performances had evolved into grander and more theatrical moments. Dave had a favourite Sondheim album that had a live-audience track. He would put it on and then run out of the room and wait for the applause to begin. As it built, he would walk into the living room with his head down and then, as the audience went wild, he would acknowledge the cheers and smile coyly at someone in the upper balcony. A friend, perhaps. Maybe Renee Atwater. She is married, and she hasn't seen him for years, and when she does, even from way up in the balcony, she thinks of what might have been and her heart breaks. Dave always dedicated the third number on the album to her. "I'd like to sing this one for someone special," he'd say. "Someone I used to sing to a long time ago."

When his son, Sam, was very young, Dave would involve him in these shows. He would hold him over his head and present him, and the crowd would go crazy when they realized he had a child. Eventually, Sam got too heavy and Dave couldn't use him in the shows anymore.

Dave kept the radio on CHUM all weekend. At night he sat in the kitchen playing old records. He was working his way back down the evolutionary chain of rock and roll. Not into the authentic blues stuff he knew he should be listening to, but down the glorious tributary where he had paddled as a kid.

Neil Sedaka's "Happy Birthday, Sweet Sixteen," the Happenings' "See You in September," Lesley Gore's "It's My Party," and, while he made supper, "Leader of the Pack" by the Shangri-Las. Dave was in pop heaven. It all sounded good to him. His sense of discrimination and good taste had been blown away by a primal memory that was almost physical. He was in the elevator of adolescence, and it was descending—dropping deeper by the hour. Twenty, nineteen, eighteen, seventeen, sixteen! He was dancing around the kitchen singing, "Dook, Dook, Dook, Dook of Earl."

He was banging his hand on the steering wheel. Geez, he was having a good time.

On Monday and Tuesday the whirling feeling in his stomach was with him all day long. He was moving in a kind of dopey haze. He wasn't paying attention to any details. He was . . . grooving. Suddenly, his life was coloured only in primary colours.

———

Debbie Anderson, the girl who came in on Wednesday and Friday nights, had, since he hired her, been his favourite part-timer. Debbie had short blond hair, an elfish smile, and big brown eyes. She went to the University of Toronto. She wanted to be a phys-ed teacher.

On Wednesday night, when they were closing, Dave said, "Have you had dinner? I'm going to El Basha for falafel if you want to come. Morley's away," he added.

"I have to study," Debbie said. "I have a physics test tomorrow."

———

On Thursday, Dave woke up at six-thirty without the alarm. He felt bright and alert. It was the second day in a row that had happened. Didn't the Monkees have a song about that? It wasn't even seven, and he was . . . excited.

He turned on the radio. The Lovin' Spoonful, "Younger Girl." He thought about Debbie. He wished she had gone to dinner with him. He imagined the two of them walking down the street together. Wondered what it would be like to hold her. Maybe he would ask her again on Friday.

———

On Friday morning, while he was shaving, he was surprised to see a blemish on his cheek. A small red dot had appeared on his face overnight. He didn't pay any attention to it at first, but as he was leaving the house, he thought about it again and went back to the bathroom to check. A pimple? He hadn't had a pimple in years. He got to the front door again and was about to pull it shut behind him when the thought crashed down on him. He was forty-five years old. Forty-five-year-olds don't get pimples. They get skin cancer. He was back in the house in a flash. He found Morley's magnifying makeup mirror. Was that how it happened? You woke up one morning and you had skin cancer?

Dave couldn't get the blemish out of his mind. He checked it three times before lunch. He thought about phoning Dr. Freeberg and having her look at it, but what if it was a pimple? He didn't want to risk sitting in the doctor's office and hearing her tell him that. He wished Morley was home so he could show it to her.

Like many men, Dave had a complicated relationship with his body. He inhabited it the way a nervous traveller settles into a commercial airliner—carefully monitoring every arrhythmia—continually aware that only through a force of his will does it stay in the air. When Dave and Morley got married, Dave's friend Dorothy suggested the minister change the marriage vow for Dave, from "in sickness and in health" to "in sickness and in remission."

Funny, said Dave, very funny. He couldn't help what his mind did with a list of symptoms.

The cancer, as he had come to think of it, preyed on his mind all day. By closing time, he had decided to treat it symptomatically, like a pimple. If it wasn't better by the time Morley got back, he'd go to the doctor. He wasn't going to show it to Morley. She wouldn't take it seriously.

He had planned to hang around until closing. He had

planned to ask Debbie out for a drink. Instead, he asked her about the blemish.

"Do you think this is skin cancer?" he said.

She looked at Dave and then at the spot on his face. Then she laughed and said, "Oh, yeah. All the skin cancers I've seen started out like that."

Dave left at six. Alone.

He went to Lawlor's drugstore and picked up a tube of Clearasil. As he headed toward the cash register, he looked around to see if he knew anyone. He felt like he was buying a pack of condoms, and he wanted to do it privately. He walked around to make sure he was safe.

His heart froze when he saw the blood-pressure chair. It was in the corner at the back of the store. Over the years Dave had had his blood pressure tested on a number of occasions. Dr. Freeberg had always reported a more or less normal reading. Dave suspected that these normal readings were not an accurate reflection of reality. They were always taken after he had been left in the waiting room for twenty, thirty minutes. Why shouldn't he be relaxed? He suspected that the normal readings were, in all likelihood, abnormal. Sometimes, when he was upset, he felt his blood pounding in his ears. Surely that wasn't normal. He decided his blood pressure was variable and dependent on stimuli beyond his control. He had never had an opportunity to check his theory.

That was why the chair terrified him. It was one thing to suspect you had high blood pressure. It was another thing to know it. Dave didn't want his body to know its own blood pressure. He didn't want his body to be given strategic information at the cellular level that it could use against him. He suspected that if his body knew how close it was to making the leap from borderline to hypertense, it would abandon everything else—all the various viruses and bacteria—and launch a frontal assault on his circulatory system.

The blood-pressure machine looked like a self-service electric chair. There was a slot on the armrest to slip your arm through, and a cuff that presumably inflated when you started the machine.

Dave was aware that if he sat down and surrendered his arm to the machine, horrible things could happen. Someone who knew him could waltz in as the machine was printing his score. The idea of Dorothy Capper knowing that his diastolic blood pressure was north of 180 horrified Dave more than the implications of the information. He knew it didn't make sense, but he felt that if no one, including him, knew what his blood pressure was, then it didn't count. It was like cheating on a diet.

There was a stack of instruction pamphlets beside the machine. Dave slipped one into his pocket. He didn't read it until he was out on the street. It opened up a whole new realm of possibilities, including step-by-step instructions of what he should do if his reading was zero over zero. Something even Dave had not imagined. He forgot about Debbie Anderson. He went out to supper; then, instead of going home, he went back to the drugstore and cruised by the chair the way he had cruised by Renee Atwater's house when he was a teenager. He felt the same way. Oppressed, anxious, hopeful, hopeless.

Just thinking about the chair raised his blood pressure. He knew he was going to try it. He knew he wouldn't be able to stop himself. He knew he was doomed. He also knew he would have to try it when there was no possibility of anyone seeing him.

He decided early morning would be best.

The drugstore opened at nine.

Two days later, Dave showed up ten minutes before opening time.

He waited on the far side of the street.

He felt like a bank robber.

When they unlocked the doors, he was the first person in the store. It couldn't take over a minute to do the test, he thought. He could be gone before anyone saw him. He went right to the chair. He rolled up his sleeve. He sat down. He put his arm through the metal slot. He pushed the large green button that said BEGIN TEST. He felt the rubber cuff inflate and tighten around his forearm.

He felt his heart pounding.

And then he felt an excruciating pain run down his arm.

Sweet Jesus. He was having a heart attack.

The machine was squeezing him tighter than he thought it should. Surely it shouldn't feel like this. Surely it shouldn't hurt.

He tried to pull his arm out of the cuff.

It wouldn't come.

He pulled again.

Still it wouldn't budge.

He looked at the black screen. It was like the screen on a bank machine. It began flashing his score in bright red numbers: 130/75. Not bad. Better than he had thought. Well, within normal limits.

Okay, thought Dave. Now let me go. But it didn't. It wouldn't.

Dave felt panic surge through him. He was trapped in the chair. He pulled again, more vigorously this time. Still nothing. He looked at the screen. His blood pressure had risen to 135/78.

He tried to relax.

Then he jerked his arm violently.

Still nothing.

Now his blood pressure was 140/80. That was borderline hypertense.

Oh God, he thought. This is crazy. He tried to calm himself again. He sat for a full minute without moving. He tried to figure out what was wrong. Something had happened to the machine. The rubber cuff would not deflate. And until it deflated, the metal slot that was holding his arm to the chair would not release him. Maybe there's some button I'm supposed to push, he thought. Maybe there's a release button somewhere.

He couldn't see a release button. He pulled his arm again. Still nothing. He didn't know what to do. Collect your thoughts, Dave. What is the worst thing that could happen?

Someone could see him. Someone he knew could see him.

No. The store could catch fire.

He wondered if he could stand up and hump his way out of the store with the chair attached to him. He imagined getting as far as the checkout counter and then getting wedged in the aisle by the cash register. He thought of dying of smoke inhalation by the cash register, with a blood-pressure chair attached to his back like a tortoise's shell. It was the kind of trivial death that Dave had always feared. Like being hit by a diaper truck. The kind of death after which his friends would gather quietly in some solemn funeral parlor until someone started to giggle. He didn't want people giggling at his funeral. He wanted a death with dignity.

He began to struggle so violently that the chair started rocking.

He heard a man's voice say, "What's going on over there?"

Dave looked at the screen. The red numbers were blinking

like the clock on a broken VCR. Except they were ascending. His blood pressure had sailed through borderline and was now firmly entrenched in hypertense: 160/93.

Dave looked up and saw Doug Lawlor, the pharmacist, heading toward him.

To his horror, behind Doug, he saw Debbie Anderson.

He felt his heart accelerate.

He glanced at the screen: 172/90.

This was a nightmare. He had the blood pressure of a seventy-five-year-old man.

He twisted desperately in the chair and reached for the screen with his left hand, trying to cover the blinking red numbers the way a man caught outside his house with no clothes on might cover his groin. He felt naked, exposed, humiliated. Debbie and Doug Lawlor arrived at the chair at the same time.

"Hi," said Dave, smiling weakly, still trying to cover the screen. "I'm stuck. I can't get my arm out."

Doug was staring at Dave as if he had asked for spare change.

"See," Dave said, rattling his arm. "It won't come out."

He could feel the blood pounding in his ears.

He felt like he was going to faint.

I am not going to faint, he said to himself.

"Hi, Dave," said Debbie cheerily. Then she said, "Your nose is bleeding."

Dave's left hand involuntarily flew away from the screen. He brought it up to his face, and when he took it away, he saw blood on his fingers.

And then everyone turned simultaneously from his red hand to the red numbers blinking on the now uncovered screen. The numbers reminded Dave of the digital displays

in an elevator. Sadly, the elevator was going up. The three of
them watched the screen blink from 172 up to 181.

"Geez, Dave," said Doug Lawlor. "Are you okay?"

"I can't get my arm out," said Dave for the third time.

He felt a drop of blood land in his lap.

"I'll get you some Kleenex," said Debbie.

The fire department arrived forty-five minutes later. By then
Dave's blood pressure had settled at 178/95.

"Geez," said the fire chief, looking at the screen. "Are you
okay?"

The drugstore had taken on the festive feel of an accident
scene. There were about fifteen people standing in a circle
around the chair. Every few minutes someone new arrived.
There was a blush of whispering as they asked what was
going on.

After twenty more minutes of fiddling with the chair, the
chief sent a man out to the truck to get the jaws of life. They
were going to cut Dave out.

"Wait a minute," said Doug Lawlor. "You're going to wreck
the chair."

"For Pete's sake, Doug," said Dave. "I'll pay for it. Just get
me out of here."

It took five minutes. Everyone applauded when Dave stood
up. He rubbed his arm carefully and said he was fine and
looked at his watch and said he had to go. People slapped
him on the back as he pushed through the crowd, as if he had
just won a race or something.

Debbie Anderson said, "I'll see you Wednesday."

Dave's family came back two nights later. He drove out to
the airport to pick them up. He left the headlights on in the
parking garage, and by the time they had corralled their suit-

cases and gone to the washroom and everyone got out to the car, the battery was dead. It took Dave half an hour to find someone to give them a jump.

After they got the kids to bed, Dave said to Morley, "I have something to tell you. Something you better hear from me."

He never took Debbie Anderson out to dinner. He still liked her, but he felt old whenever she was around. The red blemish on his face disappeared a week after Morley got home. He never mentioned it.

Burd

Early on a Saturday morning in May, Dave slipped out of his house while his family was still asleep. He was wearing a faded green sweatshirt, jeans with a rip at the right knee, and sneakers with no laces. He hadn't shaved. He closed the door carefully behind him so he wouldn't wake anyone and surveyed his backyard. The morning light was soft and silky, lending a yellow wash to the greenery of the garden. But Dave was more interested in the hedge in the shadows than he was in the rest of the garden. He stared at the hedge for a few minutes, and then he walked toward the bird feeder in the centre of the backyard. When he got to the feeder, he stood on his toes and peered over the lip. There was a yogurt lid in the far corner. He brushed the birdseed away from the edge of the lid. Then he picked up the lid and carried it carefully to the picnic table by the fence. He dumped the contents of the lid onto the table and sat down. He was looking at a pile of mealworms about the size of a hockey puck. He frowned as he pushed at them with his finger. He counted the worms carefully . . . thirty-three, thirty-four, thirty-five, thirty-six. The exact number he had put out the night before when he came home from work.

"Damn," he said. He shovelled the worms onto the ground with the lid. One of them landed in the V between two seat

87

planks. He tried to pick the worm out and then, thinking he might squish it, he went back inside and got a pencil and used it to work the worm carefully along the groove. He didn't want squished worm on his hands.

He went back inside, made coffee, and took the newspaper upstairs to bed. Arthur, the dog, who was splayed out on the couch, opened one eye to watch him pass and then fell back asleep.

———

Dave and Morley gave the bird feeder to Stephanie last Christmas. Who knows? They thought it might distract her— get her involved in the greater world around her. It was an unqualified failure. When she opened it on Christmas morning, Stephanie squinted at the bird feeder, frowned, then checked the gift tag. "Is this a mistake?" she asked, without a trace of enthusiasm.

So it was Dave who ended up assembling the feeder and it was Dave who filled it each day. Every day through the dark mornings of January and February, when the snow and ice were piled up in all the provinces, it was Dave who beat the path from the back door to the bird feeder on the pole in the centre of his backyard.

At first the only birds interested in his efforts were a thuggish gang of sparrows. They flung Dave's birdseed onto the ground, where it was pecked over by a bunch of pigeons. The pigeons had begun to hang out under the feeder like a squad of squeegee kids.

"It's more like a shelter for the homeless than a bird feeder," said Morley.

The only member of the family who displayed any real passion for the feeder was the cat. Galway spent hours perched on the kitchen radiator, her face against the back window, her tail twitching in frustrated concentration. There were not only birds to lust after but squirrels, too.

The squirrels appeared on Boxing Day, an hour after Dave got the feeder up. They spent the week between Christmas and New Year's trying to shinny around the squirrel guard. They would get halfway up the pole and then drop to the ground like plates of china. One by one they gave up, leaving the only squirrel who was not a quitter. If anything, its determination grew. Having failed from below, it shifted strategy and began hurling itself at the feeder from rooftops, the fence, a tree, and Dave's television antenna.

Dave would be washing the dishes, and there would be a blur of grey in his peripheral vision, and he would turn just in time to see the squirrel ricochet off the barbecue. Galway studied each of its attempts with the intensity of a general studying military history.

One afternoon Dave and Galway watched the squirrel haul itself, upside down, along the clothesline—paw over paw to within a few feet of the feeder before it lost its grip, hung from the line for a moment by one leg like a doomed mountain climber, and let go, its tail flailing in the air as it tried to right itself for landing. As it dropped, Galway, who was sitting in Dave's lap, dug her claws into his leg. Dave flew out of the chair, unsure if Galway's reflex was in sympathy for the squirrel or out of the forlorn realization that this, too, was a lost opportunity.

"Wouldn't it be simpler," said Morley one lunchtime as the squirrel bounced off their compost bin, "to take the winter off? Isn't hibernation an option?"

In the New Year, Dave added a blue jay and a Junco, and then a gang of chickadees and some birds who seemed to be travelling with them. But the vast flocks he had imagined filling his backyard were avoiding it. Short of amusing the cat, the feeder seemed to be filling no real need in the universe— and certainly none in the bird universe.

Then, on a chilly grey Saturday in the middle of the month, something came. Dave pointed it out to everyone at lunch.

"Over there," he said. "See. In the Lowbeers' pine tree."

No one was particularly interested.

It was not a big bird—not as big as a robin—with olive green above its wings and dull yellow below. It seemed to favour the evergreen hedge that bordered their backyard. It would flick out of this thicket and peck at the seeds in the feeder tray, then vanish into the hedge again.

Dave watched it for a week before he asked Gerta Low-beer if she knew what kind of bird it was. Gerta brought over her three bird books and her binoculars. She said, "It looks like a tanager. A female summer tanager. But a summer tanager is not supposed to come this far north." Gerta's finger was moving along the small print of her bird book. "In January a summer tanager is supposed to be on a beach in Mexico or Brazil."

Dave was watching his bird through Gerta's binoculars. He had never seen it so close. It had a stubby bill, almost swollen—not pointy, like a robin's.

"And it shouldn't eat seeds," said Gerta. "A tanager eats insects and wasps. It's a carnivore."

When Gerta left, Dave put out a few pieces of tangerine. The sort of thing you might expect to eat if you were used to wintering in Brazil. Then he drove to a pet store to see if he could buy his bird some insects and wasps. He settled for a bag of crickets.

The bird fell on the crickets as if she hadn't seen a decent meal in months. That bird was starving, thought Dave. For two hours straight, she flicked back and forth from the hedge like windshield wipers. But as happy as she seemed with the crickets, Dave could see that they weren't going down easily. She was having trouble with the shells.

It was now a quarter to six.

Dave returned to the pet store and came back with a bag of mealworms. He set them on the counter and wondered how he was going to get them to the feeder. The idea of dipping his hands into the seething bag revolted him. He tried a pair of Morley's oven mitts, but they were too large and clumsy to work with. He imagined sucking them up with the turkey baster, and experimented with the barbecue tongs. He settled on the flour scoop.

The bird didn't stop eating until nine-thirty that night. She's going to be sick, thought Dave.

Then he looked at his nearly empty bag of mealworms and thought, I'm going to be eaten out of house and home by a bird.

He went back to the pet store first thing in the morning.

When he came home at supper, only half the worms he had put out that morning had been eaten. The rest were frozen to the feeder.

It took only a few days for the bird to train Dave.

By the end of the week, they had worked out a routine that seemed effective. A scoop of worms at breakfast, a scoop of worms at lunch, and a scoop of worms at dinner. It meant Dave had to come home at noon.

"I don't mind," he said.

And he didn't. He would fix soup and cheese, or a sandwich, and would sit at the table and watch his bird through the sliding glass doors that led out to the backyard.

She was not a spectacular bird; she didn't have the blood reds of a cardinal or the rich yellows of a fall warbler. On dull days she almost looked dingy. But in some lights, she was beautiful. If the sun was low and the light warm, she would glow with a reddy hue. Almost gold.

Usually, she spent only a moment or two on the feeder, preferring, it seemed, to eat her worms in the obscurity of the hedge, but one sunny afternoon she sat on the feeder for nearly five minutes, looking around and singing softly.

Dave knew that if Gerta was right, the bird would die if he stopped feeding it. By February he had bought so many mealworms that the pet store was giving him a discount. He felt a sense of pride about what he was doing—he felt honoured that the bird had chosen him.

———

It was not long after Valentine's Day when Gerta mentioned the bird to her friend Nick, who, she said, was a bit of a birder. She brought Nick over that evening so he could see it for himself. Nick watched for half an hour and said, "I'm not sure. Do you mind if I call my friend Bob?"

Bob was there in under an hour. He was wearing camouflage pants and a heavy sweater with a high neck. He was carrying a pair of binoculars in a canvas shoulder sack. He took one look at Dave's bird and asked if he could use the telephone. He didn't even use his binoculars.

"I'm phoning from Toronto," he said into the phone, his right foot bouncing up and down excitedly. "I'm in some guy's kitchen." He smiled at Dave, then looked at him quizzically. "About fifteen minutes from downtown. Right?"

Dave nodded.

"You aren't going to believe this," he said into the phone. *"Summer* tanager."

When he hung up, he turned and smiled at Dave and Sam. "That's the bird of the winter you've got there." He pulled out *his* bird book—the *National Geographic Field Guide to the Birds of North America*—and flipped it open and pointed at a picture. Dave peered at the page and nodded.

The man said, "There are a few of my friends who would love to see it. Would that be okay?"

———

Morley came home at seven.

"Guess what we have in the backyard," said Sam.

"What?" said Morley, throwing groceries on the kitchen counter.

Sam looked at Dave.

"What?" said Morley.

"The bird in the backyard," said Dave. "The one I've been feeding worms . . ."

"It's *cosmic,*" said Sam.

"It's a summer tanager," said Dave.

———

That night as Morley was brushing her teeth, Dave said, "Some people might drop by in the morning."

"Who?" said Morley.

"To look at the bird," said Dave.

"What bird?" said Morley.

"The bird I feed the mealworms to," said Dave. "It's supposed to winter in Brazil."

"It chose our backyard over Brazil?"

"So people want to see it," said Dave, "because it's a rarity. It'll be okay. These are birders we're talking about—nice people."

"I don't want people poking around our backyard in the morning," said Morley. "Can't they wait until the weekend?"

———

It was so early that the sun wasn't up when Dave heard the noise. He listened for a moment and then he thought, Raccoons. And he went back to sleep.

When he woke the second time, Arthur was beside the bed, whingeing—padding to the window and back again. Raccoons aren't that noisy, thought Dave dimly. Then it dawned on him: Someone was stealing the bikes. He leaped out of bed and opened the curtains and squinted into the backyard. There was a smudge of grey on the horizon. When his eyes focused, he gasped and stepped back from the window and said, "Sweet Jesus on a bicycle."

There were maybe fifty motionless men lined up in the shadows behind his house—strung out along the alley, leaning over his back fence, and scanning his backyard with large binoculars. Dave inched forward and peeked out again. Then he pulled the curtains shut and sat on the edge of his bed.

"Houston," he said softly, "we have a problem."

Morley mumbled and rolled over. Dave said, "Don't wake up. I need a plan before you wake up."

He wasn't saying these things out loud. He was saying these things in his head. It was the closest he had come to prayer since last Christmas morning when he defrosted the turkey with the hair dryer.

He needed to wake up. "Coffee," he said prayerfully.

It was only when Dave was downstairs, standing in the middle of the brightly lit kitchen, scratching, that the enormity of his problem struck him. As far as the fifty men in his backyard were concerned, he was standing on a spotlit stage. He stopped scratching. Then he turned off the kitchen light.

It was six-forty-five A.M.

Fifteen minutes later, Sam's clock radio snapped on. Here we go, thought Dave. Liftoff. He was sitting at the kitchen table, not sure what he should do. Before he could do anything, the phone rang. It was Carl Lowbeer.

"Dave," he said. He was whispering. "There is something terrible going on outside."

Not as terrible, however, as what was going on at the Turlingtons'. Two doors down, at the Turlingtons' house, Mary, Bert, and the Turlington twins were lying on the floor of Mary and Bert's bedroom with their hands over the heads.

At six-fifty-five A.M., Rachel, one of the twins, had looked out her bedroom window to see if it was good snowball snow. When Rachel saw the men with the binoculars, she ran to her parents' bed and said, "The house is surrounded by police. I think it's the swap team."

Bert, who is not what you'd call a morning person, nearly stroked out when he saw the men in the dark jackets with their binoculars trained at his kids' window. His first thought was the carpet installers who had been accidentally shot dead through their motel-room door by overzealous police in the Eastern Townships of Quebec. It was a case of mistaken identity—as this obviously was, too. Bert dropped to the floor and crawled around his house, waking everyone up.

"We're surrounded," he said. "Get into our bedroom. Fast."

And now the whole family was there except for Bert's fifteen-year-old son, Adam, who had locked himself into the upstairs bathroom. Bert wormed his way into the hall and pounded on the door.

"What are you doing?" he howled.

Adam, who had never got up so fast in his life, was desperately trying to flush the first marijuana he had ever bought down the toilet. He had bought it three weeks before from a kid at school. Afraid to smoke it, he had hidden it in an old pair of sneakers in the back of his closet. Now the marijuana kept floating to the top of the toilet. And the police were here to arrest him.

Bert inched his way back to the bedroom and pulled himself up to the window to peer over the sill. There were cars everywhere, parked on both sides of the street and pulled up onto the sidewalk. Bert's heart was pounding. There were men who looked like they were carrying telescopes running down Dave's driveway toward his backyard.

High-powered rifles, thought Bert.

The Lowbeers' dog was barking.

A man came running out of Dave's yard and pointed directly at Bert's house. Bert gasped and dropped to the floor.

"Blessed Mother of Mercy," he said. "We are going to die."

————

Twenty minutes later, Dave was still trying to explain things to the neighbours standing on his lawn.

"It was announced on some birders' hotline," Dave was saying, when there was a sudden commotion at the Turlingtons' house.

Dave stopped talking, and everyone turned just as the Turlingtons' front door flew open and the entire Turlington family burst out of the house. They had wrapped themselves in a large white sheet and were moving down their sidewalk like a bunch of Shriners in a horse costume. They all had their heads low, even Bert, who was leading the way, waving his hands in the air and screaming, "Don't shoot! Don't shoot!"

Arthur, sitting at Dave's side, began to bark furiously and pull on his leash.

————

That night at eleven-thirty, Dave was standing on a ladder in his kitchen, tacking a sheet over the sliding glass door in the kitchen.

"It'll be over soon," he said to Morley. "There can't be that many birders in the city."

The phone rang at midnight.

Dave and Morley stared at each other.

Dave picked it up.

"Yes?" he said.

There was a pause, and he said it again, "Yes."

Then again.

"Yes."

And again.

Then he said, "You're welcome," and he hung up.

"Who was that?" said Morley.

"Some guy from Halifax asking if the bird is still here."

"Halifax," said Morley.

"He said he'd be up on the weekend. He said he heard it was a mega-twitch."

———

The next morning Arthur began barking at six-thirty. When Dave opened the door to pick up the paper, two men passed him on their way down his driveway toward his backyard.

"Morning," they said in unison.

"Morning," said Dave.

It rained on Friday. One of those unpleasant February rain-storms.

When Dave lifted the sheet in the kitchen to look outside, there was a group of seven men standing in his driveway star-ing back at him balefully. They were looking at his coffee. He let the sheet drop. "It's not my fault it's raining," he muttered.

———

Saturday morning at nine-thirty, when Dave came down-stairs, there were already fifteen people outside. Sam was heading out the front door with a hammer and a large piece of cardboard.

"Where are you going?" said Dave.

Sam stopped. As he flipped over his sign, he dropped the hammer. SEE THE BURD, it said in large hand-painted letters. Under the writing was an arrow that Dave assumed would soon point down his driveway.

"We're going to sell hot chocolate," said Sam.

By ten o'clock there were close to a hundred people milling around Dave's house. Arthur was beside himself. He spent the morning throwing himself around the house, barking from window to window. By eleven o'clock he was getting hoarse.

"Shut up, Arthur," said Dave.

Even though all the birders were within twenty yards of the bird feeder, they had ringed it with binoculars and telescopes, many on tripods. One man was peering through a camera with a lens as big as a toilet bowl.

At noon, when Dave stepped outside with fresh worms, he heard someone whisper, "Feeding time." He sensed the crowd stirring. He felt like an aquarium showman. Maybe, he thought sourly, he should climb onto the feeder and hold the worms between his lips so the bird could pluck them out on the fly.

After lunch Dave watched a woman pushing a man up his driveway in a wheelchair. The man had an IV drip in his arm. The couple were arguing. When she got him to the end of the driveway, the woman stormed to her car and drove away without looking back.

––––––––

Early on Sunday a man arrived in an airport limousine, ran into the backyard, saw the bird, jumped back in the limousine, and headed back in the direction he came from. He never even closed his door. The limousine never shut off its motor.

"Not unusual," said an older man near the end of the day. Dave recognized him as one of the group who had been standing in his driveway the morning it rained. He was wearing sneakers and a rumpled canvas hat. He gestured over his shoulder where the limousine had been.

"We call them twitchers," he said. "When they get close to whatever bird it is they're trying to add to their list, and they aren't sure if they're going to see it or not, they start to twitch."

It was getting chilly. Only this man and Dave were left in the driveway.

"They can pretty much tell as they drive up the street," said the old man. "If everyone is looking through their binoculars, then they know they're all right. They can relax. But if people are walking around . . . that's when they start to twitch. Because they know as soon as they get out of their car, someone is going to say, 'She was here two minutes ago, but you missed her.' "

"You watch her long enough," said Dave, "and you get to know her habits."

"She likes to fly in from the right," said the old man.

"Out of the hedge," said Dave. "She comes every fifteen minutes or so."

As they stood watching, the little bird flicked out of the hedge and landed on the feeder. She looked around rapidly, knocked back a few worms, and flew off.

"She feeds more in the morning," said Dave.

The old man nodded.

The bird flew back.

"This is a crippling view," said the man.

"Would you like to come in?" said Dave. "Have a coffee?"

The man held out his hand. "My name is Norm," he said.

It was like that for three weeks. But instead of trailing off, it got worse. Someone from one of the television stations did a feature on Dave's bird. The following weekend, when Morley was coming home from grocery-shopping, she was stopped by a policeman a block from her home. "You can't go down that street," said the cop. "Some idiot put up signs all over the place about a rare bird."

"But I live down there," said Morley.

The cop waved her through. There were cars parked everywhere and people walking in the middle of the road.

Sam was standing at the front door. He was wearing a pair of oven mitts that made his hands look ridiculously large.

"We dropped a pot of hot chocolate on the stove," he said. "It put the flame out, and the stove won't go on again. It smells of gas."

That was the weekend when people who weren't even interested in birds started coming. They wanted to be there because they had heard a lot of other people had been there, and they didn't want to miss anything.

One of the men who had come in from the suburbs chewed Dave out. "It doesn't look so special to me," he said. "I drove all the way from Brampton. It's not like it's an eagle or anything. I'll bet that bird has never killed anything in its life."

The second time that happened, Dave called the hotline and said, "The bird has gone. Could you take it off your list, please."

Then he went outside and took down Sam's sign and put up a new one. THE BIRD HAS GONE, it read.

That was at the end of March. The bird hadn't left, of course. Dave continued to feed her three times a day. He spent over two hundred dollars on mealworms during the winter. He came to know her well.

She was a woodland bird in the middle of the city, way off course, and she had landed at *his* feeder. He felt proud that he had seen her through the frigid months, that he had kept her alive. He felt affection for her. He felt that she belonged to him somehow. He knew this was sentimentality. He knew the bird didn't feel anything about him. If anything, he was just another intruder in the backyard, and God knows there were enough of those.

———

But on that fresh, soft morning in May, when Dave slipped into his backyard and counted the worms and found none missing, he knew she was gone, and he felt sad—although he realized the bird had probably migrated and that was the best thing for her.

Some of the birders told him they thought she had been blown north in a storm. But the old guy, Norm, who had come in for coffee, said he didn't accept that theory. He said sometimes something happens to a bird's wiring and it shows up in the wrong place. He said that birds who show up in wrong places have a way of doing it again.

So Dave sat in bed with the unread paper beside him early on that quiet Saturday morning and wondered if maybe he would see his bird again in the fall. He imagined that whatever else she had felt, she had felt a sense of home. She could have left anytime she wanted. And now she had. Just like everyone who has ever had a home, she had followed that universal urge to leave.

Dave picked up the paper. Then he put it down and got out of bed and stared out the window. He was thinking of the mysteries of migration. He was thinking that of all the mysteries, maybe the one true thing we know and share with the animals was this sense of seeking, finding, leaving, but above all, of returning home.

Emil

It was the mulberry spring. The spring the mulberries were fatter and juicier than anyone remembered. The sidewalk under the mulberry tree on the corner was stained deep purple for weeks. The birds got fat. Three times, Morley sent Sam out with a chair and a bowl. Three times in two weeks, she baked mulberry pie, the juices bubbling over the piecrust like wine.

It was the spring when rain only came at night. The spring of damp earth and blue skies. The spring of fat worms.

It was the spring when gardening became so popular that even criminals got into it.

"I don't believe it," said Morley, standing on her front lawn, waving at her garden. "They took two ornamental cabbages, my hens-and-chickens, and the smoke bush. I loved that smoke bush." She was pointing at the hole between the forsythia and the Siberian iris. "It was purple. My aunt Muriel has a huge one in her backyard."

Each plant had been excised with medical precision. Morley kicked the only thing that the thief had left behind, a melon-sized pile of earth on the edge of the lawn where the roots had been shaken clean. Whoever it was had made off with everything, roots and all.

"Surely," she said, "surely, you would notice someone

walking down the street with a smoke bush. Do you think we should call the police?"

When someone you love is upset enough to suggest calling the police over a missing smoke bush, you have two choices. You can, if you don't care how the rest of the day goes, say, "The plant police? We should phone the plant police? Are you out of your mind?" Or you can muster as much affection as possible and say, as Dave did, "You stay with the plants. I'll call the police." Then you go inside and stand in the kitchen for what feels like the appropriate amount of time before you come back outside and lie. You say, "They are sending out a car. And if they see *anyone* with a smoke bush, they are going to stop them. On the spot." Dave considered adding something about how they were going to check the florists in the area, but the thing about a successful lie is not going too far.

——————

That night, as she sat in bed with gardening magazines fanned around her like playing cards, Morley said, "I'm going to get him." She meant the thief.

It took her three weeks.

She got lucky one night. She woke up at three-fifteen A.M. and couldn't get back to sleep. It was hot, and she was restless, and because she didn't want to wake Dave, she got out of bed and wandered absentmindedly to the window. It was a beautiful night. The moon was shining, and the white flowers of the nicotiana held her eye. The small fragrant petals, outdone in the light of day, were radiant in the moonlight.

"To every thing," said Morley.

She frowned. Something was bothering her. Gradually, she became aware of what it was. There was movement across the street. Someone was on their hands and knees in the Schellenbergers' garden. And it wasn't Betty Schellenberger.

When you witness a crime in progress in the middle of the night, the only thing to do is to phone the police. Unless, of course, instead of being in the hands of reason, you are in hands that control more satisfying emotions—like rage and revenge. If you are being moved by hands of rage, you grab your robe, and one of your socks, and one of your husband's socks, and you pull on the mismatched socks as you hop-skip toward the stairs, and you race out the front door in the frayed robe that you would never, under ordinary circumstances, wear outside, and you dash across the street into your neighbour's yard without stopping to think.

Morley stormed into the Schellenbergers' garden. When she saw the man on his hands and knees digging up Betty Schellenberger's gold-flame spirea, she stopped dead. She thought, I should have woken Dave.

The man must have heard her, because without warning, he stood up, whirled around, and gasped. He looked frighteningly like Rasputin—bearded and dirty, wild and crazy. He took a step toward Morley, but she stood her ground, her hands folded across her chest, holding her robe closed.

"Hello, Emil," she said. "I see you're doing some gardening."

Emil began breathing rapidly, panting almost. Wringing his hands as if washing them. "I am going on vacation," he panted. "I am going to . . . Greece. Have you ever been to Greece? They have castles there. I am going on a charter flight, but it will be safe because they line the planes with lead. Before, they didn't, and the rays got you and that's how you got cancer. Did you know that? Eh? Did you know that?"

Morley had met Emil three years before. He showed up one morning in front of her husband's record store wearing a pair of ripped pants and slippers and stood on the sidewalk for two weeks.

"He's making me crazy," said Dave. "He's driving away business."

"He is *not* driving away business," said Morley.

"I've asked him to go somewhere else," said Dave. "But he's back every day. He can't just stand around on the street like that."

Morley looked at her husband carefully. "Why not?" she said.

Emil had appeared at a bad time. He had appeared only a week after the notorious Flick Lady had disappeared from the neighbourhood.

The Flick Lady had marched into Woodsworth's bookstore out of the blue one day, gone to the history section, and begun flicking the covers of all the political biographies, snapping her finger on the jacket photos and making her disgust clear with each flick: *yech, yech, yech.* After two minutes she walked out of the store. She did this every afternoon, usually between two and three.

Dave tried to convince Dorothy, who owned Woodsworth's, that the Flick Lady was harmless. And probably politically sophisticated. He held his position until she added the Vinyl Cafe to her afternoon rounds. The Flick Lady came into Dave's record store one afternoon and picked up an album and held it to her chest as she sang a tuneless rendition of "Downtown." After three months of these daily visits, she stopped as mysteriously as she had started. Disappeared. But now there was this man. Standing in front of his store like a rain cloud.

———

One morning at breakfast, Morley said, "What is his name?"

Dave was holding up a jar of peach jam, squinting at the list of ingredients. He said, "What?"

Morley said, "The man on the sidewalk with the pants. What's his name?"

Dave said, "I have no idea. What is pectin, anyway?"

Morley was pouring herself a cup of coffee. "Don't worry," she said, "it's natural." She reached out and took the jar from Dave and made him look at her. "You can't expect him to listen to you if you don't even know his name, Dave. You should introduce yourself."

And that was how Morley came to know the name of the man in the Schellenbergers' garden. Emil.

After Dave had introduced himself, Emil had moved across the street. For the past two years, he had sat in the stairwell next door to the Heart of Christ Religious Supplies and Fax Services. The stairwell had become his place in the world. And slowly, he had become part of Dave and Morley's world, too. They didn't know where he slept, but they knew before he slept, he went to Beaver electronics and watched television on the set in the store window. He liked baseball games. He owned a universal remote control and could change the channels. And he would raise the volume loud enough to hear the games through the window.

The first time Morley gave Emil money—she gave him five dollars—Emil said, "That's too much." He gave her two dollars' change.

Other times he wouldn't take her money. "I don't need it," he would say. "I have enough. I have enough."

Sometimes he was too agitated to speak. Morley would see Emil standing on a corner somewhere, his shirt out, his belly showing, the bottom of his pants ripped and grubby. He would be lost in some world, staring at his feet, talking to himself. He wouldn't even notice her. Other times he would see Morley coming and would brighten and say hello as if they were old friends, as if he had been waiting for her.

When Morley tried to give Emil food, he wouldn't take it. The first time he said, "I can't take your sandwich."

Morley said, "Well, I'm not hungry." She put the sandwich she had bought for him on top of the newspaper box on the corner. When she came back an hour later, it was gone.

––––––––

One day Emil showed up at the Vinyl Cafe with a shopping cart full of books. They were old library books he had bought for twenty-five cents each at a library sale: maths texts, novels by unknown authors, books of language instruction, romances.

"If you want to take out a book," said Emil, "you have to take out a membership."

Dave had been spending the morning slipping 45-rpm records into plastic envelopes that said VINYL CAFE on them in large red letters. Underneath, in blue lowercase, it said, "We may not be big, but we're small." Dave had thousands of 45s, and normally, he didn't pay much attention to them. He sold them like vegetables. There was a roll of plastic bags on the wall near the bin of records. You would put five 45s in a bag for ninety-nine cents. But he had been slowly working his way through the bins, pulling out the good ones, struck by the wonderful artwork on the labels: the flowing silver script on the Mercury label, the fat happy letters on the Dot.

When Emil walked in, Dave had just picked up "California Dreamin' " by the Mamas and the Papas. The moment he saw the record, he remembered that he owed Denny Doherty three hundred dollars. He was wondering if Denny remembered the weekend he had lent Dave the money. They had gone to Jamaica with Carl Wilson. Or was it Mustique with Al Jardine? Carl or Al? That was what he was thinking when Emil walked in and said, "If you want to take out a book, you have to take out a membership."

Dave slipped the record under the counter, separate from the others, and said, "How much? How much is a membership in your library, Emil?"

Emil shook his head and laughed. "Don't be crazy, Dave. Everyone knows libraries are free." He said it as if he were talking to a child.

Dave wrote his name and address on a piece of paper Emil tore out of his book. Dave picked three books out of the shopping cart, and Emil said, "You can't take out more than two books at once, Dave."

Dave settled on a western and a high-protein cookbook called *Liver with Love.* He put the books in a drawer under the counter—or thought he did.

He forgot all about them until Emil appeared a month later and said, "Did you know your books are overdue? You owe five dollars in fines, you know."

Emil then reached into his jacket pocket and pulled out the piece of paper Dave had signed when he had joined his library. Dave stared dumbly at the paper, wondering where Emil had kept it for the month.

Dave said he was still reading the books and would pay the fines after he finished. He said, "Come back in a few days, Emil."

He looked for the books at home and again at the store, and then he had to admit to himself that he had probably lost them. It bothered him that Emil could keep track of the scrap of paper, and he couldn't keep track of the books. What bothered him even more was the disturbing feeling that he had lost something else—something he couldn't even remember losing.

Emil came back two more times, each time pushing the shopping cart. The first time he told Dave his fine was up to seven dollars; on the second visit, he said it was up to ten; and then, just as Dave had hoped, Emil forgot about the books and the fines.

———

Dave didn't believe in giving Emil money. He had argued with Morley about this.

"If he gets money," he said, "he buys cigarettes and lottery tickets. And I'm sure he loses the tickets. Why would you give someone money so he can throw it away on lottery tickets he's going to lose?"

"I don't care what he does with the money," Morley said. "He doesn't take it if he doesn't need it. Sometimes he won't take it."

Dave wasn't listening. He had suddenly remembered why losing Emil's books bothered him so much—remembered the object that had been gnawing at the edge of his consciousness. He had bought a lottery ticket the weekend the prize had gone over ten million dollars. And he had no idea where he had put it. He had read that it was not unusual for winning tickets to go unclaimed because people lost them. In the middle of his conversation with Morley, he abruptly turned and went downstairs and rummaged through the laundry hamper, knowing he was never going to find the ticket, wondering if it was one of the winners and exactly how much money he had thrown away.

———

And that was why Morley felt so let down last month as she stood on the Schellenbergers' lawn at three-fifteen in the morning—that of all people it would be Emil standing there with the Schellenbergers' gold-flame spirea at his feet.

Instead of getting angry, she said, "Is that for your garden, Emil?"

Emil said, "Did you know the moon is a hotbed of hostile alien activity?"

Morley wasn't falling for that. She said, "That's crazy talk, Emil. I want to know what you're going to do with that plant. Do you have a garden?"

Emil looked up at her, and for an instant he was clear and she could see him—the real person.

"Yes," he said softly.

"I want to see your garden," she said. "Will you show me your garden tomorrow?"

Emil blinked and said, "Oh." Then he hung his head and said, "Yes."

Morley drew her robe tighter around her and said, "Good night," and turned to walk across the street, noticing for the first time that she wasn't wearing shoes.

The next day at lunch, Morley went to the stairwell beside the Heart of Christ Religious Supplies and Fax Services.

"I have come to see your garden, Emil," she said.

"There," Emil replied.

He was pointing at one of the large concrete boxes lining the street. Sure enough, nestled around the trunk of the stunted ginkgo tree that the city planted, and occasionally watered, were Morley's hens-and-chickens.

"I have another box," said Emil.

"Near the TV store," said Morley.

"At night I take the plants with me," said Emil.

"You can keep your eye on them that way," said Morley.

"So no one can touch them," said Emil.

At supper that night, Morley told everyone what had happened to her plants.

"What would you do about that?" she asked.

Sam said, "Call the police. Call the police and send him to jail. He stole."

Stephanie said, "He's retarded—just take the plants back."

Dave said, "What *did* you do?"

Morley said, "The ornamental cabbages have aphids. I took him stuff for the aphids."

————

All June, Emil kept busy with his garden—moving his plants back and forth among various concrete boxes around the city. He moved the smoke bush twelve times. He carefully noted each move in his book.

The garden, however, was not the biggest thing that happened to Emil that spring. The biggest thing happened on the last Saturday of June, when Emil won the lottery, not the big prize, but big enough—ten thousand dollars.

Emil went to the lottery offices on Monday morning with Peter from the Laundromat where he had bought his ticket. But they wouldn't give him a cheque because he didn't have two pieces of identification.

"I don't want a cheque," said Emil. "I want the money."

It took several weeks for Emil to get a social security number. When he got it, he took it to the lottery office, and they gave him the cheque.

When he took the check to the bank, the teller, Kathy, took him into the manager's office and tried to talk him into opening an account. She said maybe it was not a wise decision to walk around with that much cash. "Why don't you take forty dollars?" she said. "You could come here anytime you wanted and get more money." All the time Emil was in the manager's office, the assistant manager was watching warily from the door.

It took Emil half an hour to convince them to give him his

money—they said they were worried that people would take advantage of him. He said he knew what he was going to do. He left at noon with ten thousand dollars in twenty-dollar bills. They put it in a vinyl burgundy pouch.

He took it to his spot in front of the Heart of Christ Religious Supplies and Fax Services, and he gave away seven thousand dollars—actually, he misplaced two thousand five hundred dollars, so he ended up giving away four thousand five hundred dollars. He had three thousand left at the end of the day.

He didn't hand the money to just anyone who walked by. He gave it to his regulars—people who gave *him* money. Or stopped to talk to him.

They were awkward transactions. Emil tried to slip them the money surreptitiously, the way you might tip a head-waiter who had led you to a good table. Most people didn't like being that close to Emil, and as he tried to give them the money, they would back away. When they realized what he was trying to do—*he was trying to give them money!*—every one of them tried to refuse it . . . backed away as if he were offering them a religious tract. But Emil was persistent.

He gave Morley five hundred dollars.

"It would have been patronizing not to take it," she told Dave. "It would have been an insult." They were across the street in the record store. "I had to take it. But I know what I'm going to do with it."

"What?" asked Dave.

"I'm going to give it back to him," said Morley, "bit by bit."

"It'll just go back to the lottery," said Dave.

"Dust to dust," said Morley. "It's his money."

As soon as Morley left, Dave phoned Dorothy.

"He gave me five hundred dollars," said Dorothy. "Kenny Wong got seven hundred and fifty."

Dave hung up and headed across the street. He was sure Emil would offer him money, too. After all, he had known him as long as anyone else. By the time he was out the door, he knew what he was going to do with his share. You could still find things that paid eight percent. If everyone did that, Emil could have fifty or sixty dollars a month.

Emil was standing in the middle of the sidewalk looking around as if he was supposed to meet someone; as if this person were late.

"Congratulations, Emil," said Dave. "I hear you're a big winner. When do I get my share?"

He meant it as a joke, but Emil took him seriously.

"No share for you, Dave," he said. "You still owe your library fine."

———————

Dave and Morley aren't sure what happened to the money Emil didn't give away. They know he had a haircut and a shave. He looked great for a week. So good that Dave didn't recognize him the first time he saw him. Emil bought himself a portable battery-powered television and a chair, and all July he sat on the chair in his stairwell and watched his TV. The chair was eventually stolen, and he lost the TV, or someone took it from him. Or maybe he gave it away.

Emil wasn't sure, when Morley asked him about it. "It's okay," he said. "The battery was going anyway, and it only got Canadian channels. You can't get cable on those small sets."

It was all gone by the end of July. Well, not all gone. Because Morley still had four hundred and twenty-five dollars that belonged to him. She kept it in a glass in the kitchen, in the back of the cupboard behind the canned soups. She had already given him fifty dollars in cash. Spent twenty on sandwiches and coffee, which she left on the newspaper box on the corner. And she bought some feverfew and gave it to him to plant in his box. It's an herb that looks like a daisy, and people say it can cure fevers—it's a pretty plant, and the leaves smell good when you work around them, and best of all, it seeds itself, which means it will grow again next summer. It would need to be tough to live in a concrete box all winter—along with the Coke bottles and the straws—but the feverfew is a tough little thing and not without dignity.

On the last weekend in September, Morley will spend another five dollars while she is grocery-shopping. She'll buy a box of grape hyacinth bulbs, and she will plant them one night when Emil has left—thinking as she scrapes at the hard dirt in Emil's box that they will sprout in the spring and surprise him.

When she finishes, she will lift the watering can she has carried all the way from home and drain the last of it onto the dry soil. Then she will button her sweater and set off down the street, savouring the thin chill of the night air, the feel of earth on her fingers.

The Birthday Party

On Thursday morning, on his way to work, Dave passed Emil standing in the doorway of the Heart of Christ Religious Supplies and Fax Services. Emil was rocking back and forth with a vacant expression until Dave said, "Hello," and Emil stopped rocking and cheerfully said, "Morning." Dave was headed across the street to his store. He was halfway there when he remembered he was supposed to buy a bottle of wine. He frowned and slowed down as he tried to remember why—there was an occasion, but he couldn't remember what it was. All he could remember was that he wanted to buy something special.

This had been happening frequently to Dave. Often in the morning as he was about to leave for work. One moment he'd be standing by the front door; the next, galloping up the stairs on some vitally important mission, the purpose of which escaped him once he was standing in the bedroom. All he could do was stand by his bureau like one of those poor dumb moose who wander into subdivisions, moving his eyes woefully around the room, looking for a clue to the urge that had sent him there.

The moose end up in the suburbs when a parasite moves into their brain. As far as Dave could figure, whatever had moved into *his* brain had been marching around with a clipboard and a ladder unscrewing lightbulbs. More than once, in the evenings, Dave had stood up abruptly—right in the middle of a television commercial—and walked into the den because . . . well, that was the problem. He couldn't remember why he was in the den. The dog followed Dave around at night—in case it might be time for a walk—so the two of them would stand there, Dave and the dog, both of them staring at Dave's desk with the same perplexed expression.

It was five past ten when Dave saw Emil and remembered that he was supposed to buy the wine. He hesitated in front of his record store. He couldn't remember what the wine was for, but maybe, he thought, he should go and buy it before he forgot altogether.

It was a fifteen-minute walk to the wine store. It was a beautiful morning. The idea of staying outside pleased Dave. The walk would do him good.

There were no other customers when he got there. Just three clerks leisurely restocking the shelves and chatting among themselves.

Dave was feeling pretty leisurely himself as he wandered around the aisles. He still couldn't remember why he wanted wine, so he read a lot of labels and, to be safe, chose four bottles—two white and two red. Two Canadian, a Californian cabernet, and an Australian merlot.

There were four cash registers at the front of the store, but nothing to indicate which one was open. There wasn't a clerk at any of them and no signs or gates to suggest a course of action. Dave chose the cash register nearest the door.

He set his four bottles of wine on the counter and got out his wallet and put down his credit card beside them. Sometimes when you aren't in a hurry, waiting can be a pleasant experience. An opportunity to prove how mellow you can be. Dave wasn't in a hurry. He thought of the different kinds of people who came into his record store. He was pleased that he hadn't begun tapping his credit card on the counter, or clearing his throat, or shuffling his feet, or any of the other irritating strategies customers resort to when they are trying to attract attention. By standing quietly at the counter, Dave was displaying his solidarity with his fellow retail workers. After a moment, his patience was rewarded. Dave saw one of the three clerks stand up. Then he watched the clerk languidly drift to the cash register farthest from where he was standing.

Dave didn't move.

The clerk looked over at him and, in a tone Dave would later describe as a combination of disinterest and aggression, said, "Over here."

Dave said, "I have four bottles of wine and my credit card. Could you come over to this one?"

The clerk shook his head. He said, "This is the one that's open."

Dave felt all the goodness that had accrued to him during the morning evaporate. He felt his mellowness fade away. Felt himself slip into an elbows-up mood. Indignant that he, of all people, should be treated like this. Dave felt himself switching from compatriot to customer. He heard himself say, "Well, I'll come back when *this* one is open." He walked out of the store and into the sunshine. He squinted at the men and women walking to and fro on both sides of the street, wishing they knew what he knew—what he had just done for them. He was feeling pretty darn good about himself. Pleased because the line had come out so fast, and pleased because he had not been rude, and pleased, most of all, because he had struck a blow for all customers looking for good service and courtesy. He didn't have the wine he had come for, but he had something else—a good feeling—and it stayed with him until he got a block and a half away from his record store.

It stayed until the little voice inside his head that had been so busy congratulating him suddenly said, I don't think you have your credit card, Dave.

Dave froze in midstride. He knew right away that he hadn't put the card back in his wallet. He thought perhaps he had slipped it into one of his pockets, and hope flared. He stood on the street patting himself. He checked all of his pockets twice, even the pocket in his shirt where he never put anything. Knowing he should turn around and go back to the liquor store, he walked, with a sinking heart, in the other di- rection. He knew he should retrieve his card. But how could he face the clerk?

A few moments ago Dave had felt so sure that the clerk had been rude to him. So sure that *he* had been courteous. Now he wasn't so certain. Had he really been courteous?

Instead of going back and claiming his card, he walked to the Vinyl Cafe. When he got there, he took off his jacket and sat down behind the counter. He had to think about this. The more he thought about it, the more he realized that he was far more tense about what awaited him at the liquor store than he was about losing his credit card. He could imagine himself standing in front of the liquor-store clerk with his baseball cap in hand. He got up and walked slowly toward the front of his store, trailing his hand along the piles of records. He gazed at the little mound of handwritten notes Scotch-taped to the back of the front door. He pulled off one that read, *Back in thirty minutes.* He winced. He was too proud to do it. So he did the only sensible thing he could think of doing. He picked up the telephone and called the bank.

"I would like to report a stolen credit card," he said.

He should have said "lost," a lost credit card, but theft seemed to have more dignity, and Dave was feeling woefully low on dignity.

If he had remembered at that moment that Saturday was Sam's birthday, and the reason he had wanted the wine in the first place was so when everyone was in bed, he and Morley could quietly toast the anniversary of the birth of their second child—if he had remembered these things, Dave might have acted differently.

But he had forgotten the birthday. He had forgotten that ten of Sam's friends had been invited for supper and a sleep-over that very night. Forgotten that he had agreed to run the party, to order the pizza, to buy a cake, and to get a video. Forgotten that Morley was going shopping for presents that morning.

In fact, at the very moment Dave was reporting his stolen card, Morley was wheeling a shopping cart containing the Bat Cave Deluxe toward the cash registers at a suburban toy store. Five dollars' worth of extruded plastic that was about to cost her forty.

———

Birthdays have always been a problem for Morley. She finds it stressful to have her house full of children expecting to be entertained. She has tried, over the years, to cope with her anxiety by careful planning. When Sam and Stephanie were little, Morley spent days preparing prizes for games and wandering around stores, loading up on cheap but interesting things to put in loot bags.

But no matter how hard she tried, there was always a kid who did not want to play the games she had planned, a kid who thought the prizes were stupid, a kid who hated the food. And for all her efforts, at some point the strain of the party inevitably rendered her children, the same children she was doing this for, tearful.

Morley was a scarred birthday mom. So when Sam said that for his ninth birthday party he wanted "a major sleepover, with all my friends, with pizza and a movie," Morley blanched. She knew there was no reason not to have ten boys ransack her house for twelve hours, but she didn't know if she was up to it.

Dave had agreed to run the party. Morley would organize things, but when it was time to man the battle stations, she was, for the first time in sixteen years, stepping aside. She was going to a movie with Gerta Lowbeer while the kids had supper—this was Dave's idea—and he was in charge.

If Dave had remembered any of this, he might have, probably would have, *certainly* would have, swallowed his pride and returned to the liquor store and retrieved his credit card. But he didn't. So he reported the card stolen, and the woman on the phone typed his report into the bank's computer.

———

It is amazing how fast computers work these days. Morley, who was feeling both pleased and slightly resentful about the Bat Cave, had just begun to unload her shopping cart when Dave hung up the phone.

Morley didn't notice that the clerk was having difficulty with her purchase. Didn't notice anything was amiss until a man materialized and invited her to accompany him to the security office.

It took twenty minutes and two phone calls before Morley convinced the manager that she had not stolen the credit card. After twenty minutes he apologized to her. But he didn't give back the card. Morley had to watch him take a pair of scissors from his desk and cut up her credit card in front of her.

"Policy," he said.

When Morley got home, there was a message from Dave. It said, "Phone me before you use the credit card."

Because she loved her husband, Morley decided to wait until after lunch to call him.

In fact, she didn't call until late in the afternoon.

Dave said, "Of course I remembered the birthday party. Why do you think I was at the liquor store?"

Then Dave said, "Of course not for the kids. I was getting the wine for us."

And then he said, "Of course I'll get the pizza . . . Yes, and the movie . . . Yes, and the Bat Cave."

Then the line went dead, and he looked around and said, "Of course, I have no money."

Which wasn't completely true. Dave had nearly twelve dollars in his wallet. And forty-seven dollars in the store's till.

Dave looked at his watch. It was four-fifteen. His bank was closed. He realized that without his credit card, he had no little plastic key to any more money. He had to move fast. He went outside and unlocked the six-foot wooden kangaroo that stood on the sidewalk in front of his store. HOP ON IN, it said on the pouch. Dave wrestled the kangaroo in and then carried out a chair and unscrewed the two speakers that hung over the front door. He was moving so fast that he hadn't turned off the record player. Frank Sinatra began to sing "I Get a Kick Out of You" as Dave lifted the first speaker out of its brackets. It was an odd sensation to cradle the speaker in his arms as Sinatra sang. The speaker, thought Dave, was probably about the size of Sinatra's head.

He had both speakers stashed behind the counter and was standing in the store with his hand on the light switch when a big guy in a wool toque stuck his head in the front door. "Are you open?" he asked.

"Just closing," said Dave.

The man was wearing grey sweatpants and a Road Runner T-shirt. He had about ten albums under his arm.

"I was wondering if you wanted to buy these?" he said, holding up the records.

Dave had already flicked off the lights in the back of the store and was about to say "I've already closed the till" when he spotted the album on the top of the pile. It was the original RCA Victor Living Stereo copy of the sound track from *Casino Royale.*

His hand stopped in midair on its way to the last light switch. He invited the guy into the store with a wave of his hand, locked the door behind him, and said, "What else have you got there?"

What the guy had was the motherlode: *Harry Belafonte Live in Concert at the Carnegie Hall.* A sealed copy of Simon and Garfunkel's *Wednesday Morning, 3 A.M.*, and best of all, the *Bonanza* sound track with Lorne Greene singing the theme.

Dave whistled. "Where'd you get this stuff?" he asked.

The guy pulled a crushed package of Camels out of his pants pocket and looked at Dave questioningly. Dave nodded. "Go ahead," he said.

The guy said, "My brother used to collect them. But he's been in Australia for eighteen years, and I'm getting tired of having his stuff filling up my apartment. He said I should just sell them."

Dave had been looking for the Simon and Garfunkel album for a year. He had never even dreamed of seeing a *sealed* copy.

"How many?" Dave said. "How many records in all?"

"There are hundreds," said the guy.

Dave said, "I can give you two dollars for each album and four for Simon and Garfunkel. That's what? Ten albums? Twenty-two dollars. I'll make it twenty-five."

The guy looked disappointed.

Dave said, "Look. I'll sell these for about six dollars each. I'll come over to your place tomorrow and look at the rest. If there are five hundred albums, that's good money."

He glanced at his watch as the guy thought it over.

Dave had thirty-four dollars left in his wallet when he finally locked the store.

As he walked by Emil, he considered asking for a loan. Instead, he found a toy store downtown that took a cheque for the Bat Cave.

He stopped at a phone booth and called his friend Kenny Wong. He said, "Tonight is Sam's birthday party. There are kids coming over, I need food."

Kenny said, "You got it."

Dave got home at five-fifteen. Stephanie was in the living room watching *The Simpsons*. Dave said, "Please turn that down."

"There's a note on the refrigerator," said Stephanie.

The note said, *Birthday party instructions.* Dave glanced at it.

He said, "Stephanie, I want you to go and get a movie."

Stephanie said, "When this is over."

Dave said, "Now."

Sam emerged from under a piece of furniture and said, "I want to go and get the movie."

Dave said, "No way."

Sam started to argue. Stephanie was still glued to the television.

Dave said, "Stephanie. Go and get a movie for the party."

His daughter stood up slowly and held out her hand. Dave said, "I don't have any money. Do you have money? I'll pay you back. Tomorrow." Stephanie rolled her eyes. Before she left, she made Dave sign an IOU. On her way out the door, she looked at Sam and said, "I'm going to get *The Little Mermaid.*"

Sam screamed, "I hate you."

When Dave came into the room to see what was the matter, Sam screamed, "I hate you, too. I don't want a party." He ran upstairs. His bedroom door and the front door slammed in unison.

It took Stephanie almost an hour to return with the movie. Unfortunately, she didn't get *The Little Mermaid*. She got *Night of the Zombie* instead.

The kids had arrived and were bouncing off the basement walls. Dave was trying to ice the cake, something he had never done in his life. He was trying to spread icing from the fridge onto a cake he had just taken out of the microwave. He was too busy to ask about the movie. The cold icing was ripping hunks of cake the size of golf balls away from the surface. When he finished, the cake looked like it had been iced with a chain saw.

Dave stared at what he had done and poured himself a drink.

Which was when Kenny Wong arrived. Kenny was wearing a pair of green tartan pants and a bright yellow T-shirt. The red letters across the front of the T-shirt read, WONG'S SCOTTISH MEAT PIES—GOOD ENOUGH TO EAT!

He threw two plastic bags of meat pies onto the kitchen table.

Dave said, "There's only ten kids."

Kenny said, "It's a party. They'll be fine. I'll be right back. I'll have Scotch."

When he came back, Kenny was carrying a large cardboard pastry box. He set the box down on the table and motioned at Dave to open it. "What do you think?" he said.

Dave peered in the box. It looked like an order of fried fish.

"What is it?" he asked.

"Deep-fried Mars bars," said Kenny. "There are two dozen. I made them myself."

Dave frowned.

Kenny pointed at the lumpy cake on the counter. It looked like a grade-five geography project—a papier-mâché model of a mountain range. "What's that?" Kenny asked.

"The cake," said Dave. "I made it myself."

––––––––

The kids took one look at the meat pies and rolled their eyes.

"I thought we were having pizza," said Sam.

"They were out of pizza," said Dave.

Only Terrence was interested in the pies. Terrence, the smallest kid at the party, with a little round face and dark grubby hair hanging to his shoulders, said, "Please, can I have two?"

The other kids disappeared into the basement with hunks of cake and two Mars bars each.

Terrence was back in five minutes. He said, "Could I have two more pies, please?"

Ten minutes later, Terrence was back for a third helping. He had ketchup all over his hands and T-shirt. He said, "These pies are good."

Kenny reached out and rumpled Terrence's hair. When he removed his hand, it was streaked with ketchup.

––––––––

When Morley came home at eight-thirty, the front door was open and the house was deadly quiet.

She walked into the kitchen and saw Kenny heading out the back door with a garbage bag.

"Be careful," said Dave from under the kitchen table. "We've had a little ketchup accident."

Morley looked at the meat-pie crusts piled on the counter.

"I thought you were getting pizza," she said.

"They were out of pizza," said Dave.

Morley stared at him for a moment and then said, "What did you give Terrence?"

Dave looked at her.

Morley said, "The O'Connors are vegetarians—it's on the note—Terrence has never eaten meat."

Dave looked at Kenny.

Kenny grinned at Morley. "He has now," he said.

Morley was hoping things would be cleaned up by the time she got home. However, it wasn't the state of her kitchen that was bothering her. What was bothering her was the silence.

She looked at the basement stairs. "It's awfully quiet down there," she said. "Are they watching TV? I thought they were going to play baseball."

Dave said, "We got a movie."

"What movie?" said Morley.

Dave crawled out from under the kitchen table holding a red sponge. "I'm not sure," he said. "Stephanie got the movie."

Morley went downstairs.

The kids were on the floor, a mound of goggle-eyed nine-year-olds, their faces bathed in the eerie glow of the television set.

No one moved as Morley stepped into the room. She could see that some of them were already in their sleeping bags. "I thought you guys were going to play baseball," she said.

"Sshh," said ten boys as one.

They were on another planet. They didn't want to have anything to do with her. She was from the wrong planet. If she persisted, they would turn on her. The last thing they wanted to see was the light of day—not when they could see real life on a screen.

As she turned to go, Morley stepped on an unopened bag of chips.

"Sshh," said the boys again.

Her eyes were beginning to adjust to the gloom. She noticed that the floor was littered with empty chip bags, half-filled glasses of pop, candy wrappers, and popcorn. There was popcorn everywhere. Arthur, the dog, was over by the sofa licking at the floor. Morley stepped over the boys to see what he was eating. When she got within a few feet, Arthur turned and bared his teeth and growled. The basement felt like one of those abandoned warehouses full of squatters. She had been gone only a few hours. Could things fall apart that fast? It was bad enough that she would be pulling food out of the basement for weeks. She didn't have to stay and watch the accident in progress.

Morley wanted to leave, but she began to feel herself sucked into the movie.

It was night. A young mother was putting some children to bed. She seemed to be at a cottage.

Morley noticed some of the kids were gripping onto each other.

"What is this?" she asked.

"Sshh," said Sam.

"The zombie is coming," said Terrence. "He has an axe."

There was a chilling scream.

Walter Colbath emerged from a sleeping bag and crawled over to Morley. "I'm scared," he said.

Later, Dave worked out that everyone had been enjoying *Night of the Zombie* until the zombie started losing limbs. First a finger fell off, followed by his left ear, which Walter earnestly explained had been devoured by a Jack Russell terrier before it hit the floor. Apparently, every time the zombie lost a body part, it left a gaping sore that began to pulse and ooze some sort of material that Sam said looked like melted cheese. Within a few scenes, the zombie had been transformed from a mild elementary school teacher to a waddling sore, with arm enough still for what Dave referred to as "the knife scene."

Except it wasn't really a knife scene; it was more of a cleaver scene. It was the moment when the zombie lodged the cleaver into the skull of the young scientist—the man all the kids had assumed was going to stop the zombie from doing what he'd done to the kindly old crossing guard.

It wasn't just the violence of the scene that had upset the kids, but the morality of it.

"Why did he do that to the crossing guard?" whimpered Scott at midnight, as Dave tried to coax him from behind the sofa.

As Dave reached for Scott, he rested his knee in something greasy. It slid out from under him, and he fell forward and hit his chin against the arm of the sofa. While he lay on the floor wondering when this was going to end, the dog began to lick his knee. Dave reached out and fingered his pants—the remnants of a half-eaten Mars bar. When he stood up, the dog began barking.

"Excuse me," said Bill. "I have a headache. I want to go home."

Timmy said, "My tummy hurts. I want to go home, too. Please could you phone my parents, please?"

———

Phoning a family at two in the morning to ask if they would mind dropping over to pick up their child because you have just shown him *Night of the Zombie* is not the easiest thing in the world to do. But Dave had no choice. It didn't take longer than fifteen minutes for the parents to begin to arrive. Everyone was polite, but Dave knew what they were thinking. They were thinking their kids would never come to this house again. Certainly not on a sleepover.

When Terrence's parents came, Terrence said, "I ate meat. I ate meat. They made me do it."

"It was textured vegetable protein," said Dave glumly. "It just looked like meat."

Everyone was gone by two-thirty.

All except Walter Colbath.

Walter was a thin boy with a perpetually runny nose. He was always worried that someone was breaking the rules.

Walter Colbath's parents weren't home. Or if they were, they weren't answering the phone.

"Maybe they turned the ringer off," said Dave. "You just stay. They'll be here in the morning."

Walter said okay, and Sam and Walter, the last remaining warriors, headed off to bed together, Walter chewing his nails. Finally, the house was quiet.

Dave had just drifted off to sleep when Sam appeared by his side, poking him, saying, "Walter is crying. He thinks there's been a fire at his house and his parents are dead."

At three-thirty Dave agreed to drive Walter by his house so he could see that it hadn't burned to the ground.

"You don't have to get dressed," said Dave as he struggled into a raincoat. "We're not going to stop. We'll just drive by. Just put on a sweatshirt over your jammies. And your sneakers."

It was chilly outside. Dave had to turn on the wipers to clear away the dew.

"Please, God," he said quietly as they rounded the corner. "See?" he said. "Your house is still standing. No fire." He still didn't know why the Colbaths weren't picking up the phone.

"Maybe they've been murdered," said Walter. "By a zombie or something."

"Your mom and dad are up north," said Morley to Walter

softly. He and Dave had woken her when they got back. "They're coming home tomorrow."

"I know," said Walter. "But I'm afraid that the zombie got them."

Morley looked at Dave. She put her arm over Walter's shoulder and said, "You come here with me. You can sleep with us in here."

When Dave woke up at six-thirty, it was with Walter Colbath's feet sticking in his back. Walter was sleeping diagonally across the bed, his feet drilling into Dave's kidneys, his head where Morley's should have been. Morley was nowhere to be seen.

Dave got up and went downstairs. Morley was snoring softly on the living room couch.

Dave went into the kitchen and put some coffee on. He went to the front door and picked up the morning paper.

He looked at Arthur, who still had chocolate smeared around his mouth, and said, "What was the point of all that?"

The dog seemed to shrug.

"Pride before a fall," muttered Dave as the coffee began to sputter. If he had only gone back for his credit card, none of this would have happened. He wouldn't have had to send Stephanie for the movie . . .

Was that what he had learned? Or was it simpler than that? Maybe the lesson was supposed to be . . . don't put your credit card down anywhere.

Arthur shook, and the jingle of his tags echoed in the quiet morning. Nothing else stirred.

Dave carried his coffee to the table.

He opened the paper.

Then got up and took a meat pie out of the fridge and dropped it in the dog's dish.

"Happy birthday," he said.

Summer

Driving Lessons

Morley was telling her friend Nicky about her mother's accident. They were both fixing supper as they talked on the telephone.

"Just a second," Morley said. "Wait a minute. Wait a minute. Shoot."

There was a crash as the receiver snapped off Morley's shoulder.

Nicky winced. "What's the matter?" she asked. It sounded like the phone had fallen into the blender. "What's happening?"

What was happening was that the receiver was snaking across the kitchen floor. The dog was chasing it.

"Morley?"

There was another clatter. Then Morley came back on the line. "Sorry," she said.

"What happened?"

"The potatoes were boiling over. Where was I?"

"Your mother."

"She rear-ended someone. It wasn't her fault. Someone jumped out in front of the guy, and he slammed on his brakes."

"Was she hurt?"

"No. No. She's okay."

"What about the other guy?"

135

"No. Everyone was okay. It was Friday night. She came here after it happened. Dave and I were supposed to be going out. She got here the same time as the babysitter."

"How?"

"How what?"

"How'd she get there?"

"She drove."

"Did you go out?"

"Yeah. It was her second accident since Christmas."

"What did you do?"

"What do you mean what did we do?"

"Where did you go?"

"We went to a movie. I'm worried she's going to kill someone."

"I wish *my* mother could still drive. What did you see?"

"I don't remember. Damn. What did we see? The one with the guy and the bomb. Where the father gets blown up. You know, that's the problem. Everyone is so impressed because she's eighty-two years old and she still has her mind. She also has cataracts. She can hardly see, Nicky. She's going to kill someone."

"Don't they have to take the test when they're over eighty?"

"She took the test. She's waiting for cataract surgery, and you know what the guy said? He said, 'I am going to retire in seven years, and if I can drive as well as you can when I'm sixty-five, I'll be happy.' "

"He passed her?"

"Yeah, he passed her."

"So don't worry."

"She's had two accidents since Christmas."

"You said it wasn't her fault."

"Still."

———

"If you're so worried, why don't you call the police?"

Morley and Dave were lying in bed.

"She's my own mother. How can I turn my mother in? I can't rat on my own mother. What if I call and she finds out about it?"

"What if you don't and she kills someone?"

"Thanks, Dave. That's a big help. Thanks a lot. Why don't *you* call the cops."

"She's not my mother."

"Great. That's great. That's really great."

Morley was picking up her pillows and heading out of the room.

"Well, she isn't," said Dave as she disappeared.

———

Dave said, "I'm sorry."

Morley didn't say "It's okay."

Dave said, "Listen. She hardly drives anymore. What does she do? She goes for groceries. How far is it to the grocery store? A quarter of a mile? Two turns? She goes to bridge. Those are the sort of trips you could do in your pyjamas. Who's going to see you? What's going to happen?"

"I know what's going to happen," said Morley. "She's going to kill someone, Dave. That's what's going to happen."

"She's not going to kill someone going to the grocery store."

"You know what happened last month? She got lost. You know where she got lost? She got lost in Scarborough."

"Scarborough?"

"She went to dinner at Norah's house, and she got lost coming home. She said she didn't know where she was. She said she couldn't see the numbers on the houses or read the signs. She said she was so scared, she was shaking. And then she got on the highway, don't ask me how, somehow she found the highway, but she didn't know where she was going. And you know what she told me? She said she must have been driving funny, because someone stopped and helped her. Someone stopped, Dave. She said they told her she was going the wrong way."

"I thought she didn't drive at night."

"How else was she supposed to get there?"

"She could have taken the subway. The subway goes to Scarborough."

"She hates the subway. The stairs are too hard."

"But she figured it out. Anyone could get lost in Scarborough. She got home. Right? She's fine."

"You know what scares me, Dave? She said she was heading the wrong way. I don't know whether she meant she was heading in the wrong direction or driving on the wrong side of the highway."

"Did you ask her?"

"I was too scared to ask her. Somebody stopped. What do you think?"

———

Dave was reading the paper. Morley was knitting.

Dave said, "Did you know some guy in Kansas, some eighty-year-old guy in Lawrence, Kansas, has Albert Einstein's brain in a pickle jar in his apartment?"

Morley said, "No. Mom phoned today."

Dave said, "The guy was a pathologist. And he was on duty when Einstein died, so he did the autopsy and kept the brain to study it. What did she want?"

Morley said, "Nothing. Every time she leaves a message on the machine, I feel guilty erasing it."

Dave said, "Listen. 'The most celebrated brain of the twentieth century resides in Apartment Thirteen on the second floor of a nondescript brick apartment building here.' Here is Lawrence. Kansas. The guy has it all cut up. He says he's two thirds of the way through studying it."

Morley said, "I keep thinking it'll turn out to be the last thing she ever says to me, and I will have erased it."

Dave said, "He keeps it in his hall closet."

Morley said, "I invited her for dinner on Friday. It's Dad's birthday."

Dave said, "Friday?"

Morley said, "When did Einstein die, anyway?"

Dave said, "Nineteen fifty-five."

Morley said, "How?"

Dave said, "Automobile accident. He was hit by an old lady."

Morley said, "What?"

Dave said, "Just kidding. It doesn't say. It just says he was seventy-five."

———

There is a picture of Morley's father on her bureau. It is in a gold frame. It was taken in Florida ten years ago. Roy was seventy-six years old. He looks impossibly young and vigorous. The sun in his face, the wind tugging at his hair. He is squinting.

"Thirty years as a copper," he used to say, "and the payoff is I get to go to Florida and squint for three months."

Ten years ago Helen and Roy used to drive to Florida and back and didn't even think about it. Nobody thought about it.

They brought back pictures of their friends, all of them holding drinks, standing around someone's mobile home— "It's not a trailer park," Helen used to say, "mobile homes, mobile homes."

Six years ago, in January, he collapsed. Helen phoned Morley and said, "You better get down here." She said it was like someone had unplugged him. Dave said, "What do the doctors say?"

Morley had phoned the hospital in Clearwater and spoken to a doctor. He said, "You have to be philosophical about this; he's had a good life." Morley and Dave rushed down and put the trailer up for sale and sold some stuff and left the rest for whoever bought it, for whatever they wanted to pay.

After two weeks the doctors said Roy could travel. Dave had already left with the car. Morley flew back with her parents. She couldn't believe how old Roy looked. He could walk, but he was walking old. He didn't seem to be paying attention to anything. He didn't want to eat.

Roy had always been so strong.

————

When he was a young man, he played hockey. In 1927 he played centre for the Toronto Granites. It was three years after the Granites won the gold medal at the Winter Olympics.

He was a born athlete. He used to go and watch the Maple Leafs play baseball at Hanlan's Point Stadium. He took his glove. If he got there early enough, they would let him shag flies during batting practice.

He quit school when he was sixteen and worked on an ice truck. Two years later, the hockey team got him a job at the Inglis factory on Strachan Avenue. He stayed there, working in shipping and then on the line, for almost fifteen years.

When he and Helen got married, they got a place in the suburbs. He used to run a mile every morning to the end of the streetcar line so he wouldn't have to pay two fares. In those days, when you changed cars, you had to pay a second fare.

He got a weekend job with the Mounties, and when the war came, they hired him full-time. They gave him a rifle and one bullet and sent him to Port Colborne to guard the

Welland Canal. He wasn't allowed to put the bullet in the rifle in case he might hurt someone. He used to say it was the most boring job he'd ever had.

Dave tried to tease him about it once. He said, "But you must have been good at it, Roy, you must have done a great job. At no point in the war did the Nazis make it anywhere near the canal." Roy looked at him like he was nuts. He wasn't going to let anyone say the job was unnecessary.

After the war, Roy left Inglis and got a job with the North York police force. It paid less than the factory, but it was with the township, and that meant job security. There were only fifteen other men on the force when he joined. When he retired, there were three hundred, and he was an inspector.

———

When they got back from Florida, Morley took Roy to see Dr. Freeberg, who said, "I want you to go and see a blood specialist." The blood specialist asked Roy to walk across the room, and he diagnosed the problem before Roy got to the other side. It was his thyroid. The specialist wrote out a prescription and said, "Take these and you'll feel better in three days." Roy took his first pill at the drugstore and started feeling better on the way home.

———

But Roy was never the same. He was like a balloon with the air slowly seeping out of it. Sometimes when he and Helen came for dinner, he would sit in the living room as if he were the only one there. Other times he was bright and chatty, telling them what was in the paper, what he had seen on the news. He still did the crossword every day.

He kept driving, but he was nervous about it. He got a speeding ticket—forty-five in a thirty-five zone. He was incensed. It was his first violation. Ever.

One day he and Helen were in the garage, on their way to

the supermarket, and he was revving the engine. Helen said, "What are you doing?" He said, "I'm backing out. Why?" She said, "Why don't you put it in reverse first?" It was just a lapse. He was thinking about something else. But it worried him. "I want to keep driving," he told Dave. "I couldn't stand it if I couldn't drive."

Another time he was pulling into the parking lot at the back of the apartment, and he hit one of the huge plastic garbage cans lined up in the alley.

Dave said, "I could have done that, Roy. Don't worry about it."

But he worried.

———

Then one day he phoned Dave at work and said, "I'm at the liquor store. You better come and get me."

Roy had gone to the store to pick up a case of pop and a dozen eggs and some orange juice. When he was pulling out of his parking spot, he put the Buick into reverse instead of forward.

"I don't know," he said. "I just did it."

When he pressed the accelerator, the car lurched backward instead of going the way he expected it to go. Roy said it felt like the car had been possessed by a demon, and the only thing he could think of was to press harder on the accelerator. He didn't figure out what had happened until he hit the car behind him. It was a little red Honda.

Instead of getting out of his car and checking the damage, Roy took off.

"I don't know," he said. "I guess I was thinking they might take away my licence or something. All I could think about was that I had to get out of there. If I had stopped . . ."

"I know," said Dave.

When he pulled up to the stop sign at the parking-lot exit,

Roy checked his rearview mirror and, to his horror, saw that the Honda was right behind him. And the guy in the Honda was shaking his fist.

"He wasn't thinking straight," said Dave to Morley. "He was scared of losing his licence. He was scared of being old."

"I know," said Morley.

As soon as there was a break in the traffic, Roy had roared onto Dupont Avenue.

"I never drove that fast in the city in my life," he said.

"Even when you were a cop?" said Dave.

"I don't know," said Roy.

When he checked his mirror and saw that the guy in the Honda was still behind him—and not just following him but right up against him—Roy thought, The bugger thinks he can tailgate me. I'll show him. He took the corner at Howland Avenue almost on two wheels. The Honda came screaming around the corner right on his bumper. Roy thought, This is crazy. He sped up.

He kept checking the mirror as he went down Howland, and that was when he noticed the guy in the Honda was still waving at him. In fact, he wasn't only waving, he was pounding on his windshield. With both hands. Roy thought, How's he doing that? Driving so fast and so close to me without using his hands. Which was when he realized the guy in the Honda *wasn't* driving. *Roy* was doing the driving. The Honda was hooked onto his bumper. Roy was dragging the Honda through the city like a fish on a line.

Instead of stopping, Roy decided to try and shake him loose.

"I turned around and waved at him," Roy told Dave. "Then I gave him the thumbs-up and started weaving from side to side. Jerking the wheel, like. Slowing down and speeding up."

"You waved at him?" said Dave.

"And smiled, like," said Roy.

"He must have thought you were crazy. He must have thought he was going to die."

"I think that's when he started honking the horn," said Roy.

The two cars finally separated when Roy took the corner at Barton. He saw the Honda fly off across the sidewalk and stop against a tree.

"He didn't hit too hard," said Roy.

"Was he hurt?" asked Dave.

"I don't think so," Roy said.

He hadn't stopped to check.

Instead of hanging around, Roy drove to the liquor store and bought himself a pint of Jack Daniel's and phoned Dave and said, "You better come and get me." When Dave arrived, Roy was sitting in the passenger seat. Dave watched him for a moment—saw him take a swig of the Jack Daniel's—watched him fingering the dashboard as if he were saying goodbye.

When he saw Dave, Roy handed over his keys and said, "You drive it home."

———

Morley said, "You know what I thought today? I thought I should get a tape recorder and leave it by the phone so I could record all her messages before I erase them. Then I wouldn't have to worry."

Dave said, "About what? What messages?"

Morley said, "My Mother's messages. I could record them all on a tape. Then I wouldn't feel bad erasing them. I could keep them all on a tape. It would be like a diary."

———

Roy died in 1987. And still, all the time, Helen caught herself thinking, I have to tell Roy that. She would see something, or read something, and think, Roy would like that. And then she would remember, Roy is dead. It was such a black, empty feeling.

On Friday when she came for supper, she said, "I saw a program about the invasion. On TV. When you hear that the invasion was fifty years ago, you just don't believe it. It feels so strange."

Stephanie said, "What invasion?"

Sam said, "Can I be excused?"

———

After supper Helen wanted to help with the dishes, and Morley let her, even though Morley knew they'd fight about it. Knew she would hand something back and say it was still dirty and her mother would get huffy. Morley promised herself not to do it, but when Helen handed her a plate that was so greasy Morley couldn't bear the idea of wiping it with the towel, she said, "Mother, could you rinse that a little more, please?" She tried to be offhand about it, but Helen said, "I know how to wash dishes. You don't have to tell me how to wash dishes."

When she was young, Morley could be as mean to her mother as she wanted. It was part of her job description. Now Helen was more fragile. Delicate. The repercussions of anger were much greater than they used to be.

"I washed more dishes in my life than you'll ever wash," said Helen, rubbing the plate harder than necessary.

She's scared, thought Morley. She feels like she's losing control. That's why she gets so angry. She doesn't even know how she's behaving. If I get mad back, it will feel to her like my anger has come out of nowhere.

———

Their roles were changing, and both of them resented it.

The first time she noticed it, two or three years ago, Morley had gone to Helen's apartment to pick her up. They were going to meet Dave for dinner and then to a show. Standing in the hallway holding her mother's coat, Morley saw a stain on Helen's green dress. Helen couldn't see it, but she would have been horrified to know it was there. Morley didn't say anything.

She is my mother, thought Morley. I am not supposed to look after her. She is supposed to look after me. Except Morley didn't want a mother anymore. Bristled every time Helen told her how to do something or kissed her good night. And found it maddening when Helen wouldn't accept her help.

"She wants to be independent," said Dave. "She doesn't understand dependency."

That was what the car was all about. If Helen stopped driving, her world would become smaller. And it would never become larger again. Morley wanted her mother's world to become more restricted. But she understood why it terrified Helen.

When Roy had given up driving, Morley had tried to persuade Helen to quit, too.

Helen had said, "How would we get around? I don't walk well anymore. My back bothers me. I can't walk and carry stuff at the same time."

Dave said, "What about the subway?"

Helen said, "I can't take the subway. All those stairs."

Morley said, "Sell the car. With the money you save on insurance and gas and repairs, you could afford to take taxis anywhere."

"How would we get to the supermarket?" said Helen. As if it couldn't be done.

"Taxi," said Dave.

"But how," said Roy triumphantly, "would we get home?"

To a man who used to run a mile every day to save a five-cent streetcar fare, the idea of taking two taxis in one day was unthinkable.

————

Helen stayed over at Morley and Dave's on Friday night. After she helped with the dishes, she watched television.

"I saw a special on the invasion the other night," she said again. "It's so hard to believe it was only fifty years ago. Roy would have liked the show."

————

It was two months later that Helen found the old clipping. She was in a sorting mode, going through some old papers, when she came across an announcement that someone had clipped from the police newsletter. At first it confused her. It said that her father had won the Policeman of the Month Award. But it wasn't her father who had won that—it was Roy. She couldn't make sense of the clipping. Had she got her father and her husband mixed up in her mind? She started to get scared. Then she saw the date on the clipping. April 1912. She suddenly understood that both her father and Roy must have won the same award, at different times. She remembered when Roy had won. They had gone out to dinner at a restaurant, and a man had taken their picture at their table. She wondered what had happened to the photo. God, she wished Roy were here. She wanted him to know this. She wished they could tell her father. She looked at the clipping again and felt her heart sink. There was no one left to tell. No one who would appreciate it. Anyone who knew her father would know what a thrill it would have given him to know this. He was so proud when Roy had joined the force. She thought, I hope he knows. She thought, I hope he and Roy both know. She started to cry. She thought, I wish I had someone to tell.

————

She phoned Morley and said, "Can I come over? I have something I want to show you."

She didn't say what it was.

It was four o'clock.

The early-spring sun was low in the sky. As she turned west onto Roxborough, she squinted and reached for the visor. When she came to the crosswalk, the sun was still in her eyes, and she didn't see the man step off the sidewalk, his arm extended. Only heard the sickening thump when she hit him. Only saw him lying in a heap on the road in the rearview mirror. She stopped the car and struggled with the seat belt and ran back to help him, but some young men had appeared from somewhere and pushed her away and said, "We don't need you here." She felt sick. She felt faint. She went back to her car and started to cry, and a nice woman came and sat beside her. She said, "Could I call someone for you?" Helen said, "No, it's okay." The woman stayed with her until the police came. Helen told her the story of the clipping. Told her how both her husband and her father had won the same police award and that neither of them knew it. All the time she kept twisting in her seat, trying to see the man. Wishing he would sit up. She started to shake when she saw them take him away in an ambulance. A policeman came over, and she said, "My husband was a policeman. Is the man all right?" The policeman didn't know. He said he wasn't going to take her licence. He said she might have to take the test again.

She made herself drive to Morley's. After dinner Dave phoned all the hospitals, and they said there had been no serious accidents. That gave her hope.

She stayed two days. She fussed a little in the kitchen, but mostly, she watched television. She didn't talk a lot.

"I'm worried," said Morley.

"She'll be okay," said Dave.

On Wednesday, when Dave came home from work, Helen had gone home.

"She left this afternoon," said Morley. "She came down after lunch and said she had to get going."

"Did you drive her?" said Dave.

"She drove herself."

"Huh. I didn't think you'd let her."

"She said she was scared to drive. Then she said, 'But old age isn't for sissies.' What could I say to that, Dave?"

Summer Camp

The fact that he hated his niece, and had from the moment he met her, bothered Dave. He felt it was wrong to dislike, let alone loathe, a thing that stood no taller than three feet; and in this case, because the thing was his sister's child, he felt it was shameful. But he loathed Margot, and he had loathed her since she was four years old.

That was when they first met. She was walking down the arrivals corridor at the airport, holding a white vinyl purse in one hand and a large doll in the other. Annie had broken into a broad, toothy grin when she spotted her brother. She dropped her suitcase and held out her arms.

"It's so good to see you," she said.

Dave had hugged his sister, and then he had bent down, with love in his heart, and smiled at Margot. But before he could say anything, she said, "You're late. We've been waiting. You were supposed to be here to meet us."

Annie had left her husband, whose name Dave always had difficulty recalling: Peter? Paul? It was one of the disciples— Matthew. *Matt*. Annie had left Matt that spring and was bringing Margot to Dave's for Easter.

They had stayed a week.

"We should have done this years ago," Annie said. "It's good to see her with the kids. It's important."

Margot tagged around Sam and Stephanie like a pet. Margot and her doll. The kind with the string in the back that you could pull when you wanted it to talk. A Chatty Cathy.

"Have you noticed," Dave said to Morley at the end of the first night, "how the doll is always interrupting me?"

They would be drinking coffee in the kitchen, talking, doing the dishes, and Dave would say something, and the doll would jump in: "You could feed me now. Oh, I love you *soooo* much."

He hated the doll's whiny voice. And he hated everything it had to say—eighteen different statements. He knew them by heart by the end of day two.

"Ohhhhhhh," he said to Morley as they went to bed. "I love you *soooo* much."

The summer he was seven, Dave sneaked one of Annie's dolls outside on a Saturday afternoon and sat it in the middle of the sidewalk in front of their house. Then he got his sister's tricycle and took a run at the doll from down the street. There was such a satisfying crunch that he set up the doll again and then again, until it was first a collection of limbs and finally just a pile of plastic. Unable to stop himself, he went upstairs and collected an armful of her dolls and began running over them, one by one. When Annie saw what he was doing, she started to cry hysterically. He calmed her down and convinced her to join in. "You can be the nurse," he said. She was four. He had her stand on the lawn and throw her dolls in front of his bike as he flew by. "As if they jumped," he said.

As he was putting the car in the garage, Dave imagined running over the Chatty Cathy in the driveway. *"Oh,"* he said softly, "I'm *soooo* sorry."

———

The next time Dave saw Margot, she was six. He'd been in Halifax at a convention. He had brought Margot a Barbie doll. He wanted to make up.

"Thank you, Uncle Dave," she said flatly.

But she didn't play with the Barbie.

"She's off dolls," said Annie.

Margot didn't watch television, either. Or do anything Dave's kids did.

"It's all dumb programs," said Margot when Dave asked about her favourite show.

After dinner she was doing schoolwork. She looked at Dave and said, "Why is the sky blue?" When Dave said he wasn't sure, she rolled her eyes and disappeared into her bedroom.

"It's okay," said Annie. "She can look it up."

An hour later, Margot was out again.

"Uncle Dave," she said, "how many moons does Jupiter have?" Dave was sure she already knew the answer. It felt as if she was tormenting him.

He stayed three days.

He was determined not to leave without breaking through.

As he was going, he hugged Annie and then picked up Margot by her wrists.

"I'm getting on an airplane," he said, spinning Margot around and around.

"Put me down," screamed Margot.

But Dave kept spinning, making airplane noises, Margot flying around parallel to the floor until her foot smacked the kitchen table and she yelped with pain.

He stopped turning and set her down. She cried, "I hate you," and then turned to run. But she was so dizzy that she hit the kitchen counter with her forehead and fell down.

They were supposed to come with him to the airport.

"I'll just go," said Dave. "I'll go. You stay."

"What?" said Annie. Margot was screaming. Dave didn't bother to repeat himself.

At Christmas, Annie wrote that she was going to France for the summer. She had a six-week tour with a Gaelic group.

Morley said, "Why don't we take Margot? Give Annie some time off."

Annie wrote back in a week. *Are you sure?*

Margot arrived on July 1. She flew from Halifax by herself.

"You wouldn't let *me* fly to Halifax alone," said Stephanie to Dave as they drove to the airport.

Margot, who was now ten, arrived sullen and grumpy.

"She wanted to come to Paris," said Annie to Morley on the phone. "I'm sorry. Will you be all right?"

"She'll be fine," said Morley, not knowing that at that moment Dave was standing by a luggage carousel at the airport, trying to coax the colour of her suitcase out of his niece.

"Is it that one?" he said.

"I don't know," said Margot. "I told you. Mommy packed. I haven't the foggiest what colour it is."

Stephanie, who had refused to come into the airport, was lying in the backseat of the car when they got there. She was wearing a Walkman and had her eyes closed, her feet tapping on the passenger door window. She didn't acknowledge their arrival until Dave reached into the backseat and removed her headphones.

"Hey!" she said.

Margot watched carefully.

She was growing up to be a serious and intense little girl. Stephanie, six years her senior, was clearly the most interesting thing to have entered her universe in a long time. Here was a gateway into the world of teenage femininity. Margot wanted as much of it as she could get. She was attentive to everything that Stephanie did, the music she played, the way she used the telephone, what she watched on television, and especially, the nightly application of unguents and balms. When she learned that Stephanie and Sam were about to leave for two weeks at camp, Margot was distraught. "What about me?" she said.

When Annie had asked, Margot had rejected the idea of camp. "Summer camp is for *children,*" she said. Now, however, as Stephanie's departure drew closer, Margot wanted to go to camp, too.

She became increasingly difficult. "There is nothing to do," she said. "I'm bored."

Morley gave her the Camping Association booklet and said, "Maybe there's a place you'd like."

Margot took the book to her room and came back in an hour, pointing to "The Crystal Lake Thespian Experience: Artistic Direction and Creative Encouragement for Young Actors."

Morley phoned the camp the next morning. It was full. That night she handed the camping booklet to Dave and said, "This is your job."

These were the sort of decisions Dave normally tried to avoid. He preferred the conceptual over the practical. But the possibility of two weeks without Margot—without, in fact, any children—delighted him.

"There must be a camp with space somewhere," said Dave.

Dave had spent only one summer at camp himself. He had been hired as the arts and crafts director. Before he left for camp, he was seized by some primitive and unfamiliar wilderness spasm and bought a book on plant identification. It featured pencil sketches of flowers, trees, and shrubs. Dave had the idea that he would spend his free time poking around in the forest. He believed that if he applied himself, by the end of the summer he could become an accomplished woodsman. Maybe by August, some kid hanging around the Hike and Trip Office would poke his buddy as Dave swung by and say, "That's Dave." The kid would say it with the same reverence he might say, "That's Pierre Radisson." Dave planned to forgo the pleasures of the Red Pine Inn, where the other counsellors went to drink at night. He would get up with the sun and go to bed at dark. Born to television, bred to the automobile, he would become Wilderness Dave.

As arts and crafts director, Dave had a two-room cabin called the Wigwam, near the hospital. He set off from his cabin at rest period on his second day at camp, armed with his plant book.

Somewhere between the chapel and the rock where the trail angled up toward the Indian Council Ring, Dave found himself staring at a shrub with three leaves and prominent veins. It looked like the first picture in his book, an Indian turnip.

The way you identified Indian turnip, said his reference, was by its white root. Dave reached out and plucked the plant from the ground. To his great astonishment, he was holding something that looked like an albino carrot.

Dave still finds it difficult to understand what happened next. Perhaps the word "turnip" was what confused him. Perhaps he was just swept away by the moment. Without pausing to think, he wiped the end of the root on his jeans and sank his teeth into it. He had already swallowed a large mouthful before it occurred to him that this might not have been the smartest thing he had ever done. That was when things started to happen in the back of his throat. The first thing was a mild burning sensation. The second felt like the detonation of a small nuclear device somewhere in the vicinity of his tonsils. As Dave stood on the chapel trail, clutching the stump of the Indian turnip, wondering what would happen next, he noticed that his lips had gone numb. Soon his entire mouth had begun to tingle, and the tingling was crawling down his oesophagus toward his stomach. It didn't take Dave long to realize that eating the root had been a terrible mistake.

Turnip in hand, Dave made his way back to camp.

If he was going to lapse into unconsciousness, he wanted to do it where someone might help. Once back at camp, however, Dave felt too foolish to turn himself in to the nurse. How could he go to the nurse with the turnip and say "I ate some of this"?

He went back to his cabin and lay down on his bed. It occurred to him that if he passed out, no one would know why. He got up and put the turnip on his desk and wrote a note. The note read: *I ate some of this*. Dave figured if he made it to dinner, he could destroy the note and no one would know anything. If he blacked out, someone would surely find him, read the note, and organize the appropriate treatment. Dave lay down again and prepared to die. During the hour he spent on his bed, he came as close to embracing Christ as his personal saviour as he had in his life. After the hour of prayer and wild promises, it occurred to him to have another look at his plant book.

The information on the Indian turnip was continued on page two. In his original excitement, Dave had failed to read the whole story.

Indian turnip, he read, *is a close relation of the horseradish. When cooked, it is a mild and pleasant vegetable. When eaten raw, it is the hottest plant known in the northern woods. Indians used to feed it to settlers as a joke. Painful but not poisonous.*

That night Dave got drunk at the Red Pine Inn. He gave the plant book to the hike and trip director.

———

After the kids were in bed, Dave came downstairs with the camping booklet. "There are camps with rifle ranges," he said. "We're not sending Margot to a place where they arm the campers."

"I knew you could handle this," said Morley.

He chose a camp that didn't have power boats. "No water-skiing," he said to Margot. "No horses. A small quiet camp. With a lake and sailboats. A summer place."

What Margot really wanted was to go with Stephanie.

But Stephanie was going to a teenage camp and, for the first time ever, to a camp with boys.

They all left the same Monday morning. It was as chaotic as Christmas. Sam packed all his comics and no clothes. He was being driven to the bus by neighbours. His first time at camp, and he ran out the front door without saying goodbye. "Hey!" said Dave. "Come back."

Stephanie thumped downstairs with a trunk and a suitcase and a sports bag full of stuff—including, hidden in her sleeping bag, the family's only hair dryer and a handful of makeup she had swiped from her mother's bureau.

She wasn't talking to anyone. She was mad about something—mostly nervous, probably. Dave looked at her across the table, scowling into her cereal bowl, and his heart went out to the boys into whose lives his daughter was about to march. Somewhere, he thought, some poor kid who has no idea what is heading his way is calmly eating breakfast.

Margot was last to leave. After lunch, Dave drove her to the parking lot of a suburban shopping centre. She was wearing flared blue shorts, a white T-shirt, and a scarf in her hair.

She left on a bus with a lot of other kids and a handful of counsellors wearing tie-dyed T-shirts. The last Dave saw of her, Margot was sitting alone at the back of the bus. All of the other kids were clapping and singing. Margot had her hands in her lap. She was staring dead ahead.

———

For the first few days the kids were gone, Dave was edgy. "I don't get it," he said. "Margot's the one I'm worried about."

In the morning he'd wake up and say, "I wonder how she's doing?"

Morley would say, "She's doing fine." This would make Dave feel better. But it didn't last. An hour later, he'd be worried again.

By Thursday, though, he was enjoying an unfamiliar sense of freedom. That night he and Morley wandered out to a local restaurant for supper. Afterward, on impulse, they went to a movie. On Friday morning they slept in.

"This is kind of nice," said Dave. "What do you want to do tonight?"

The first letter arrived at noon:

Dear Uncle Dave,

This place is torture. Get me out of here. The meals are horrible. I haven't eaten anything for two days. They serve old oatmeal in the morning. My counsellor's name is Phyllis. She looks like Igor. Except meaner. I hate the kids in my tent who are all weird. I got bit by a weird looking bug and my arm is swelling up and turning red. I hate this camp. Why did you send me here to this place? This place is despicable. When is my mother coming home? I can't stand it. I might kill myself.

Love, your niece,
Margot

Dave was horrified. "What are we going to do?" he asked.

"I thought we'd go to another movie," said Morley.

"About Margot," said Dave, pointing to the letter. "What are we going to do about Margot?"

"Nothing," said Morley. "She's fine. She'll be fine."

"What if she's not fine?" said Dave. "If it's such a great place, why did they have spaces available in the middle of July? What if the kids *are* all weird? What if her counsellor *is* meaner than Igor?"

"Dave," said Morley. "She's fine."

At dinner Dave said, "What if they have guns and she gets a gun and shoots someone? Her counsellor. What if she shoots her counsellor? What if she shoots herself? She sounded pretty desperate. How am I going to explain that to my sister?"

"Dave," said Morley. "They *don't* have guns."

"Maybe," said Dave, "it just wasn't in the brochure. Maybe they knew better than to put it in the brochure."

That night as he was getting undressed for bed, Dave said, "What if she gets so hungry she goes into the woods and eats a poisonous plant? What if she starts eating plants that make her sick?"

Morley, who was already in bed, didn't even pretend to stop reading. "What," she said, "are you talking about?"

Dave said, "Margot. I am talking about Margot. What if she gets a book on plant identification and pulls up a poisonous plant and eats it?"

Morley closed her book carefully and glared at her husband. "Dave," she said, "only an idiot would go into the woods and pull up a plant and eat it."

———

On Monday, when he came home at lunch and saw the envelope addressed in Stephanie's handwriting, Dave's heart was filled with the milk of human kindness. Stephanie had been gone nine days, and to Dave's surprise, he missed her. He carried the envelope to the kitchen table, sat down, and held it up to the light. Then he got up and poured some juice. He was savouring this. He sat down, had a sip of juice, and opened the letter.

> *There are boys everywhere,* it began. *Boys! Boys! Boys! This camp is boy! heaven. Mostly they are dorks–real geeks– except this guy Larry, who is 23, and a lifeguard, and a hunk, and last night . . ."*

Last night?

Dave stopped reading and stared out the kitchen window.

This letter seemed to be heading to a place he didn't want to go. He didn't want to know about *last night*.

He glanced down at the pages on the table in front of him. He began to read it again. From the beginning.

July 7,
Dear Becky,

Becky is Stephanie's best friend.

Dave stared at the greeting as the awful truth slowly came into focus.

His daughter had put the letter she had written to her friend Becky into the envelope she had addressed to her parents. It was seven pages long.

I don't need to read this, thought Dave. This letter was not meant for me. Please, Lord, give me the strength not to read this letter. Lead me not into temptation. Stop me from reading any further. Deliver me from evil.

His eyes flicked down at the page in front of him. He thought he saw the word "tongue."

He looked away quickly. Lord, why are you testing me like this? Why are you doing this to me?

It has been Dave's experience, through many confusing years, that Oscar Wilde had it right—the best way to get rid of a temptation is to give in to it. He fingered the letter without looking at it and thought of his little girl, as sweet as summer. Don't give in, darling, he thought. Please don't let bad things happen. Then, not sure at all that he was doing the right thing, he put the letter back in the envelope and carried it to the garbage can. He held it away from his body the way he might have carried a dead mouse. And he never mentioned it—not to his wife and not to his daughter. Sure of only one thing: If he was doing the right thing, he was doing it for the wrong reason, acting out of cowardice, not courage.

He drifted around the house aimlessly. Picking things up. When he got to the bathroom, he leaned on the sink and stared at himself in the mirror. Then, without thinking about where he was going or why, he wandered into Stephanie's room and sat on her bed. It was not a big room. Years ago he and Morley had framed a collection of family photos and hung them on the wall at the foot of her bed. Dave's father and mother; Roy and Helen; Stephanie in a stroller, on skates, at Halloween with her friend Becky. There were about ten pictures. They were the only things in the room that Stephanie hadn't redone. The other walls were covered with pictures she had cut out of magazines. The collage, which had begun with rock stars and lately grown to include a collection of models who didn't eat enough, had begun over her desk and moved up the wall, across the ceiling, and down to where he was sitting. Three walls and half the ceiling were completely covered, but still, the wall with the photos was untouched. As if she didn't want to hurt their feelings.

Dave bent over, picked up a sneaker, and looked around for its mate.

Instead, he found a paper bag with the two bottles of sunscreen he had bought for her to take to camp. He picked it up and looked around for somewhere to put the bottles. He tried to clear a space on the table by her bed, but all he managed was to push a bottle of lotion on the floor. He picked up the lotion and put it back where she had left it. She would soon be seventeen. This was her room, not his.

That night, as Morley and Dave were watching the news on television, Dave said, "You know, I'm still worried about Margot."

Morley said, "Margot is fine," and would have continued, but Dave stopped her and said, "No. Listen. We don't know anything about that camp. Maybe she's miserable. She *is* only ten. That's young. And Annie is in Paris. And God knows where Ralph's gone—or whatever his name is. Why did she marry that guy, anyway?"

Later, Morley said, "If you're so worried about Margot, why don't you phone the camp and ask them how she's doing?" Then she rolled over, set her book on her night table, and put her head under the pillow.

Dave phoned the camp from work the next day.

A woman answered.

Dave said, "I'm phoning about my niece. I was wondering how she's doing. She's in Igor's tent."

The lady at the other end of the phone said, "What?"

Dave hung up.

On Wednesday, Dave couldn't stand it any longer. "I'm going to drive up to see her," he said.

Morley said, "They aren't allowed visitors for two weeks. It's against the rules. It makes them homesick."

"I've thought it out," said Dave. "She doesn't have to see *me*. I'm going to take a paddle. I'm going to say she forgot her paddle. I'll say I was in the neighbourhood and thought I'd drop it off. I'll see *her*. But she doesn't have to see *me*."

Morley said, "If it makes you feel better. But I'm not coming with you."

Dave said, "That's okay. I can go myself." He didn't think she would let him go.

———

The camp was two hours north of the city. He parked his car in the visitors' parking lot at the camp gate. There were no other cars. He got his prop—the paddle that he had bought just that morning—out of the trunk and started off down the dirt road. There was a lake beside the road on his left. There was a forest on his right. It was a beautiful summer afternoon. The sky was blue. The clouds white and cottony. And there was wind. A soft breeze off the lake. Dave felt like he was taking a wind bath. The city was so hot, so sticky. He could hear children playing ahead of him.

There was a bend in the road. As he came to the bend, Dave saw a beach and a group of girls swimming. The road he was walking on dipped down a hill and wound to the beach. From the top of the hill, Dave could see the length of the lake, the shadows of the clouds on the water. It was beautiful. More beautiful than he had imagined. Dave stood there and drank it all in. He was about to walk down to the beach when he recognized one of the bathing suits. It was Margot. Margot standing at the end of the diving board. Margot laughing and pointing at a teenager in the water. That must be Igor. Margot running along the diving board and hurling herself into space, grabbing her feet and tucking herself into a cannonball, exploding into the lake a few feet from the older girl. Dave stepped off the road so no one could see him. He stood behind a tree and watched his niece play for fifteen minutes. Watched her get out of the lake all legs and arms and tighten herself into a towel and pick her barefoot way along the road Dave was standing beside.

Dave was overwhelmed by the urge to leave his tree and tell his niece he was there. He wanted to walk up to her and pick her up and say, "Here I am. I just drove two hours to see you. I drove all the way from the city because of you. Because I was worried about you." He wanted to say, "I love you, Margot, and if you are unhappy here, you can come home. And if you are ever unhappy anywhere else, all you have to do is call and I'll come."

He knew she wouldn't come with him. He knew she would want to stay. He felt stupid for being here. He understood that something important had happened. His family was growing up. His little sister's kid was doing fine at camp.

He jumped when he heard the man's voice.

"This is private property. What are you doing here?"

Dave stepped out from behind his tree.

The man was older than he was. Maybe fifty-five. Wiry. Tough-looking. Like a farmer.

God, thought Dave, what *am* I doing here? "Hello," he said, trying to be pleasant, trying to be nonthreatening.

"What are you doing here?" said the man again. Threateningly.

"I was watching the kids," said Dave.

"This is private property," said the man. Moving in front of Dave so he couldn't get past.

Dave said, "Uh. It's not what it looks like. I'm a parent. My kid is down there." Dave thought trying to explain it was his niece would be too complicated. "I was bringing her this paddle." Dave held up the paddle. "I didn't want her to see me. They're not supposed to have visitors." He held out his hand. "My name is Dave," he said.

The farmer didn't move. He didn't want to shake hands.

"You work at the camp?" said Dave.

"I'm the caretaker," said the man. "Maybe you better come to the office."

"Wait a minute," said Dave. "I really don't want to go to the office." Dave did not want a scene. He did not want his niece to know he was there. Did not want them to phone Morley. "Have you got kids?" said Dave. "A week ago I got a letter from my kid. She's the one in the bright blue Speedo. In the letter, she said she was unhappy. She said she hated it here. I needed to see if she was all right. The paddle was just an excuse." Dave held out the paddle. "Take it," he said. "The camp could probably use it somewhere. I really don't want to go to the office."

The caretaker sized Dave up and took the paddle. "Visitors' day is on Sunday," he said.

"Yeah," said Dave. "I know. Listen, I'm sorry. Thank you."

The caretaker stood back and let Dave pass. Watched him walk down the road. Dave turned around once and waved awkwardly and then didn't turn again, walking with the strange self-conscious roll that comes when you know someone is watching you.

———

He picked up Margot a few weeks later. He met her at the same parking lot where he had dropped her off. Sam was already home—minus most of the clothes he had left with, but not the comics. Stephanie was coming that evening. As they were walking into the house, Margot turned.

"Uncle Dave," she said, "do you know what it is we breathe in?"

"Oxygen?" said Dave.

She nodded and took a step and stopped again. "And what about what we breathe out?"

"Carbon dioxide?" said Dave.

"Huh," said Margot.

"Why?" said Dave.

"I didn't think you were that smart."

Dave winced for only a second before he laughed.

Road Trip

By the end of August, summer had settled so lazily upon the city that it was hard to imagine a different season. It confirmed itself every night, in the clutter spilling from the sidewalk cafes, in the chatter of neighbourhood baseball games, in the nighttime hiss of a thousand water sprinklers.

Across from the Vinyl Cafe, two young men, both wearing beards and assorted earrings, had erected a scaffold and were painting a mural down the empty brick wall of an old theatre.

In Jim Scoffield's backyard, the last of the raspberries were barely hanging on to the raspberry bush. Jim brought Morley a bowl of berries, and they had them for breakfast the next morning. Sam spent one morning following the water truck around the neighbourhood on his bike. He rode in the rainbow at the back of the truck—in the driver's blind spot—enjoying the sweet iron smell of cold water on hot pavement, the spray licking at his pedals. There were worse places to be, in the dog days of summer, than back in the city.

Dave was not unhappy to be at home, pleased that the summer had been declared a success. It was a far cry from last summer, when he had taken his family on a road trip—something he might not have tried if he had read the survey that said forty percent of children claim they would rather clean their room and eat vegetables every day than go on a family holiday.

The survey hadn't been published when Dave and Morley were planning last summer's vacation. Dave had always wanted to drive west with his children, and Stephanie was almost sixteen. She would soon be too old for family trips. They were running out of summers when they could travel together.

"We could go around the Great Lakes," said Dave. "Maybe into Saskatchewan." Dave wanted to show his children the beauty of the prairies. Imagined his family in a campground in the valley of the Saskatchewan River. What could be better?

Morley said, "We are not going to put the cat in the car again, Dave. If the cat's in the car, I'm not coming."

Dave said, "We'll find someone to look after the cat."

―――――

The cat had once belonged to Dave's sister, Annie.

Dave and Morley took it the spring Annie moved back to Nova Scotia from Boston. She was planning to leave it behind.

"I don't know," she said when Dave offered to take the cat.

"What do you mean?" said Dave.

"I feel stupid," said his sister. "I don't like to say it out loud."

"Say what?" said Dave.

"Whenever the cat is around, things seem to go wrong."

Dave said, "Don't be silly. We can look after a cat."

―――――

Annie brought the cat in a cage. As soon as they were in the house, Dave knelt down and wiggled a finger through the bars. "Puss puss," he said.

"Galway," said Annie. "After the poet Galway Kinnell."

The cat was beige with black spots, lean and rangy.

A female.

"Galway Kinnell is a man," said Dave.

"I know," said Annie. "But we were big fans."

Dave started to fiddle with the latch on the cage door.

"Wait," said Annie, holding out an envelope. But she was too late. Dave had already flipped the latch open.

"Here, puss," he said.

The cat shot out of the cage as if she had been spring-loaded.

"Oh," said Annie.

"Oh," said Dave.

They were both off balance, staring at each other and then at Galway, who had sailed over Dave's shoulder and landed in the middle of the hall with the sureness of a dancer.

"It's okay," said Dave. Thinking maybe it was not okay at all.

"You should have read this first." Annie was gesturing with the envelope. "Before you let her out."

As Dave took the envelope, Arthur, the family dog, ambled through the dining room door. When Galway saw Arthur, she hissed. Arthur jerked to a stop.

"Arthur," said Dave, "this is Galway. Galway is a cat."

Arthur took a cautious step forward, wagging his tail tentatively. Galway sank to the floor and began to lower her ears—they folded back on her head like bat wings—until they were flat and she looked like she was wearing a helmet. Arthur bared his teeth, and a sound that was more a rumble than a growl began to emanate from deep inside of him. The cat and the dog stared at each other for a moment, and then Galway flicked her tail. Arthur abruptly stopped growling, looked pathetically at Dave as if to say, "Why are you letting this happen?," and slunk into the kitchen.

Annie looked defensive.

Dave said, "I'll read this later." He stuffed the instructions in his back pocket.

He forgot about the letter until that night. When he pulled it out, he wondered how his sister could have written three pages about a cat. Typical of Annie to fuss like that. He took the letter and went into the den. Arthur, who was curled up on the couch, lifted his head, furrowed his brow, slid onto the floor, and mooched out of the room, throwing a doleful glance over his shoulder. Dave shut the door. He had come into the den because he didn't want to read Annie's letter in front of Galway, so he was startled, when he turned around, to find she was sitting on top of the bookshelf.

"She was threatening me," he said to Morley the next day.

Instead of reading Annie's letter, he took it downstairs and put in his briefcase. Then he went to bed.

He was pretty sure he had put it in his briefcase.

"Maybe you threw it out," said Morley. "It was garbage day."

"I didn't throw it out," said Dave. "The cat took it out of my briefcase."

"Probably," said Morley.

"She did," said Dave. "Look at her. She's smirking." At that moment Galway turned and walked away, her tail in the air.

"See?" said Dave. "She didn't want us to read the letter. It said something about the cage. About keeping her in the cage."

"Probably," said Morley. "That's probably it. The hair dryer is missing, too. Do you suppose she has the hair dryer as well?"

———

It took Arthur and Galway about a week to work out an uneasy truce. For the first week, the cat barely set foot on the floor. She moved around the house from chair back to table-top, often settling somewhere above Arthur, gazing down at him threateningly. Dave came home one night in the second week, and the cat had descended. Morley said, "See? They're fine now."

Dave wasn't as sure. "Watch," he said. "Whenever Galway comes into the room, Arthur gets up and leaves."

One day Dave came home at lunch to check the mail. It was garbage day, so instead of going through the front door, he picked up the empty garbage can and lugged it down the driveway. As he passed the dining room window, he saw movement in his peripheral vision. He turned just in time to see Arthur hurtling through the dining room with Galway clinging on his back as if she were riding a bucking bronco.

A moment later, they came back, Galway barely clinging to Arthur. Dave watched her slide off as Arthur spun wildly into the kitchen. He watched Galway jump onto the dining room buffet and perch there, her eyes glued to the kitchen door.

No wonder Arthur had seemed so tired.

———

That summer Dave had made the mistake of trying to take Galway with them on a weekend trip to the Muskokas. This was what Morley was remembering when she said she would not travel with the cat again.

The car was all packed. Sam, who was two at the time, was already strapped into his car seat, and already crying, when Dave tried to put Galway back into the cage. Getting the cat into the cage was like trying to fold a large spring into a tin can. Galway kept popping free, then hiding—behind the fridge, under a bed. Dave chased her around the house, hu-miliated, thinking that when he was young, fathers knew how to do things like change the oil in their cars, solder things together, clean fish. Surely he could put a cat into a cage. He needed to show his family he could do this thing. It was driving him wild.

Out in the car, Stephanie was throwing a tantrum. Morley, who was feeling irritable herself, said, "Stay here. I'm going to get your father."

When she found Dave pulling Galway through a radiator by her tail, Morley said, "What are you doing? Why do we have to use the cage? Why don't we let her free in the car?"

"That's why," said Dave five minutes later, as the family stood in the driveway beside their packed car, watching Galway disappear over the backyard fence like a burglar. There was a set of red scratches that looked like skid marks running up Dave's face and over his forehead.

"You better have those looked at," said their neighbour Jim Scoffield, who had been watching. "They can infect."

"What?" said Dave.

"Cat scratches," said Jim. "They get infected easily."

"She didn't have to do that," Dave told Morley as she wiped his face with hydrogen peroxide. "She had to go out of her way to go over my head. It was deliberate. It was malicious."

It started to rain. They never got to the cottage.

———

Last summer Dave said, "I'll get Kenny to look after her. We'll leave her here, and Kenny can come over and feed her. It's just two weeks. Kenny can do that."

Dave knew Kenny would be delighted to have a key to his house. To a television set with cable.

Dave was prepared to leave Galway in the house by herself, but not Arthur. Jim Scoffield had offered to look after the dog.

Usually, Arthur was anxious when he sensed he was being left behind, and Dave felt like a traitor when he led him over

to Jim's house. But when they got there, Arthur seemed . . .
relieved. Almost delighted. When Dave took him off the
leash, he bounded around Jim's house. When Jim leaned
over to pat him, Arthur licked his face with enthusiasm.

"That's odd," said Dave.

———————

They left on a glorious Monday morning in August. They
drove north, stopping for hamburgers after two hours on the
road. Stephanie walked into the restaurant after they had
found a table and sat at the counter by herself.

They made supper in a provincial park on the shores of
Georgian Bay.

"This is what Canada is all about," said Morley. "This is
the heart of our country."

"It's too windy," said Stephanie. "It's just trees."

They drove aboard the ferry to Manitoulin Island in the
morning. "First on, first off," said Dave.

Halfway across the lake, the sky abruptly darkened, and
the ferry started to roll in the chop. Dave said, "I don't feel so
good. I'm going to the car to get a sweater." Down below, he
had to pick his way along the length of the ship to where he
had parked at the front of the line of cars. First on. First off.
The rumble of the ship's engine and the greasy smell of
motor oil didn't make Dave feel better. He was standing
alone among the parked cars, like a wonky scarecrow, wondering what he should do if his stomach got worse, when he
opened the trunk. He was preoccupied and totally unpre-
pared for what happened next.

He squinted into the dark trunk and leaned forward, feeling for his sweater. In the darkness, his hand brushed against
something soft and wool-like on top of the picnic basket.
He tried to pick it up, and then, with a shock of adrenaline
rushing through his body, he let it go—knowing this thing he

had touched wasn't a sweater-thing but something that could breathe, it was a breathing-thing. At this point, Dave lost conscious awareness of what was happening. The adrenaline hit some primal gland, and he became Cro-Magnon Dave. Knowing only that the thing-that-wasn't-a-sweater, the breathing-thing, was big enough to be a life-threatening sort of thing. Not cougar, but maybe wolverine. Cro-Magnon Dave made a grunting prehistoric sound that twentieth-century Dave had never heard before but immediately understood to mean get-me-out-of-here.

When you reach into any dark place, a place you can't see into, even an innocuous place like under-a-sofa, when you reach under-a-sofa expecting to come up with something like a newspaper and hit, instead, something soft, like the family guinea pig, or worse, something you can penetrate, like a piece of rotting fruit, even these innocuous objects can kick the get-me-out-of-here gland into action.

So it is, when you reach into your trunk in the darkness of a ferry expecting to grab a sweater, and wrap your hand instead around something that can breathe, you do exactly what Dave did—you jump back and smack your head on the roof of the trunk. A split second later, when the breathing-thing—which some part of Dave's brain noticed bore an amazing resemblance to Galway—when this *living creature* explodes out of your trunk, you instinctively grab it by the tail as it sails by you, and you swing it in the air.

Galway landed on the roof of the car. Dave stood there, the blood pounding in his ears. Heard an announcement over the speakers instructing passengers to return to their vehicles. Saw his wife and children coming toward him.

"Now, Lord," he said. "Take me now, Lord."

The family seemed more concerned, *were* more concerned, about Galway than they were about Dave.

"Is she okay, Daddy?" said Stephanie.

"What happened?" said Sam.

"How did *she* get here?" said Morley.

As the ferry docked, the kids ran to the cafeteria. They came back with a tuna-salad sandwich and a pile of coffee creamers.

"She hasn't eaten all day," said Sam.

Galway spent the next half hour in the backseat, between the kids, lapping up the tuna sandwich and innumerable creamers. By the time they reached Sault Ste. Marie, she had settled comfortably in what became her favourite car place— curled under Dave's seat, where she could reach out whenever she felt like it and take swipes at Dave's ankles.

"Tough," said Morley.

She didn't say "Sorry." She didn't say "We could stop and get a cage." Just "Tough."

———

There were some nice times: an afternoon at Science North in Sudbury, the morning the truck driver took their picture beside the giant goose at Wawa.

"I was once stuck here for two days," said Dave. "Trying to hitchhike to Vancouver."

But it wasn't the vacation Dave had imagined. He had envisioned himself in the early evening, drinking a beer in a lawn chair beside the pool of some seedy motel, watching the kids swim. He had imagined baskets of fried chicken, strange television shows, roadside theme parks.

Mostly, it was a dark and sorry week.

He had not considered flat tires, "No Vacancy" signs, lost sunglasses, and a worn-out alternator. He left the headlights on one afternoon in a mall parking lot outside Schreiber, Ontario. They had to phone for a jump.

Mostly, it was thumping west along the Trans-Canada

Highway to the constant buzz from Stephanie's Walkman. Mostly, it was Morley and Dave barely talking, Sam and Stephanie talking only when they needed to point out where their side of the seat began or ended. Every night Dave locked himself into the motel bathroom and dabbed at his shredded ankles with hydrogen peroxide. There was no air-conditioning in their car, and each day it seemed to get hotter.

On a Sunday when they woke up sticky and got stickier as the day progressed, Galway started to behave oddly. She moved out from under Dave's seat and began pacing around the car.

"I think Galway is sick," said Sam.

"She looks weird, Daddy," said Stephanie. "There's white stuff around her mouth."

Galway wasn't sick. She had just been heated up hotter than a cat should be heated. Dave said, "We'll get off the highway. There must be a back road."

The temperature in the car *was* unbearable. They couldn't open the windows for fear Galway would jump out. Dave was thinking, We'll stop for ice cream at the first place we see.

And then, suddenly, they were in a traffic jam.

On a Sunday? thought Dave. In Atikokan?

"I need a drink," said Stephanie. "I don't feel so good."

Dave said, "Hold on," and turned abruptly onto a side street. He had no idea where he was going. He just knew that he had to keep the car moving until they got somewhere. Anywhere. He didn't want to be stuck in traffic. He drove halfway down the block and, to his horror, saw there was a barrier at the end of the street. He could feel the car closing in on him.

"I don't believe this," he said.

He stopped short, throwing the kids against the front seat and Galway into his ankles.

"Cool," said Sam.

"Dave," said Morley, "take it easy."

But Dave was way beyond easy. He put the car in reverse and began backing up the street faster than he should have. Swinging from side to side.

"There's an alley," he said. "I saw an alley."

He turned into the alley and too late saw that a block away, where the alley rejoined the street, there was a crowd of people standing with their backs to him, blocking his way. He honked. When nothing happened, he honked again. He kept driving down the alley. Honking. No one moved until he was close, and then a man, holding two children by their hands, turned and looked. Only then did the crowd part, parents tugging children out of the way.

Then they were out of the alley and turning onto the main street. Dave hesitated and turned right because everything seemed to be moving right. He thought, At last.

And Morley said, "Dave?" It was a question.

Dave noticed the sidewalks were lined with people—not just across his alley but all up and down the street—on both sides.

Stephanie said, "Why is everybody waving?"

And Morley said, "Because this is a parade. We are in a parade."

Dave started to feel sick himself.

"This is pathetic," said Stephanie as she slipped out of sight on the seat. Before Dave could think what to do, there was an explosion, like a cannon or a rocket.

Loud and close. And another . . .

It was a bass drum. Dave looked in the rearview mirror and saw that there was a band right behind them. He watched as the man in the bearskin hat leading the band, about ten feet behind their car, hurled a silver baton high into the air. When he caught it, the band began playing. Dave didn't know marching bands sounded so loud when you were that close to them, and then he couldn't see them anymore because the mirror was suddenly filled with the image of Galway hurtling from the backseat toward Dave's head, like a jet plane. Dave ducked. The car lurched momentarily toward the sidewalk. Dave slammed on the brakes. But he had to start up again quickly, jerkily, or the marching band was going to march right over them.

So they drove on, Galway ping-ponging around the car, over all of them. Front seat. Backseat. Ricocheting off the windows. Flecks of foam flying from her mouth. She settled abruptly in Sam's lap.

Sam said, "Cool." He held the foaming cat up to the window, waving her paw at the crowd.

A clown appeared at the side of the car, jogging along beside them, knocking on Morley's window, waving. Morley looked straight ahead.

Sam said, "This is *really* cool."

Dave smiled weakly at the clown and waved at a little girl who was pointing at him. He was looking for a street he could turn onto.

But there were no streets to turn onto.

"Well," he said, leaning in to the driver's door, trying to be comfortable with this, "it could be worse."

Which was when Galway vomited.

Into Morley's lap.

———

They turned around that night.

They were sitting in the parking lot of a doughnut shop somewhere between Atikokan and Fort Frances. It was eight-thirty at night, and they couldn't find a motel.

Morley said, "Dave, do you want to go home?"

"Is this Saskatchewan?" asked Sam. "It looks just like Scarborough."

They got home three days later.

As they drove under the warm orange glow of the lights that hung over the expressway, Morley felt as though she were being wrapped in a blanket. She turned to Dave. "If you had to," she said, "how would you categorize this holiday?"

Dave looked at his wife. She was smiling.

He felt a wave of relief wash over him. "Catastrophe," he said.

"I thought for a while," she said, "that you were . . ."

"Catatonic?" said Dave.

She laughed. "It's good to be home. It wasn't a complete . . ."

"Cataclysm?" said Dave. "Next year," he said, "no car. We'll fly to the . . ."

"Catskills," said Morley.

"And eat the flesh of large, dumb, slow-moving animals," said Dave. "Meat that will block our arteries and make us fat."

"What?" said Morley.

"Elephants," said Sam.

"Cattle," said Stephanie.

It was good to be home.

There was a pile of mail on the dining room table.

"I'm going over to Jim's," said Dave. "To get Arthur. I'll be back in a minute."

It was Morley who found the note from Kenny on the kitchen counter.

Didn't see the cat for the first day or two, so I put the food on the porch and she started eating it. She finally came in

*after a couple of days. I didn't let her out again. I think she
missed you. She's been scratching the furniture a bit.*

Dave walked into the living room with Arthur the same
moment Galway came pounding down the stairs with a huge
orange tabby on her tail. Galway, a step ahead of the tabby,
leaped onto a bookcase and spun around to face the intruder.
There was an instant of perfect silence. Dave standing at the
doorway with Arthur at his side, Morley on her way from the
kitchen with Kenny's note in her hand, Stephanie reaching
for the mail, Sam about to turn on the television. All of them
frozen for a moment, their eyes on this monstrous cat they
had never seen before.

Arthur was the first to react.

He growled, and as everyone turned to look at him, the
growl changed to a bark. He jumped into action, his feet
windmilling on the hardwood floor; barking, growling, he
chased the orange cat once around the dining room and then
out the front door.

It happened so fast no one had a chance to say anything.

Before anyone moved, Arthur was back, wagging his tail.

Galway jumped down from the bookcase, and Arthur
wagged up to her and licked her face.

"That's so cute," said Stephanie, turning back to the mail.

"They're happy to see each other," said Morley.

It was only Dave who noticed Galway's ears flattening
ever so slowly; Dave who recognized the look of despair descending on Arthur as he tucked his tail between his legs and
loped toward the kitchen, his dark woeful eyes glancing back
over his shoulder at Galway as he went.

Autumn

The Pig

The guinea pig was losing hair. Not shedding it; losing it. Morley said, "You better take her to the vet." Dave said to his wife, "I know."

The neighbourhood vet said she didn't do pigs. She told Dave he'd have to take her to a clinic that specialized in small animals. Dave wasn't sure how to move a sick pig across the city. He settled on the bus and a wooden fruit basket filled with wood chips. The pig didn't seem to mind the excursion. Neither did Dave.

The pig was Dave's job. He cleaned her cage, he fed her, and since she was sick, he accepted that it was up to him to make her better. The pig was his son's pet, but when he bought her, Dave knew that caring for her would eventually fall to him. He didn't enjoy cleaning the cage two nights a week; often he resented it, but he never expected it to be any other way. The pig, after all, was his idea. Why shouldn't he look after her? Once it occurred to him that he did a better job caring for the guinea pig than he did for anyone else in his life—not that he cared for the pig more than his wife or kids; just that looking after her was clearer. He could see when her cage was dirty, and when it was, he knew what to do about it.

When he got to the vet, a young receptionist asked him

questions and typed his answers into her computer. When she asked for the pig's name, Dave said, "Doesn't have a name."

Not liking the look that crossed her face, he added, "We call her, the Pig . . . sometimes just Guinea." Dave, who had always felt naming animals was a questionable practice, thought naming a rodent was foolish, and he hadn't encouraged the idea. But standing in front of the receptionist, he felt shabby about owning an unnamed pig. As if that told her all she needed to know about him and his family and the way they cared for animals. As if it were suddenly obvious why the pig was sick.

Dave is foggy about the rest of the visit. But he can remember snatches of it. He remembers the receptionist ushering him into another room. He and the pig. He remembers being left alone until another young woman walked in. In his memory, she is wearing a white lab coat. She looks much too young to be a doctor. When she plucks the pig out of its basket and holds her up confidently, he thinks, Must be just out of school.

The young woman is asking him questions. She is poking the pig, petting her. She is taking her away. Dave waits in the front room with the receptionist.

When the young vet, whose name is Dr. Percy, calls Dave back into the examining room, she tells him that she suspects the pig has a tumour. Suspects. She can't be sure. Not without tests.

"We don't see a lot of guinea pigs," she adds.

Then she hands Dave a yellow piece of paper that he still has in his wallet. He has been showing it to everyone who lingers by the cash register at his store. At the top of the page it says:

ESTIMATE
GUINEA PIG—UNNAMED

What seized Dave's attention the moment Dr. Percy handed
the estimate to him, and why he has been showing it around,
is the figure at the bottom of the page.

ESTIMATE TOTAL: $563.30
The ESTIMATE is carefully itemized:

Guinea pig examination and assessment	$37.00
4 days hospitalization exotic level 2 @ $21.50/day	$86.00
Vitamin C injection	$12.00
Fluids, Reglan injection additional @ $6.00 each	$12.00
Exotic anaesthesia induction fee	$30.00
20 mins. Isoflurane anaesthesia @ $120/hr	$40.00
15 mins. Surgery minor category @ $200/hr	$49.95
Radiograph split plate	$62.00
CBC—done with profile	$25.00
Clinical chemistry 1 profile	$47.50
Cortisol (3 tests)	$75.00
Miscellaneous charges if needed (medication at home, etc.)	$50.00
7% GST to be added to final bill. Estimated to be	$36.85

The figure that galled Dave was the $21.50 a day for hospi-
talization. How could it cost $21.50 a day to feed and lodge a
guinea pig? He himself had stayed in motels for under $21.50
a night. How much could a guinea pig eat, especially after
surgery?

At first he thought the estimate was a joke. Or maybe a
mistake. Then he realized it was neither, and he felt trapped.
If he signed the estimate and handed the pig over to the vet,

he could imagine what they would have to say about him at closing time. What kind of person, he could hear the receptionist ask, would spend five hundred dollars on a guinea pig? A four-year-old sick guinea pig. A guinea pig that was going bald and could soon look like a worm with legs. A pig that was clearly playing on the back nine of pigdom. On the other hand, if he were to walk out, wouldn't that confirm everything that the receptionist had thought about him?

He asked if he could phone his wife. She wasn't home. "I have to speak to my wife," he said as he left with the pig. "I'll phone you tomorrow."

———

Everyone he has asked says he did the right thing. Brian, who opens the Vinyl Cafe on Saturday mornings, said so. Morley said so, too. "Are you crazy?" she asked. At supper she made hair-replacement jokes. She said if the pig lost all its hair, she would knit her a little sweater.

Dave's friend Al suggested he take the pig for a walk in the rain. "That'll fix her," Al said.

Dave didn't try to explain what he was feeling. He knew it was crazy to spend $563.30 on a balding guinea pig that had cost $30. But when you are standing in a vet's office holding a life in your hands, it is easy to imagine yourself spending the money. It was, after all, a life. And it was, after all, in his hands.

———

The next evening, after everyone else was in bed, Dave poured himself a beer and sat down at the kitchen table. He began writing a list of animals whose deaths he had already caused.

　　l. One hamster. Not really his fault. She had died from chewing the wood in her cage. Dave's grandfather

had built the cage. And it was his grandfather who
had painted it yellow. It was the lead in the paint that
had killed the hamster. Dave remembers the night
the hamster died. He remembers his mother feeding
his hamster brandy from an eyedropper. What he
can't remember is whether the hamster had a name.

2. Frogs. Too many to count. He had never actually
killed a frog himself. But he had been present when
frogs were killed. He must have been twelve when
his friends had found the swamp. They went there
and killed frogs in all sorts of fiendish ways. They
tied rocks to the frogs' legs and threw them into the
water so they drowned. Dave remembers watching
one frog, weighted down, its front legs pawing at the
water, trying desperately to swim to the surface. He
couldn't remember whether he had said anything.
Whether he had stood up for the frog or not.

Years later, he went to Honolulu and toured the
wreckage left from the attack on Pearl Harbor. The
guide explained that the destroyer the glass-
bottomed boat was gliding over had flipped during
the Japanese raid, trapping hundreds of men in air
pockets when it sank. The guide said that for one
week, rescuers could hear the trapped men tapping
on the hull of the sunken boat. The guide said there
was nothing anyone could do for them. Dave
squinted into the Hawaiian sun and remembered the
way the frog's front paws had worked the water.

3. Starlings. When he was duck hunting. He went duck
hunting only the one time. All morning there were
no ducks. Nothing in the water. Nothing in the sky.
Just heavy grey clouds, a smudge of sun at the end of
the lake. Just before dawn, a flurry of starlings flew

overhead. Dave can't remember who was the first to shoot into the flock. He remembers lifting his borrowed rifle. Remembers the wonder he felt as the starlings tumbled out of the sky. They hit the water like stones.

4. One groundhog. It was summer. He was a university student. He was working on a dairy farm in the Ottawa valley. He loved the job. He was driving tractors and cows. Every night after supper, he took a .22-calibre rifle and walked through the fields. He watched the sun go down and smoked an Old Port cigarillo. He had the gun because he was supposed to shoot groundhogs. They dug tunnels in the fields, and the tractor might tip into the tunnels. It made Dave feel important. The evening he saw his first groundhog, she must have been a hundred yards away. She was sitting up in her hole like a prairie dog. The sun was behind him. He dropped to his knees and brought the rifle up to his shoulder. He squeezed the trigger. He was mortified when the groundhog dropped out of sight. She was lying on the ground when he walked up to her. There was a small red puncture in her side as if someone had driven a nail into her. Every time she breathed, an awful sucking sound came out of the hole. Dave fumbled with the rifle. The bolt jammed. He couldn't get another bullet into the chamber. And the groundhog wouldn't die. Dave started to cry. "Die, dammit," he yelled as he turned the rifle upside down and hit the groundhog with the butt. It was the last time he had ever shot a rifle.

5. One baby raccoon. Maybe two. It was night. He was driving his family back from a week's vacation by

the ocean. They had just crossed the Appalachian Mountains. They were in a valley, on a two-lane highway. He was driving too fast. He saw the eyes glint in the darkness well ahead of him.

"Watch out," his wife said in the seat beside him.

"I see it," he snapped, impatiently.

Saw with plenty of time to slow down. Instead, he veered to the right. He still remembers the surprise, the shock, when he heard the thump on his right bumper.

He had seen the flash of the mother's eyes in his headlights; what he hadn't seen were the babies following her across the highway. He plowed right into them. He wanted to stop, but his wife told him to keep going. The kids were in the backseat.

That was as far as Dave got on his list. It was after midnight. Everyone was asleep except for the pig, who, not accustomed to having the lights on at this time of night, began to whistle from her cage on the counter. Dave got up and took a carrot out of the fridge and dropped it through the door on the top of the cage. The pig sniffed the carrot and settled down to it.

"Pig," said Dave out loud with great affection.

"Pig," he said again quietly to himself on his way upstairs to bed.

Labour Days

On the first Tuesday in September, Morley flew through the back door and said to whoever was in the kitchen, "Sorry I'm late." Whoever turned out to be Arthur, the dog, sitting expectantly by his dish, his tail wagging to see her. It was six-fifteen. Morley had meant to be home before five-thirty. She had thought *everyone* would be waiting, *everyone's* tail wagging, *everyone* expecting supper.

"Dave?" she called as she kicked her shoes off on the back steps and headed for the kitchen. She hesitated in front of the refrigerator for the briefest instant, like she might hesitate at the side of a lake or a swimming pool, pushing the hair off her face and then taking a deep breath before plunging in. She was on her knees rummaging around for something fast and easy to make for supper when Dave walked in.

Before he could say hello, she said, "Potatoes or rice?" Before he could answer, she did. "Rice," she said. Kicking the fridge closed, she headed for the cupboard. "Anna Lindquist asked me to go with her to L.A. for the weekend."

Dave opened the fridge and pulled out a beer and said, "Why not? It couldn't cost more than a few thousand dollars."

"It's Emma Thompson's birthday," said Morley. "Anna invited me to go with her to Emma Thompson's birthday dinner. In L.A."

"We could put off fixing the car," said Dave helpfully.

"She says she doesn't want to travel alone. Emma Thompson, Dave. The movie star."

Dave said, "When she invited you . . . did she mean you . . . you? Or you . . . and me?"

Morley was standing by the sink, rinsing the rice. She screwed up her face in concentration and said, "This is ridiculous. I can't afford to go to L.A. for the weekend. She knows that. That's why she asked me."

Morley and Dave had talked about Morley going back to work once the kids were grown. She never thought she would stay away from the stage so long. It was hard to believe it was almost twenty years. She was busy, and she was happy with what she was doing. But when the Century of Wind theatre company asked her if she would work for them as general manager, she realized it was the right time.

She was feeling defeated by the Sisyphean nature of her life—washing the same dishes, doing the same laundry, over and over again. She was jealous of Dave's engagement with the world. Even around the house, he always took on the big industrious projects—rewiring the basement might be hard work, but she suspected it was a lot more interesting than organizing the winter clothes again.

When they offered her the job, however, no one mentioned that the British actor Anna Lindquist had been signed to a six-week contract—due to arrive in town on August 22 to begin rehearsals for the role of Madame Arkadina in Anton Chekhov's *The Seagull*. In her darker moments, Morley suspected maybe someone had thought better of mentioning it. Anna Lindquist is what is known, in the theatre business, as "high-maintenance."

As it turned out, Anna Lindquist arrived in Toronto two days early. It was Morley's first week at work.

"Darling," Anna said when she phoned from the airport, "surely you don't expect me to take"—her voice dropping an octave—"a taxi?"

"She did this last time," said Robert, the stage manager. "She does it to put everyone off balance. I can't stand it." And he started to cry.

As Morley rushed out to the airport, she wondered if she would be able to recognize Anna Lindquist from her publicity photos. As it turned out, she needn't have worried.

Anna was sitting in the arrivals level with a little white dog in her lap. She was holding a lit cigarette in a long tortoise-shell holder—under a NO SMOKING sign. She was by far the most colourful thing in sight. Her heels were high, her skirt was short, her nails were long, and her hair, under the glare of the bright neon lights, was a shade of red Morley had never seen before.

Morley introduced herself and asked about luggage.

"I don't know, darling," said Anna, frowning. "I haven't the foggiest."

There was, she said, a matched set of three suitcases, and a hatbox. "In canary yellow, darling. I bought them in Mustique."

While Anna stayed in the lobby, Morley found a cart and wheeled the suitcases across the airport. "If you'll wait here," she said, "I'll get the car."

Morley had been too panicked on the way to clean out the candy wrappers, coffee cups, and the stack of vinyl Dave had left in the front seat.

She rolled the baggage into the elevator and wheeled

around the ramp to the parking lot. She threw the suitcases and the records into the trunk and cleaned up the car as best she could.

Ten minutes later, she led Anna out the airport door to where she had parked illegally by the curb. She ran around to the driver's side, jumped in, and noticed Anna standing on the sidewalk looking vague. At first Morley thought Anna was looking for the limousine. Then she realized she was waiting for Morley to open the door for her.

When Anna finally settled into the front seat, she said, "I was actually expecting a car and driver."

Morley drove directly to the apartment the theatre had rented for Anna Lindquist. It was on a lovely tree-lined street. The uniformed doorman, who had a nose for these things, immediately opened Anna Lindquist's door and led her into the foyer, leaving Morley to struggle with the luggage.

The apartment had the deep tranquility of serious money —thick carpeting in the halls, heavy oak doors, the burnish of old brass, and a lobby mirror that really was antique.

Anna Lindquist peered in the open third-floor apartment door, her feet firmly planted in the hallway. "I can't possibly stay here, darling," she said. "The walls are green. They remind me of vomit. I'll stay at a hotel until you can find something suitable. No need to drive me, darling . . . I'll call a taxi."

———

After supper, a week after Anna Lindquist arrived, Morley said, "The roughs for the posters came in today. Anna was upset because her name was below the title."

Dave was reading a music magazine at the kitchen table. "Gerta phoned," he said. "She's going to some new discount mall on Saturday."

Morley was spreading newspaper on the table. She was

going to waterproof a pair of boots. "Chekhov is the only name above the title. I told her, 'You can't be above Chekhov.' "

Dave said, "Gerta wants to know if you want to go with her—to the mall."

Morley said, "You know what happened then? She said, 'Chekhov's been dead for ninety-three years, darling. What could he possibly care about where he is on your silly poster?'

"Then she started talking about the size of the type. She wants her name in bigger print than Martin's."

Morley glared at her husband. "It's like working with a five-year-old. I went back to work because all I was doing was picking up after children, and I end up picking up after a fifty-five-year-old."

Dave said, "You should go. It'll be fun."

"This is my life?" said Morley. "Shopping for bulk food is fun?"

———

Morley eventually decided she would go to the mall with Gerta Lowbeer, more to get out of the house on Saturday than anything else. Going to a bunch of discount stores in the suburbs, she decided, was the closest thing to foreign travel on the horizon.

"I'll just look," she said. "It will be a cultural experience."

She looked at the aisles of cartons, the miles of produce, and as she looked, strange and unfamiliar urges descended upon her. She came home with a camp-sized case of cereal that had to be wheeled to her car, a carton of frozen lasagna with fifty individual meals, and a case of organic all-natural fruit snacks—four bright new flavours: pear, boysenberry-mango, apricot, and very berry—for the kids' lunches.

———

Morley prepared the lasagna for the first time the next Monday night. This is easy, she thought, coming home from work. Frozen lasagna and a salad. No sweat.

She was feeling smug until Sam asked what was for dinner and then said, "I hate frozen lasagna. Can I have spaghetti?"

Just as the water for the spaghetti was beginning to boil, Dave phoned and said, "I'm going to be late."

Instead of waiting, they started without him. When Stephanie took her first mouthful of lasagna, she said, "This tastes doughy—it's not like the kind you make."

Morley didn't answer. She was watching Sam suck a piece of spaghetti up his nose. "Do that again," she said, "and I'll cut your nose off."

Sam said, "Robbie taught me."

Stephanie said, "I hate this lasagna."

Dave came through the door and said, "Hi, everybody. Sorry I'm late."

The three of them stopped what they were doing and turned toward the door in unison—Stephanie raising her head glumly from her plate, Sam with the piece of spaghetti dangling from his nose, Morley frowning. All of them staring at this inappropriately cheerful man standing in the kitchen doorway.

At some mysterious level of Dave's brain, a tiny voice was saying, Don't say anything, Dave. Just sit down and eat the lasagna. But Dave didn't hear the voice in time. So instead of sitting down, he stood in the doorway. "Kenny Wong is doing renovations. *He* got *his* belt sander, and *I* got *mine,* and we were drag-racing them around the restaurant. I lost track of time."

No one said anything except the little voice. I told you not to say anything, it said.

So Dave sat down and took a bite of supper and said, "The lasagna is kind of doughy."

Morley stood up abruptly.

And the little voice said, Uh-oh.

But Dave continued, "What's wrong? Where are you going?"

Morley snarled, "I have to go out. Sam wants to show you something Robbie taught him."

Dave twisted around in his chair. He was talking to Morley's retreating back. "It's just frozen lasagna, right? It's not like you made it. That was a compliment. You don't have to buy any more of these frozen lasagnas."

———

The next morning Morley got up and went into the bathroom, and her toothbrush was already wet.

She said, "My toothbrush is wet. Why is my toothbrush wet?"

The family gathered solemnly around her.

"See?" she said, flicking the bristles. "It's wet. And I haven't brushed my teeth yet."

Sam and Dave stared glumly at the toothbrush, full of concern. It was as if she were telling them the dog had been hit by a car.

"That's *my* toothbrush," said Stephanie quietly. "The red one is *my* toothbrush."

Morley felt her heart turn cold. "The red one," she said, "is mine. I use it every day. *You* are green."

"I am?" said Stephanie. "I thought I was red."

"Me, too," said Sam. "I thought *I* was red."

Morley screamed and disappeared downstairs.

"What's the matter with her?" said Stephanie.

———

The kitty litter was Maggie's idea. Maggie's fault.

Maggie, who has three boys. It was Maggie who told Morley that she'd had it with washing around the toilet.

"I told them if they planned to keep using our toilets, they were going to have to sit down when they went from now on," said Maggie.

Maggie's husband, Russ, said if he had to sit down every time he went to the bathroom, he would leave home. Russ said it was a humiliating thing to ask of a man.

Maggie said okay. And then she dumped an entire bag of kitty litter around the base of the toilet.

Morley said, "You're kidding."

She didn't stop to think that the difference between her house and Maggie's house was that Maggie didn't own a cat.

When Galway saw the kitty litter around the upstairs toilet, she assumed it had been put there for her.

It took Morley a day too long to figure out what was happening. Removing all the litter took nearly an hour.

Convincing Galway to give up on her new second-floor litter box took even longer. It was not until the middle of November that Morley was able to stop reminding everyone, guests and family alike, to barricade the bathroom against the cat. Even now, whenever she sees the cat slinking down the hallway toward the bathroom, Morley shouts and rushes madly after her.

———

In the middle of September, the cast of *The Seagull* moved from the rehearsal space across the street into the theatre. An outline of the set had been marked off on the black stage floor with masking tape. Without flats, and with all the curtains raised, the stage looked like an empty aircraft hangar. You could see the dirty brick wall at the back of the building and the iron stairs leading to the catwalks. Standing alone on the stage, Morley was struck, as she always was, by the space above her. The black bars holding the rows of lights seemed impossibly high.

Thursday afternoon was a technical run-through. Anna Lindquist arrived carrying a large mirror. She played the entire first act holding the mirror no more than six inches from her face. Her eyes never left the mirror.

No one said a thing. Not even Martin Tidmarsh, who was playing her young lover. He leaned forward and kissed her on the cheek, pushing his lips around the mirror as if she always carried it, as if it were the most normal thing in the world.

This was how crazy she had made them.

Ralph, the director, knew what she was doing. She was checking the lighting.

"She has approval of the lighting," Ralph said to Morley when she slipped into the theatre to see how things were going. "If she complains, I think Gordon is going to quit."

They were sitting in the middle of the empty theatre. Ralph had his feet jammed against the row of seats in front of them. Morley was holding a large green binder.

"Why," said Morley five minutes later, "is she facing *that* way? If she's talking to Martin, shouldn't she be facing him?"

Anna Lindquist had her back to the entire cast. Everyone else was stage left except Anna, who was delivering a passionate soliloquy, to stage right.

"This way," said Ralph, "her left profile is facing the audience."

"She said my lights make her look old and crumpy," said Gordon to Morley an hour later. "We don't have to take this, you know."

Morley was sitting in her office working on the first draft of the next season's budget. "Come in, Ralph," she said, flipping off her computer. "I was just going to get a coffee. Do you want one?" She could work on the budget at home.

———

Thursday night at nine, Morley went upstairs, announcing she was going to take a bath and go to bed early. As she passed Stephanie's room, she stopped and said, "Have you hugged your mother today?"

Stephanie rolled her eyes and got up from her bed and leaned her arm around Morley's shoulders and then slouched back into her room.

Dave was downstairs helping Sam with maths homework when Morley screamed.

Dave said, "Stay here," and ran up the stairs. Two at a time.

Morley was standing in the bathroom. She had her bath-robe on.

"It's happening again," she said. "There are more tooth-brushes in this bathroom than there are people in this house."

She assembled everyone and lined up the toothbrushes. "Where did this *purple* toothbrush come from?" she asked.

Nobody would look at her.

———

Friday, Dave phoned Morley at lunch.

"I think I've solved the toothbrush mystery," he said. "I think that during the day, when the house is empty, there are people coming into our house to brush their teeth."

Morley said, "This isn't a joke, Dave."

———

On Tuesday morning, Ralph came into Morley's office. He sat down beside her desk. When he began to speak, it was with uncharacteristic intensity.

He said, "She refuses to hold hands during curtain call."

It struck Morley that Ralph didn't look well.

"I am not going to tell you what she says about Martin," he said. "I am going to tell you this instead. If you don't get her to hold Martin's hand during curtain call, then I'm leaving and I am never coming back."

He stood up carefully. Morley noticed that the act of standing required more thought on his part than usual. He pushed the chair deliberately behind him. He turned at the door. "One more thing," he said.

His deliberate calmness was starting to worry Morley.

"You tell her that if she slaps Melissa for real in Act Two, I am going to press charges. No more of this 'heat of the moment' crap. And I don't care if she needs time off to be Rolfed. There is a rehearsal tomorrow morning, and if she can't make it, we'll get Joanna to play the part. And if Joanna plays tomorrow morning, Joanna opens tomorrow night."

———

Anna Lindquist opened Wednesday night. Gordon was on the lights; Ralph was in a seat at the back beside Morley.

The next morning all three papers weighed in favourably, two with raves. The play was a success. The mood at the theatre was buoyant.

Friday morning, Morley decided to stay at home. The house looked like it needed bulldozing.

Morley had been so preoccupied with the theatre and Anna Lindquist that she hadn't noticed how bad the house was.

When everyone was finally off to work and school, she wandered into Sam's room. There were dirty clothes everywhere. She felt a heaviness descend upon her as she bent over to pick up a blue sweatshirt.

By eleven o'clock she had done seven loads of wash.

One more, she thought, and maybe I'll have time for a load of my things.

She was doing fine, thought she had broken the back of the laundry, until something made her look behind Stephanie's door. She found another pile of dirty clothes.

The relentlessness of the task overwhelmed her.

She could wash everything she could get her hands on, she could clean everything in the house, and no one would ever notice, no one would thank her. They would just put on the clothes and get them dirty again.

The washing machine, open beside her, seemed to understand what it was doing. It seemed to be saying, "I'm a bottomless pit. You'll never be done with me."

Morley started to cry. And then she started to struggle out of her shirt.

"Take this," she said, throwing it in the black hole at the top of the washer.

"Have more," she said, pulling off her jeans.

She was really crying now, pulling off her socks. "Have it all," she said.

At that precise moment Dave walked in the back door.

Morley quickly wiped the tears from her face and turned slightly as Dave walked into the kitchen to find his wife standing there with no clothes on.

He had read about things like this.

A goofy, lopsided grin spread across his face.

He winked at his wife.

He started to unbutton his own shirt.

There are small moments of misunderstanding in a marriage that can be cleared up with a simple apology. There are other moments that require elaborate explanations and fast talking. And there are moments when neither an apology nor an explanation will do.

These moments require time and patience and great faith for the air to clear. Sometimes they require even more.

Morley had to get up at five-thirty the following Friday morning to take the limousine to the airport with Anna Lindquist,
on their way to L.A. for Emma Thompson's birthday party.

"I left a note," Morley said to Dave as she got out of bed,
"by the phone. The meals are all written out. They're all in
the freezer."

Dave read her note an hour after she left. He was standing
in the kitchen in his pyjamas, squinting at the paper, waiting
for the coffee to brew.

Friday night, he read, *lasagna and salad.*
Saturday, lasagna and salad.
Sunday, lasagna and salad.
I'll be home at noon on Monday.
We'll go out for Chinese.

When Morley got home, they went out for Chinese food. She
told them all about the impossibilities of travelling with Anna
Lindquist. And about Los Angeles and the birthday dinner.
She sat beside Candice Bergen. Opposite Ron Howard. She
barely said a word all night.

"Those people," she said, "they don't know a thing about
laundry or kids or running a house."

She seemed happy to be back.

"They've all had face-lifts and tucks. You know what they
served for dinner? Sunflower pilaf with guava relish."

She laughed with delight as she said it, and reached for another spring roll.

School Days

September is the most beguiling of the months. It is the month that won't let go of summer, and it is the month that calls from the crow's nest of the year and announces, in the thinning air and morning dew, that summer is gone and autumn is already here. One day September will lull you into believing that you should assemble your things and mount a picnic on a Saturday afternoon— September is made for Saturdays. But when Saturday comes, you spend the morning fumbling around in the attic, looking for sweaters, because it is raining and cold. You look at the picnic supplies you gathered and wonder how you could have been so misguided.

September is a month for plans and a month for no plans. The month of full shelves and empty fields. A time for leave-taking and taking stock. It is the end of summer and the beginning of all that is to come. It is the month that Morley still uses to mark the progress of the years.

This September, Morley had to be at work early every morning. An American production house was using the theatre to shoot scenes for a made-for-television movie. The agreement was that they would move in every night at midnight, wrap by eight, and be struck and gone by ten in the morning. On their first Wednesday, no one from the theatre was there at eight to lean on the director, and the last lights weren't packed away until after eleven-thirty, and they almost didn't have the theatre ready for a matinee of *The Seagull*.

Morley didn't mind coming in early. She liked the texture of morning—the colour of the light, the peaceful feeling of moving around the house while everyone was asleep. She bought a pastry on her way in, a chocolate croissant. When she got to the theatre she brewed tea, walked around to let everyone know she was there, then went to her office and got a start on the day.

Although she enjoyed these early mornings, it meant she missed, for the first time ever, the kids' first giddy days of school. Dave was looking after things at home. It would have broken Morley's heart to see her husband and son walking along the sidewalk every morning, hand in hand. Though she might have felt a pang of jealousy for the lost intimacy of this early-morning ritual that had always been hers, if she could have seen them walking along together, she would have also thought, I should have done this years ago. Sent them off together. Her son's canvas backpack. Her husband's leather briefcase.

The morning walks caught Dave by surprise. On Tuesday night he told Morley that walking to the school yard with his boy was like walking through a house of mirrors. You bump up against reflections of your past in the most unexpected places. You are hurrying your child to school, and you turn a corner and look across the street and see a seven-year-old version of yourself standing on the opposite corner.

———

Dave grew up in the town of Big Narrows in Cape Breton, Nova Scotia, Canada, third planet from the sun, the Milky Way, the universe, et cetera.

This September the kids in Big Narrows were picked up at their doors and bused to what Dave still thinks of as the new school—only twenty-five years old and under forty miles out of town. When Dave was a boy, he went to school in town, to the Big Narrows Elementary School on High Street. Which was not only, worse luck, the same school his sister attended, but also the school where his own mother—in one of the greatest treacheries that can be perpetrated on a child—worked as one of four teachers.

Dave had to walk the best part of a mile to get to school, and he can't remember ever walking with his mother, not once, even though for seven years they left the house at the same time and were heading for the same place. Dave had his own route, and his mother afforded him this independence. It took him down dirt lanes, through vacant lots, and along residential streets. It was a route carefully designed to pass the Pattersons' woodshed, where kids would gather every morning to talk and scuffle and sometimes smoke, if someone had cigarettes.

Because Dave was Margaret MacNeal's son, every year, on the first day of school, he would have to endure what every other kid in the Big Narrows Elementary School still remembers and cherishes as Miss MacNeal's greatest moment. Because every year on the first day of school, the entire student body—all sixty of them—was assembled in the basement lunchroom and Dave's mother climbed onto one of the six picnic tables they kept down there, and to the great amazement of the kids in kindergarten who had never seen this before, and to everyone else's delight, Miss MacNeal would burp the alphabet from A to Z.

Many of the kids in kindergarten actually stopped breathing when they witnessed this extraordinary feat. Their mothers had told them many things about school, but they hadn't told them about this *wonderful* woman. Some of them were away from their mothers for the first time ever. They would stand with their mouths hanging open and think, The world is so immense, and I have so much to learn. It was a performance that would damage live theatre for many of them. "It was good," they would say many years later of a play they had just watched—but, they would think, not as good as the morning in September when Miss MacNeal burped the alphabet. Even Nora MacDonald, who as an adult went on to play in the woodwind section of Symphony Nova Scotia, had more than once stood squinting into the audience after a concert, bowing, thinking how much better the concert would have been if Miss MacNeal could have been there. It was true art.

Every September, after she was finished, and before everyone was sent to their classrooms for the first morning of school—sent up to find their seats, to get their readers and workbooks and pencils, and to contemplate the year stretched ahead of them as fresh and full of possibility as a field of snow—every year before they went upstairs to do these things, Dave's mother would demonstrate how to burp the alphabet the way she did. They would try it in unison, the entire school together.

Most kids never got past C, although not for want of practice. It didn't in fact seem to *be* a matter of practice; it seemed to be more of a gift that would appear every few years, usually in some grade-one kid with a skinny neck and a large Adam's apple who could do it just like that, as if there were nothing to it.

If you were in kindergarten at Big Narrows Elementary, you didn't see Miss MacNeal again for five years, until you got to grade five, and then you had her for three years straight: grades five, six, and seven. And for three years you got to take part in the other ritual she is remembered for—the morning challenge. Every morning, before anyone was allowed in her classroom, Miss MacNeal wrote the morning challenge on the blackboard. When the bell rang, she expected her students to take their seats and work quietly on the quiz. Everyone did, because everyone knew that whoever scored best on the quiz would be let out of class fifteen minutes early at lunch to ride his or her bike into town and buy Miss MacNeal a package of cigarettes. They got to spend the seven cents' change on penny candy. It was a ritual that made children so happy that even parents who didn't approve of smoking didn't think to question it.

Dave never got to do this, even on the six mornings when he scored highest on the quiz. His mother did not want to appear to be favouring her son, so on those six occasions when she could have legitimately sent him, she sent the child who had come in second. Dave was once, however, allowed this—the exquisite joy of drifting along Main Street when every other kid in town old enough to have a two-wheeler was still in class—when the principal, Mr. Ormiston, sent him to the hardware store to pick up a hunting rifle he had ordered.

"We were so free," said Dave to Morley one night. "Nothing was organized. There was a creek behind the school. We spent hours catching frogs. God, that was fun."

"All I remember," said Morley, "is pain. Pain and humiliation."

———

On her first day of kindergarten, Morley was told to lie down on a piece of long brown paper while the teacher traced her outline with a thick black pencil. Then Morley was given a box of crayons and told to colour the life-size outline. Morley started with the eyes. She put the first eye smack in the center of her forehead. She knew it was the kind of mistake you couldn't come back from, and she asked for another piece of brown paper. But no matter how hard she tried to explain about the eye in the middle of her forehead, her teacher wouldn't let her make a fresh start.

Instead of turning the paper over and starting again, Morley sat on her spot on the floor and refused to do anything. At the end of the morning, when everyone's pictures were put up on the wall, Morley's went up, too, with no mouth and no hair and no clothes, just one huge brown eye staring down from the middle of her forehead and her name written at the bottom of the paper in big black letters. The portrait glared down at her every day for a month before it was removed.

"It was humiliating," said Morley, "having to look at the eye every morning. I felt like it was watching everything I did."

That, thought Dave, is the essence of elementary school. You walk around the school yard, up and down the corridors, you sit at your desk, and wherever you go, there is someone with a great big eye in the middle of their forehead staring down at you. Sometimes it's your teacher, sometimes it's your friends or your family—most often it's the quiet voice in your mind that compares you to everyone else and weighs in with its inevitable and unforgiving judgment.

———

Last year, when he was in grade three, Dave's son, Sam, had his own meeting with the unflinching eye. After Christmas each student in Sam's class was assigned a pen pal from a school in the suburbs. Sam was assigned Aidan. Most of the letters written back and forth between the classes were stiff and a long way from real, but somehow the stars were aligned when Sam and Aidan were paired. They developed that most rare of modern relationships—they became correspondents.

Through the mail, Sam and Aidan learned they liked the same television shows, played the same video games, read the same books, and felt the same way about much of it. They even had the same birthday.

"Maybe," said Sam, "Aidan is my twin brother. Maybe there was a mistake at the hospital or something."

At the end of May, the two schools arranged a field day so they could bring all the pen pals together. Everyone knew the highlight was going to be the moment when Sam met Aidan. Everyone knew how excited Sam was about the meeting, and about the plans he and Aidan had made.

"I'm going up to his cottage," said Sam. A statement of fact, not a question.

They met on the sidewalk beside a large yellow school bus.

"I'm Aidan," said the skinny, freckled eight-year-old girl holding out her hand. She had stringy straw-coloured hair that hung down to her shoulders. She was wearing a grubby T-shirt, jeans, and sneakers. She looked as if she could throw a ball. She also looked undeniably like a girl.

"I'm Aidan," she said again.

"No, you're not," said Sam.

"Aidan is a girl," sang Lawrence Hillside. "Aidan's a girl."

It was a fact beyond Sam's comprehension; outside his realm of the possible. His friend Aidan was a boy. His friend Aidan could not be a girl.

"Yes, I could," said Aidan, holding her ground.

There was a circle of kids around them.

Sam was dumbfounded. He said, "I have to go." He turned and pushed desperately through the crowd, pain on his face. He never mentioned Aidan again. Dave knows this much because he heard it from Sam's teacher.

———

"We had a fat boy in our class," said Morley. "His name was Norman Minguy. Did I ever tell you about Norman? He got along better with the girls than the boys. But he didn't get picked on. Probably because he always had lots of money. He used it to buy penny candy. The year we were in grade four, we had Mrs. Merrill, who was strict but nice. Norman sat in the middle of the class, and when Mrs. Merrill was writing on the blackboard and her back was toward the class and the room was quiet because everyone was copying what she was writing on the board into their exercise books, sometimes Norman would reach into his desk and take a handful of penny candy and toss it in the air. It was like someone had lobbed a grenade into the class—one minute dead silence and the next, bedlam. Kids on the floor, kids under desks, everybody fighting for candy. Mrs. Merrill would turn around, mystified, because except for these unexpected explosions, we were a well-behaved class. She would put her hands on her hips and ask what was going on, and of course no one would tell her. No one would turn Norman in, because no one wanted him to stop. It was too good to be true."

In the middle of her second week of early mornings at work, Morley dreamed she was sitting on a bench in a crowded waiting room.

"All the parents were there," she said to Dave on the telephone the next morning. "Everyone looked so worried. I was sitting right across from Ted and Polly Anderson. But they wouldn't look at me. No one would. Polly was wringing her hands like something awful was about to happen. It felt like we were there because we had done something terribly wrong. Do you think it means I shouldn't have gone back to work?"

Sam had never been so far out of her orbit. He was moving into a universe that soon she would hardly be allowed to visit. And he was moving so fast. Morley began to think more and more about her own childhood—to compare her experiences to her son's. It was dangerous ground: Even the happy memories could make her sad. She was feeling guilty that she was not walking Sam to school, that he was eating lunch in the cafeteria for the first time.

She kept coming back to Norman Minguy and the utter joy of those classroom scrambles. Morley wanted the same thing for Sam. And that was what led her into the school yard at six A.M. on a Monday in September with two rolls of quarters and a roll of dimes and nickels. If she couldn't lob candy around Sam's classroom, she could scatter change around his schoolyard. Morley imagined that a schoolyard full of coins—like pirate's treasure—would create the same joy for her son as Norman Minguy's penny candy had for her.

She scattered twenty dollars in loose change around the yard. Under the play structure and in the sandbox and by the toolshed and under the stairs where the little kids gathered. She felt wonderful and light and alive. It didn't matter, she thought, if Sam didn't get any of the money—although she was planning to head home as soon as she finished and do her best to get him to school early. But it didn't matter, because school yards exist in stories as much as real life, and Sam would be part of the story, and the story would become a legend, and it would grow in the telling. Before long it would be hundreds of dollars—they would talk about the morning when there was hundreds of dollars in the school yard. Kids would be at school early for weeks in the sure knowledge that it would happen again.

It did not, of course, work out like that. After she finished spreading the money, Morley went for coffee and a roll at a little place run by a Portuguese baker from Argentina. It was a happy little spot where you poured your own coffee from a pot on the counter and sat, if you felt like sitting, at one of the two tables in the rear of the store. Morley liked it there because everything was made of wood and you still got your bread in brown paper bags.

On her way home, she detoured by the school to savor the sheer recklessness of what she had done. As she pulled up to the school fence, she saw a tall, bony man with a goatee standing by the swings, wiping his brow. It was Floyd, the school janitor, who was never seen within an inch of the school yard whenever there was broken glass to be picked up. As Morley watched, Floyd bent over and began plowing around the yard like a Zamboni, sucking up every coin she had dropped. Instead of going home and waking up her son, as she had intended, Morley went to a phone booth and called her husband.

"Why didn't you stop him?" asked Dave. "Why didn't you tell him it was for the kids?"

"I was too embarrassed," said Morley. "It was too silly. I'm going to walk to work. The car is parked by the field. Will you pick it up when you take Sam?" And she hung up.

All morning Dave imagined, with growing regret, what might have happened had Floyd not stumbled upon Morley's money. By midafternoon he had worked himself into such a state that he was having trouble concentrating. He spent fifteen minutes sticking twenty-dollar price tags on a stack of albums he meant to label with two-dollar tags. It took him half an hour to peel the labels off and reprice them. When he caught himself filing *The Best of Herman's Hermits* under soul, he knew it was time to stop. It wasn't until he was almost home that he knew what to do about Morley—he was going to finish what his wife had started. But he wasn't going to fill the school yard with spare change for Floyd to scoop. Dave had a better idea. He was going to fill it with frogs.

———

"Catching frogs," he said to Morley that night, waving arms as he walked around the kitchen, "is the essence c childhood."

It had taken Dave only two phone calls to find frogs.

"I called a pet store first," he said, "but all they had was green tree frogs. For, like, pets."

"How much," said Morley, "is a green tree frog?"

"Nine ninety-nine each," said Dave. "Fifteen dollars for two."

As she stared at her husband in trepidation, Morley did the maths in her mind—six frogs . . . forty-five dollars. Surely he wouldn't spend forty-five dollars on frogs. There wouldn't be more than six.

Dave was somewhere else. Going too fast to notice Morley's growing apprehension. He was full steam ahead.

"Anyway," he said. "I had a better idea."

"*Different* idea," said Morley. "You had a different idea."

"Bait store," said Dave.

"Bait store?" said Morley.

"Leopard frogs," said Dave. "The frogs we caught when we were kids."

"When *you* were a kid," said Morley.

There was silence. Morley and Dave in their kitchen looking at each other. Dave holding a dripping dish towel, beaming and proud. A little nervous. A *lot* excited. Morley, her hands up to the wrists in a bowl of raw hamburger, fearful of what she had created.

"How much," said Morley, "are leopard frogs?"

"Only six ninety-nine a dozen," said Dave.

"How many are you getting?" said Morley, wiping meat off her fingers.

hree dozen," said Dave.

"Three dozen," said Morley, walking toward the sink.

"Maybe four?" said Dave. He said it like a question. Like he was asking permission. But he wasn't asking permission. He had already been to the bait store. He had already bought the frogs. They were out in the garage in five large plastic boxes. Ten dozen of them. One hundred and twenty leopard frogs Dave intended to set loose in the morning.

Morley might have stopped him then—should have stopped him—but he hadn't stopped her. Dave imagined the school yard full of fast-moving children; imagined boys with frogs in their pockets, girls crouched in secret councils. If she had known how it would work out, Morley would have said something. But she didn't. She was trying to be supportive.

———

Neither of them imagined Rebecca Morton, five years old, kindergarten, on the sidewalk in front of the school clutching her mother's leg, screaming loudly enough that she was heard a full block away.

"Take me home," she was crying.

Certainly, neither of them—Dave nor Morley—imagined Duncan Sheppel, grade seven, would have a Swiss Army knife in his pocket. Or that Mrs. Jenkins, on yard duty that morning, would react with what Dave later described as hysteria when confronted with a frog head.

"If she hadn't fainted," he said glumly to Morley that night, "things wouldn't have got out of hand." Even Dave had to admit things had got out of hand.

Children were running wildly over the yard, girls chasing boys, boys chasing girls, everyone chasing frogs. Rebecca Morton provided the unfortunate sound track for the whole sorry scene.

"What sort of idiot," Dave overheard Rebecca's mother saying, "would have done this?"

"Out of hand?" said an icy Nancy Cassidy, the school principal, as Dave sat across from her desk the next morning. "It was like a prison riot." Nancy Cassidy had always struck Dave as a gentle soul. Now she was reprimanding him as if he were a child.

"What on earth did you think you were doing?" she demanded. "Perhaps you would consider some form of counseling?"

Dave had already spent an hour on his knees in the school yard with Floyd, the janitor, scraping frogs up with a putty knife. Surely, he thought, this was enough. Clearly, it was not. And that was why, on the following Monday morning, the entire school gathered in the lunchroom so Dave could explain what he was thinking when he had brought the frogs. Why frogs were such a joyful memory—memories he had hoped they would capture as they went about capturing the frogs. And why it was wrong to remove a frog's head. It was his idea to make this speech. It was one of the worst moments in his life.

———

The next morning, when Duncan Sheppel saw Sam walking across the school yard, he fell in beside him and said, "Your dad's pretty cool."

Sam didn't know what to say. It felt odd to have this older boy walking beside him. He wasn't sure if the boy was teasing him or not. He looked around to see if anyone was watching. "He's all right," he said.

Then Duncan pulled out his Swiss Army knife. "I'm not supposed to have this," he said. "I'm afraid they might take it away. Could you hold it until three o'clock?"

Sam nodded dumbly and took the knife and stuffed it into his pocket. He had never had a knife in his pocket before. All day he could feel it, hard and full of potential. He returned it to Duncan after school, by the climber, carefully.

Mostly, when they pass each other in the school yard now, Duncan ignores Sam, but from time to time he nods and says, "Hi."

This is what Sam will remember of everything. Not the thrill of finding treasures or the joys of catching frogs. Rather, that his father came to school one day and talked about memories and that Duncan Sheppel, who was in grade seven, lent him his knife once, and sometimes said hi to him.

A Day Off

The *Seagull* was extended for two weeks, and might have been held over for two more, had Anna Lindquist not had to be back in London by mid-October.

The week before she left, Anna appeared in Morley's office and said she wanted to throw a cast party on closing night. She wanted a room at the Palazzo. And champagne. Could Morley help with the details?

Organizing the party gradually took over Morley's life. There were constant interruptions from Anna, and Morley ended up having to come in even earlier to keep up with her own work.

When closing night finally arrived, Morley was so fed up with Anna Lindquist, and so utterly exhausted, that she said she wasn't going to the party.

"It's her last night," said Dave. "You'll never have to see her again. Just go."

So Morley went. She spent most of the evening on the balcony, smoking Ralph's cigarettes and drinking too much of Anna Lindquist's white wine.

"At least she's paying," she said.

"I didn't know you smoked," said Ralph.

"I don't," said Morley, reaching for another cigarette.

At midnight Anna Lindquist stood in the apartment doorway, a cigarette holder dangling from her right hand, her left running through Martin's hair. Martin, who had played her young lover in *The Seagull,* was not yet thirty. Anna Lindquist was fifty-five if she was a day.

"How long has *that* been going on?" asked Morley.

"I don't even want to think about it," said Ralph. "Let me get you another drink."

It was the last time Morley saw Anna—but not the last she heard of her.

———

The next morning when Dave and Morley woke up, it was snowing. The snow turned to rain before breakfast. It was just a whiff of winter, but the warning shot propelled Morley to make the annual trip down into the basement. She headed into the darkness like a migrating goose, carrying a dim memory of Sam's snow boots, which might have been blue and maybe still fit. She waved her arm in front of her in the darkness, as if trying to brush away a spider web. She groped for the string that turned on the storeroom light, then she reached up among the pipes, praying as she did that there was a lightbulb in the socket so she wouldn't stick her finger in an empty socket and die.

Morley knew she was on a fool's mission. She knew in her heart that the boots weren't down there. And if they were, she wasn't going to find them. Not in October. She would find them in June. When she was down there looking for bathing suits. Sam's boots had probably spent the spring at the bottom of a lost-and-found box at a school he never attended. And now? They weren't in the basement. They were on the back of a shelf in a Goodwill store, miles from home.

Morley trudged upstairs. "We'll have to get Sam new winter boots on the weekend," she said.

Dave nodded.

———

On Wednesday two unexpected letters arrived at the theatre. The first, addressed to the accounting department, was from the Palazzo. It was a bill for Anna Lindquist's party—$4,700.

Morley threw the bill on Ralph's desk. "I don't believe it," she said. "It was clear from the beginning. She was paying for the party, all of it."

Jennifer, who opened the mail, wasn't sure what to do with the second letter. It was handwritten on pale blue vellum—a heartfelt thank-you from Anna Lindquist.

Dear Morty, it began.

Jennifer took it to Ralph.

"We don't have a Morty," she said. "Who could she mean?"

———

When Dave woke up the next morning, Morley was sitting in bed drinking coffee and reading the newspaper. This wasn't part of the normal routine. Dave peered at the clock radio and then at his wife.

"I'm sick," she said.

Dave propped himself up. She didn't look sick to him.

"I am," she said.

She put the paper down and stretched languidly. "So are you," she said. "I think you should get someone to open the store." Morley leaned forward and put her face close to Dave's. "I don't think you should go to work. Not the way you're feeling."

Dave reached up and touched his forehead. It was a reflex.

Morley nodded. "I think it has a fever." She jumped out of bed, wandered to the window, and stretched again. "We're staying home. We're taking a mental-health day."

Dave said, "I can't do that."

Morley said, "Yes, you can. Phone Brian. He's always looking for extra hours."

Dave said, "I've never done anything like that in my life. Ever."

Morley said, "Dave, you *own* the business. If you want to stay home, you're allowed. If you really were sick, everything would work out."

Dave said, "Yeah, but . . ."

It was not that the record store was too busy. Nor was it that Dave was the kind of man who couldn't goof off. Dave had whiled away entire mornings at the Vinyl Cafe with a Rubik's Cube, ignoring dusty shelves, piles of filing, and overdue accounts. Dave could goof off. It was his sense of himself that was affronted—his place in the world. Every morning, after he woke and showered and dressed and ate breakfast, Dave headed off to open his record store. If he didn't have to do this today, then he didn't have to do it tomorrow. Or, for that matter, ever. And if he didn't have to do this, what *did* he have to do? By asking him to stay home, Morley was calling into question his place in the universe.

She said, "We've been married fifteen years, Dave. It's time for some spontaneity. We are going to spend one unplanned perfect day together. I am going to that gourmet-food store near Thea's and buy supplies. I'm going to get some videos. We are going to eat and watch movies. And other things."

It was the "other things" that got Dave.

He shoved a wad of Kleenex in his mouth and phoned Brian and said, "I'm sick. Can you open up?"

Brian said, "Yeah. Sure. What are you eating, anyway? It sounds like your mouth is full of Kleenex."

Morley said, "I'm going to get the food and the videos. I'll be back in an hour."

———

Dave was hardly ever home alone.

He made a pot of coffee and settled down with the paper. He wondered if Morley would get some of the chocolate-covered strawberries he loved. He wondered if she would get some crusty bread and smoked cold cuts. He felt deliciously guilty. He felt free.

This *was* a good idea, he thought.

He wondered if they had any wine. Maybe for lunch he would open the bottle of Bordeaux they had bought at the duty-free shop two years ago.

The telephone rang.

Dave stared at the phone, but he didn't make a move to answer it.

He knew people who could do this. He had friends who could let their phone ring. He couldn't.

He sat at the table and stared at the phone as if hypnotized. It rang two, three, four times.

When it stopped, the house felt immensely quiet.

Dave felt wonderful.

He didn't check the answering machine.

He didn't care who had called.

No one was going to bother him today.

He got up and walked across the kitchen, moving slowly and deliberately. He poured himself another cup of coffee. He read a movie review.

It was like skipping school.

The phone began to ring again.

Should have taken it off the hook, thought Dave.

Then he thought, Maybe it's Morley. Maybe she wanted to consult him about the videos. Maybe he could ask her to get some of the black-olive paste.

Maybe if he didn't answer, she would be worried. Or angry.

In a sudden panic, he jumped for the phone. He scooped it up on the fourth ring. He was out of breath when he said, "Hello?"

It wasn't Morley. It was Morley's mother.

"I phoned a few minutes ago," said Helen. "Then I tried the store. They told me you were sick. Are you okay?"

Dave reached into his pocket, pulled out his wad of wet Kleenex, and stuffed it back in his mouth. "Just a bit of a fever," he mumbled.

"You sound horrible," said Helen. "You sound like your mouth is full of Kleenex."

Dave said, "I'm okay."

Helen said, "I wanted to see if Morley would have lunch with me."

"Morley's sick, too," said Dave. He said it without thinking. The words just flew out of his mouth. He was trying to save the day. He was trying to head Helen off at the pass.

"Can I talk to her?" asked Helen.

"Too sick," said Dave. "She's too sick to come to the phone. She's upstairs. Asleep. I don't think I should wake her."

Dave felt like he had stepped on a treadmill. Some part of him knew he should pull the brake and get off. He should tell Helen the truth. Should say, "Helen, we're not really sick. We're taking the day off. We're going to spend it together. Alone." Instead, he said, "She has fever and these little red dots." Then, for good measure, he added, "She threw up last night."

Helen said, "She has a rash. Maybe I should come over."

It was a statement, not a question.

Dave could feel perspiration gathering on his forehead. His breathing was shallow. His hands were cold and damp. He was beginning to feel . . . sick.

Dave said, "It's okay. We'll be fine."

Helen said, "I'll bring some soup for you two and fix dinner for the kids. It's no trouble. Don't worry. I'll be there in an hour."

———

Morley came home half an hour later, carrying two large brown paper bags and two videos.

"I got *Wild Orchid* and *9½ Weeks,*" she said.

Dave picked up *9½ Weeks*. "It's the original, uncut, uncensored version," said Morley. "We're going to see it the way it was meant to be seen."

Dave flipped the box over. "What's it about?" he asked.

"It's the one with Kim Basinger," said Morley. "The one where Mickey Rourke feeds her the giant chili pepper." Morley reached into one of the bags and pulled out a box of chocolate-covered strawberries. Then she walked across the kitchen and put her arms around her husband's neck. "It's a steamy story of a love affair that breaks every taboo."

Dave swallowed.

Morley laughed. "I got some of that olive paste you like. And some French bread," she said.

Dave said, "There's something I better tell you."

Morley said, "Just a second." She reached into the other bag and pulled out a handful of magazines. She was grinning. "This is going to be great," she said.

Dave said, "Helen phoned. She's coming over."

Morley said, "You can't be serious."

Dave said, "I told her I was sick. Then I told her you were sick." He pressed his hands against his forehead. His head was beginning to throb. "I didn't know if I should tell her I was faking—we were faking. I felt like an idiot."

Morley said, "That's because you are an idiot."

Dave and Morley spent the next half hour tidying up. Then Morley went upstairs and put on her old flannel nightie, which hung off her shoulders like a sack. When Helen arrived, they were both lying in bed, stiff as corpses. They weren't speaking to each other. The two brown paper bags from the food store were under the bed on Morley's side.

Helen said, "You look awful. Have you eaten? I'll make soup." She went down to the kitchen.

Dave turned to Morley and said, "I'm sorry. Come on. This isn't my fault. She's your mother."

Morley looked at him and said, "I don't believe this." Then she reached under the bed and pulled out a chocolate strawberry and ate it as if she were alone.

Dave's headache was getting worse. "Could I have one of those?" he asked.

"I'm not stopping you," said Morley.

But she wasn't offering them around, either.

Dave crawled over his wife and took two strawberries out of the bag. He was standing by the bed in a T-shirt and a pair of boxers when Helen came back in the room.

"Everything okay?" she said.

Dave rammed the second strawberry into his mouth.

"Dave?" she said.

He covered his mouth with his hand. "I think I'm going to be sick," he said, and ran for the bathroom.

"He doesn't look well," said Helen to Morley.

By the time Dave was back in bed, Helen was in the kitchen again, and the oily smell of chicken soup was drifting upstairs.

Morley said, "This is a nightmare. I hate chicken soup. I had to eat chicken soup when I was a kid. That's what she always fed us whenever we were sick. Just the smell of chicken soup makes me ill. Do something. Get her out of here."

Dave said, "How do I get her out of here? She's trying to help."

"You invited her," said Morley. "You uninvite her."

———

Helen brought the bowls of soup up on a tray.

Dave's head was pounding. His mouth was dry.

He didn't want a scene. He didn't want Morley to thunder out of bed and tell Helen he had lied. He would feel too stupid. It had gone too far. Please, God, he thought. Please let us carry the soup part off.

He smiled weakly at Morley. "Look," he said. "Dry toast. Dry toast is just what I wanted."

Morley made Dave eat her bowl of soup.

"Can't I flush it down the toilet?" he asked. "It tastes funny. I think it's off." He was starting to feel queasier with every spoonful he swallowed.

"Eat it," said Morley. "All of it." Then she got out of bed and started to get dressed.

———

Downstairs, Helen was sitting in front of the television.

Morley walked into the room carrying two paper bags. She put them down and said, "The soup was great. I feel much better. I think it was one of those eight-hour things. I'm going to go for a walk. Can you stay for a while? What I'd really like to do is go to a movie. I haven't been to a matinee for years. Would that be wicked?"

Helen frowned. "Do you really feel better?"

Morley said, "I'm fine. Could you stay with Dave? He's not looking so good. I think he needs more soup."

Helen brightened. She was watching a documentary on the grizzly bear. She saw Morley frowning at the screen and said, "There's nothing else on."

Morley picked up the two videos she had rented and

looked at them ruefully. She put them back down and gathered up the two brown paper bags.

"What's that, dear?" asked Helen.

"Oh, just some dry cleaning," said Morley. "I'll drop it off on my way to the theatre."

———

When Helen came into the bedroom, Dave was lying under the covers, staring at the ceiling. Helen was holding a bowl of soup in one hand and a video in the other. She said, "Morley thought you might like company," and then, lifting the video, she added, "I found this downstairs."

Dave's stomach began to churn. He felt as if he were strapped into the passenger seat of a car that was about to be involved in an accident. Everything seemed to be moving in slow motion. He closed his eyes. This couldn't be happening.

Helen flicked on the television and bent down and stared at the video player. She slipped the movie into the machine and pressed the play button.

She straightened up and kicked off her shoes and sat down on Morley's side of the bed, arranging the pillows so she could lean against the headboard.

"It's called *9½ Weeks,*" she said. "Have you heard of it?"

Dave shook his head numbly.

"Me, neither," said Helen. "I hope it's not full of violence."

Dave was too ill to reply.

"This is fun," said Helen. "I don't think I've ever watched a movie in the middle of the day. I should do this more often. Eat your soup."

Winter, Again

On the Roof

Betty Schellenberger and Morley were drinking coffee.

Morley said, "They've done studies. Even in families where men and women do equal amounts of housework, it's the women who organize it."

Betty nodded, her hands cradling the mug of coffee in front of her on the kitchen table.

"It's the women," said Morley, "who plan and assign. It's the women who drive the train."

Dave was washing the lunch dishes. It made him feel bad, listening to them talk. It felt personal, as if they were criticizing him. No one, he thought grimly, assigned me these dishes. He considered stopping. I wouldn't want to overstep my boundaries, he thought. Since Morley had gone back to work in the fall, Dave had been trying to shoulder his share of the chores. But Morley was right. There was no denying it. She was management. He was labour.

It was Saturday afternoon. The sky was grey and heavy. The wind was rippling the puddles on the driveway. It looked like it could snow.

The weather suited Dave's mood. When he finished the dishes, he said, "I'm going to take Arthur out."

He put on an old blue sweater and a canvas jacket, stuffed a toque and a pair of gloves in his pocket, and headed outside with the dog. He thought of loading Arthur into the car and driving to a park, or maybe taking him down to the lake. He stood on the front walk—Arthur looking up at him expectantly—then, instead of getting in the car, he headed north through the neighbourhood.

There was hardly anyone else out. There were some kids walking through the park, but no one on the playground. The abandoned swings hung on their yellow metal frame like a row of mourners.

Up ahead was a woman walking toward Dave on the same side of the street.

"Hello," said Dave as they passed. The woman walked by with her jaw firmly clenched, her eyes straight ahead. As if he and Arthur didn't exist.

There are lots of things that can give you the blues. The weather can give you the blues. Sometimes it is so grey out, it makes you feel blue inside. Your friends can give you the blues. In fact, your best friends are often better at making you feel blue than your worst enemies. Sometimes, however, it's just an overheard conversation, a stranger on the street, empty swings.

Dave had not intended to be gone long. But he kept walking. After forty-five minutes, he was on a street he had never been on before, gazing into the window of a store he had never seen: Thrift Villa—"where smart shoppers save."

He went in only to warm up, but he ended up buying two drinking glasses—sixty-nine cents each. One was a Dave Keon hockey glass with a picture of Keon on one side and a referee on the other demonstrating the signal for a holding penalty. HOLDING, it said in black letters under the referee. The lady at the cash register told him it was a peanut-butter jar from the sixties. She couldn't remember the brand name.

"I'm pretty sure it was a rodent," she said as she rolled the glasses in newspaper. "Like a beaver. Or a squirrel."

———

When Dave was halfway home, it started to snow. He pulled his toque out of his pocket and put it on, tugging it down over his ears. It was four-thirty and getting dark. He had been gone two hours. The weather was whispering warnings: Just wanted to remind you, said the snow, that you'll be walking home from work in the dark from now on. Just wanted to let you know, said the wind, that it will probably be raining.

He was cheered by the texture of the light from the houses he passed. It reminded him of winter nights when he was a boy, of afternoon-long games of hockey. Maybe, he thought, I should take everyone to Cape Breton for Christmas. He hadn't been home at Christmas for too many years.

He thought of the disaster that befell him when he tried to cook the turkey the year before. They could do worse than spend the holidays with his mother. She would be happy to see them. The kids could cut a tree on the McCauleys' farm.

That was what started him thinking about Christmas decorations. He had been late with them last year, so late that he'd ended up more or less throwing their lights over the front hedge. He had promised himself he would do better this year.

Well, it was this year now. He would get the lights up before anyone had to ask. He would beat Morley to the punch. He would be labour *and* management. He was feeling better when he got home.

———

On Tuesday, Dave came home early, determined to climb onto his roof and hang the Christmas lights. He wanted to be done before dark. But first, he had to go to Jim Scoffield's house to borrow a ladder, and they had to have a beer. Then they had to find the ladder. Dave had to replace all the burned-out bulbs. Suddenly, it was dusk.

It was dark by the time Dave stepped gingerly onto the roof and half-walked, half-crawled across the shingles to the chimney.

It was colder than he'd expected. He grabbed hold of the television antenna and carefully straightened up. He could see all over the neighbourhood. He wondered why he got up there only at the worst times of the year. I should come up here more often, he thought. He sat down with his back to the chimney and began to untangle the lights that he had already untangled before he climbed the ladder.

It took him about half an hour to attach the lights to the antenna. When he was finished, he plugged them in, and his roof was bathed in light—yellows, reds, greens, and blues. They didn't look half bad, and miracle of miracles, no bulbs had burned out since he had checked them half an hour ago. Dave shuffled back to the ladder to get a better look.

The antenna reminded him of the clothesline in his yard when he was a child. They had the kind made from one centre pole, the kind that looks like an umbrella with the fabric removed. Dave remembered the winter mornings when his mother would push him into a snowsuit and out the back door like a blimp, remembered the swishing of all that nylon material between his legs. How he inevitably needed to pee once he was stuck outside.

He looked out over the rooftops, and suddenly, as sure as if she were standing beside him, Dave could hear his sweet mother's voice fill his head. She was warning him about something. She was saying, Dave, don't lick the clothesline.

Sometimes you do things just because someone tells you not to. Sometimes you do things because you have never done them before and you want to see what will happen if you do. Sometimes it's hard to figure out why you do some things at all.

Dave had never put his tongue against a television antenna on a cold night in November, although he had a pretty fair idea what would happen if he did. But the moment his mother's voice came into his head, he could feel himself drawn to the antenna.

As he slowly crab-walked back across the roof toward the chimney to which the antenna was attached, Dave was thinking to himself, This won't happen. I won't do this. Why would I do this? I'm not stupid. I'm just trying to scare myself. Yet he felt as if he were outside of his body. It didn't seem to be him moving across the roof. It seemed to be someone else. And there didn't seem to be much he could do to stop himself.

Part of Dave was saying, I don't want to put my tongue on that television antenna, but another part of him, the part that seemed to be in control—the part his tongue seemed to be listening to—was saying, Just do it, Dave. You don't have to listen to your mother anymore. You're an adult. You can do whatever you want.

He was surprised by how unequivocally his tongue grabbed on to the metal. It was not at all uncertain about what it was expected to do. Dave himself was uncertain that he had even touched the metal. He thought there was still some space between him and the pole, and then all at once he was bonded to it. At first he was intrigued by the way his tongue stuck. Almost proud of it. It hurt a bit, but it was not an excruciating pain—more the pain of melted candle wax than molten lead.

Then it hurt a bit more, and Dave thought, Okay, that's enough, and he tried to pull his tongue off the antenna. It didn't come. He leaned forward because it hurt when he tried to pull, and then more of his tongue was stuck to the antenna, and he felt a wave of panic rush through him.

His mother's voice filled his head again. She said, I told you not to do that.

And Dave said, "Why didn't you stop me?"

Except it sounded different . . . more like "MMMMUUU-UGGGHHHH." When he said it, his top lip brushed against the antenna, and then his top lip was stuck as well as his tongue, and he knew he was in serious trouble.

Dave stopped moving. He was very still. Then he tried to lean back a little, but it hurt, and his tongue didn't want to let go.

He thought, Maybe it's like taking a Band-Aid off a kid. Maybe you have to be sure about it. Sure and fast.

So he counted. "One. Two."

Just as he was about to say, "Three," Dave heard his mother's voice again. She said, Have you thought that you could pull your entire tongue out of your mouth and leave it on the antenna? Have you thought of that?

Dave stopped counting.

That's impossible, he thought.

But it occurred to him that if he didn't actually lose his entire tongue, maybe he could lose a layer of it—the layer with his taste buds. He would never taste anything ever again. For the rest of his life, he might as well eat tofu, and it wouldn't make any difference. That scared him so much that he didn't move a muscle for a long time. He stood on the roof, sucking on his antenna, without moving.

He could see his neighbours walking up and down the street. He saw the Schellenbergers stop and look up at him. When they stopped, he began to flap his arms up and down, being careful not to move his face. The Schellenbergers watched him for a few moments, and then they said something to each other, turned, and walked inside their house.

Dave knew they weren't going to come to his rescue. They had been admiring him. They thought he was part of the display, hanging from the antenna in the middle of all the lights.

This is what happens when you do things you aren't asked to do, thought Dave.

He was filled with self-loathing. His life seemed to be a parade of similar incidents.

———

When his daughter was very small, Dave had taken her in the car on his way to a job interview. Morley was sick, and he was going to drop Stephanie at Morley's mother's house while he went to the interview.

The interview was for a job that Dave thought he wanted at the time—a buyer for a record-store chain. He had borrowed a briefcase from Carl Lowbeer as a prop.

It was not an easy drive. Stephanie cried all the way across town. Dave was desperate to calm her down. He needed to be calm for the interview. He decided that a stick of licorice might do the trick.

He pulled up in front of a corner store. As he jumped out of the car, he noticed four young thugs, wearing more than their fair share of black leather, bumping up the street. He didn't want them messing with his daughter. Better lock the door, thought Dave.

He patted his pockets looking for his keys. Silly, he thought, they're still in the ignition. Dave had left the engine running so that when he came out of the store, he could be on his way as quickly as possible. He wasn't exactly running late for his interview, but he didn't have a lot of time to spare.

No worries. He could lock the car door without the key.

Dave reached inside the car and depressed the lock button. Then he slammed the door, carefully holding the door handle so the door would stay locked.

As he stood beside his locked car and smiled at the four thugs, Dave was vaguely troubled by a feeling that something wasn't right. But he was too uptight and in too much of a hurry to worry about it. He dashed into the store and moments later dashed out again, waving the candy. When he saw his car, he stopped dead in his tracks. The doors were locked. The motor was running. His keys were in the ignition.

When Dave saw Stephanie locked in the back of the car, something inside him snapped. He was irrevocably and undeniably certain that his daughter was in danger.

He knew that people who wanted to end their lives often sat in running cars. He understood that they usually did this in garages, but he reasoned that even though his car was in the open air, fumes could still seep through the floorboards, and if they didn't kill his daughter, they could surely damage her brain.

Dave looked around for something to break a window with in case Stephanie started to nod off. He spotted a brick at a construction site and placed it on the sidewalk beside the passenger door. He sprinted to a phone booth.

Morley, who had a fever of 102, got dressed and took a taxi across town with their extra set of keys.

By the time she arrived, so had the police.

Morley still says she should have denied knowing Dave. When she tells this story, she says she should have pressed charges. "Look at the brick," she could have said, "I think he was planning to steal my daughter. "

Dave was late for the interview. He didn't get the job.

This was the life that was flashing by Dave's eyes as he hunched over his chimney. He could hear his family moving around the living room. He could hear their voices floating up the chimney. He heard Morley say, "Wouldn't a fire be nice?"

"No," said Dave. "No, it wouldn't."

Then he heard Sam. "Can we put on two logs?"

Dave and Morley burn synthetic wax logs. The moment the waxy smoke hit Dave, he needed to pee. He thought, The fumes are probably poisonous. I am being asphyxiated. My body is trying to clear the toxins.

It was like being trapped in the backyard in a snowsuit when he was a kid.

His mind began to race.

What if spring never came? What if there was never a thaw? What if he died there?

He couldn't remember the last time the chimney had been cleaned. What would happen to him if the chimney caught fire? The fumes were stinging his eyes. He needed to pee badly now.

What if he peed on the antenna?

Would that warm it up enough?

Enough to set him free?

And what, God help him, would happen if his penis touched the metal?

And then it came to him.

Why didn't he take one of the Christmas lights and hold it against his lip so the warmth from the light would melt his mouth free?

It took under five minutes.

In five minutes he was down the ladder, in the house, and peering into the bathroom mirror at his tongue. It was red but not too sore.

Sam and Stephanie were snuggled on the couch watching television, and Morley, his sweet wife, Morley, was sticking cloves into an orange as she watched TV with them. Dave thought, They didn't even know I was in trouble.

There was a commercial, and Sam said, "What were you doing up there? The picture was really fuzzy for a while. Then all of a sudden it got better."

Dave said, "I put up the Christmas lights. Come and see."

They all trooped outside.

Sam looked up and down the block. "We're the first. We beat everyone."

Morley was smiling. "I was thinking about the lights yesterday," she said.

The kids ran back inside.

Morley was still looking at the lights. "They always make me feel good," she said. Then she turned and put her arms around her husband. "I ordered the Christmas turkey today," she said. "I was thinking you did such a nice job with it last year, do you think you could do it again?"

Polly Anderson's
Christmas Party

Dave received his new driver's licence in the mail at the beginning of October. It was accompanied by a letter that began:

Dear Sir:
  We were pleased to note that you no are no longer required to wear corrective lenses.

Dave had never worn glasses in his life. Somewhere in the pit of his stomach, he felt a queasy twinkle . . . like the birth of a star in a distant galaxy.

  Before we can change the category code on your driver's licence, we must receive notification from an ophthalmologist of the change in your vision.

Dave's vision hadn't changed in twenty years. The star in his stomach was burning brightly now. Ahh, thought Dave, I know the name of the galaxy. It's the galaxy of bureaucratic misfortune—an abyss of swamps and labyrinths, a horror house of tunnels and mazes. Dealing with the letter would be like playing a real-life game of snakes and ladders. With a sinking heart, Dave finished reading the note.

*We have reissued your permit subject to the following con-
ditions.*

At the bottom of the letter, it said:

Driver must wear corrective lenses.

Dave knew this wasn't going to be easy.

"Do you have any idea," he said to Morley, "how long you
have to wait to get an appointment with an eye doctor?"

The next morning, when Morley woke up, Dave was lying
on his back, his hands cupped behind his head. He was staring at the ceiling. "This is the sort of thing that sends people
into clock towers with high-powered rifles," he said.

————

October, and then November, came and went. By early December, Dave still hadn't made even a halfhearted attempt to
schedule a doctor's appointment.

"I'm too busy," he said when Morley asked.

December is the busiest time of the year if you work in
retail, and things had been busy enough at Dave's record
store, but they both knew this was a lie. By the middle of
the month, Morley was ready to force the issue. Then she
thought, He's an adult. Why should I be the bad guy? Instead, as he left for work on Saturday morning, she reminded
Dave that they were expected at Ted and Polly Anderson's
annual Christmas party that night. As he stood at the front
door, his parka open, his hat askew, Dave gave Morley a look
that said, Please say I can stay home and watch the hockey
game?

Morley was sitting on the stairs, frowning into her open
briefcase. "Don't look at me like that," she said. "We have
to go."

Dave's shoulders sagged. "Okay," he said. "But let's go early and leave early."

And that was how Dave came to be standing in his driveway, yelling impatiently at Sam, on Saturday evening at five-thirty.

"Just come without your jacket," he said. "You don't need your jacket. The car is warmed up. Just come."

Sam bounded down the front steps, his shoelaces undone, his shirt untucked, and jumped into the car beside his father.

"Backseat," said Dave as Sam reached for the radio.

Morley was next. Slipping into the car and examining her lipstick in the mirror on the back of the sun visor.

Dave had to send Sam to fetch Stephanie.

"What's the hurry?" she said, slumping into the backseat. "No one will be there yet. This is stupid. There's never anyone my age. Do I have to come?"

They were, as it turned out, the first to arrive.

"Come in," said Polly Anderson, who hadn't finished setting things out. "It's good to see you." Looking as though it wasn't.

"I told you it was too early," said Stephanie.

"It's okay," said Dave. "We'll help out."

Five minutes later, Dave was holding an open bottle of rum in front of two bowls of eggnog. He was helping out.

"The Lalique crystal is for the adults," called Polly Anderson from the kitchen. "The glass bowl is for the kids."

Dave took a step back and peered at the two bowls. "Which is the Lalique?" he called.

The doorbell rang.

Polly said, "The Lalique is on the left. Can you get the door?"

Dave said, "Just a minute."

The doorbell rang again.

Dave frowned and thought, Glass left and crystal right . . . or crystal left and glass right?

From the dining room, Morley said, "Dave, get the door."

Dave said, "Eeny meeny miny mo," poured the rum, and ran for the door. As he left, he saw Ted Anderson pick up one of the bowls and head down to the rec room, where Sam had joined the Anderson kids.

———

Morley had always left Polly Anderson's Christmas party feeling inadequate. There was the spiral staircase, the Lalique bowls, and Polly's bonsai collection in the hall—which this year she had decorated with miniature origami birds, each one no bigger than an aspirin. Morley felt defeated by these things, and by the moment at the end of each year's party— a moment that was not unpleasant but just so perfect—when everyone gathered around the Andersons' Christmas tree (it always seemed taller and straighter than the tree Dave and Morley had found), and Ted turned off the lights and lit the real candles, and they all sang carols. Defeated by these things that the Andersons seemed to do so effortlessly. And if that wasn't enough, there were the Anderson kids—so polite and well dressed and, most galling, so clean. It all made Morley feel small.

But the thing that really ground her down was the mountain of food that Polly produced. This year it was Christmas sushi—pieces of salmon twisted into the shape of fir trees, little tuna wreaths, yellowtail angels with white-radish wings, and in the middle of the table, a seaweed manger with a baby Jesus made from flying-fish roe and three wise men with pickled-ginger robes and wasabi faces.

Then there were the crackers. Polly Anderson's crackers were better dressed than half the people at the party. It was as if Polly Anderson had Martha Stewart working for her in the kitchen, and any moment Martha was going to march out carrying something on a silver platter: a stencilled roast beef, Cajun fillets of peacock tongue, a roasted unicorn, or maybe quail, a flaming wreath of baby quail with cranberry and mango salsa.

The last time she had entertained the Andersons, Morley was so determined to measure up that she went to the library and checked out a pile of gourmet magazines. She had come home and rolled cylinders of salmon in a soft cream-cheese dip and stuck toothpicks at the end of each roll. It didn't occur to her, until Sam pointed it out, that her creation looked like a plate of miniature toilet-paper rolls. She saw Polly Anderson looking at the plate quizzically, then watched in horror as Polly picked up one of the hors d'oeuvres and it slid off the toothpicks and landed in her drink. Morley hid in the kitchen until Dave forced her to join them in the living room.

As Morley stood in the Andersons' living room, staring at Polly Anderson's Christmas crackers, she thought about the week following her own party. For days she kept coming across remnants of her toilet-paper hors d'oeuvres all over the house: under the couch, in the drawer where she kept her checkbook, in the bathroom garbage can, on a windowsill. All of them had one bite missing.

Morley was so lost in these memories that when Ted Anderson came up behind her and offered her a drink, she jumped.

"Are you all right?" he said.

Ted, gliding from guest to guest in a grey suit and ivory collarless shirt buttoned to the neck.

Morley looked across the room at Dave. He was wearing the blue sweater his mother had knitted last Christmas. It had

a map of Cape Breton on the front with a large red dot mark-
ing the site of his hometown. One side of his shirt was hanging out from under the sweater.

Morley had already had three cups of eggnog, but she just
couldn't seem to relax.

"Sure," she said, taking a drink off Ted's tray.

Morley thought the party seemed stiffer than usual, though
the kids seemed to be having a whale of a time.

Sam wound by her with a plate piled with bread and
salmon mousse.

You'd never eat that at home, thought Morley.

"This is the moose," said Sam exuberantly, pointing to the
orange spread. "And this," he said pointing to the gelatin, "is
the moose fat."

He snorted and wheeled back toward the basement where
the kids were. When he opened the basement door, the
sound of boisterous children singing Christmas carols came
wafting up the stairs.

———

Dave headed back to the punch bowl and poured himself
another glass of eggnog—his fifth. He couldn't seem to
loosen up.

Half an hour later, Bernie Schellenberger lurched by Dave
on his way upstairs. Bernie looked like he was being chased
by wolves. He was holding his five-month-old daughter in his
arms. The baby was howling.

"Every night," said Bernie.

"When you try to put her down," said Dave.

"She screams for two hours," said Bernie.

"You ever try the car?" asked Dave.

"What?" said Bernie.

Dave, who was looking for any excuse to leave the Andersons', said, "Get your coat."

———

Sam had come out of the womb screaming, and every night at bedtime, for the first year of his life, he would lie in his crib and scream.

Morley and Dave would sit in the kitchen, rigid as lumber, and listen to him. They would say things to each other like "We are not going in there. Not tonight. He has to learn."

Other parents in the neighbourhood would find excuses to drop in on Dave and Morley around bedtime, because listening to Sam scream made them feel better about their own children. If mothers were becoming short-tempered with their children, fathers would say, "Could you nip over to Morley's and see how things are coming with . . ." and they'd make something up. And their wives would go, because they knew it would do them good.

People who didn't have children were horrified with the way Dave and Morley could offer them coffee and carry on a conversation while Sam raged against sleep. They would keep glancing toward the stairs. When they left, they would say things like "That was unbelievable. Our children will never do that."

On the rare nights when Sam stopped crying within an hour, Dave and Morley would glance at each other nervously, and one of them would say, "Maybe I should check him."

As soon as they opened the bedroom door, he would start crying again.

Once, Dave crawled into Sam's room on his belly and pulled himself up the side of the crib like a snake, only to come face-to-face with his son. They stared at each other for an awful minute. Then Dave slid back down. Sam smiled and waved. Dave had crawled halfway out of the room before Sam started to cry.

They lived like this for a long time before Dave discovered the car. He took Sam with him to the grocery store one night, and Sam drifted off to sleep in his car seat. And was so soundly asleep he didn't wake when Dave got him home and carried him to bed.

The next night Dave drove around the neighbourhood for an hour before Sam conked out, but it beat sitting at the kitchen table. So every night Dave loaded Sam into the car and drove around until Sam fell asleep. He had to drive less and less each night. Soon Sam was falling asleep within a block of the house. One night he nodded off before Dave got out of the driveway. Eventually, Dave could put Sam in the backseat, start the car, and idle it in the driveway. It was something about the sound of the engine.

One night, instead of putting him in the car, Dave put Sam in his crib and said to Morley, "Watch this."

He got the vacuum cleaner and carried it into Sam's bedroom and turned it on and left the room, shutting Sam's door behind him. Five minutes later, when they opened his door, Sam was out cold.

By the time he was fourteen months, they could put him to sleep by waving the hair dryer over him a couple of times.

———

Bernie Schellenberger was standing on the stairs at the Andersons' party, his screaming daughter in his arms, listening intently to Dave's story.

"Get your coat," said Dave again. "You'll see." Then he said, "I'm going to bring Sam."

He was thinking, after all those years Sam should see what he put his father through.

When Dave went down the back staircase into the Andersons' basement, the television was on, but none of the kids were watching it. The videos Polly Anderson had rented to keep them amused were still piled on top of the TV. The TV was flickering like a yawning eye at a bunch of empty chairs. The twenty kids were at the other end of the room, pressed around the upright piano. Sam, to Dave's astonishment, had his arms draped around the shoulder of a girl Dave had never seen before. Dave couldn't see who was at the keyboard, but he recognized the tune. It was "The North Atlantic Squadron":

> *Away, away, with fife and drum*
> *Here we come, full of rum,*
> *Looking for women to . . .*

Someone noticed Dave, and the piano stopped abruptly.

Sam said, "Hi, Dad."

He jumped toward his father and caught his foot on the edge of the piano stool and came down hard on middle C with his face leading. All the kids applauded, and Sam bowed, blood dripping from his nose. He said, "Our family motto is 'There are sewers aplenty yet to dig.' " Then he wiped his nose, smearing blood across his face and shirt.

Dave said, "I'd like you to come with me in the car. Where is your other shoe?"

Sam looked around. "Beats me," he said.

Dave held out his hand. "Forget it," he said. He picked up his son and carried him out to the car.

It took only twenty minutes before the Schellenberger baby was snoozing comfortably.

Bernie couldn't believe it. "Geez. I'm going to have to buy a car," he said.

"Try a vacuum first," said Dave.

Bernie said, "We have central vac."

"Then move her crib to the basement," said Dave.

From the back of the car, Sam said, "It's the physics of baseball that has always fascinated me."

Dave looked at his boy in the rearview mirror.

Sam waved absently at his father, then pressed his face to the window and started to sing something that sounded like opera.

Carmen? thought Dave.

Then something awful occurred to him.

Dave slammed on the brakes and squealed to the side of the road. He twisted around in his seat and stared at Sam. "What have you been drinking?" he asked.

"Eggnog," said Sam.

"From which bowl?"

"From the bowl in the basement, of course," Sam replied.

Uh-oh, thought Dave.

Bernie Schellenberger said, "Dave?"

Dave looked at Bernie, then he looked at Sam, then he looked at Bernie again. Bernie was pointing. Dave peered into the darkness and spotted three police officers standing on the edge of the road half a block away.

They were manning a roadside check for drunk drivers, and Dave had just fishtailed to a stop in front of them. The cops all had their hands on their hips. The streetlight shining from behind them made them look ominous. The only thing Dave could do was put his car into gear and creep toward them.

Sam pulled himself forward so his head was beside his father's. "This," he said, "is an area of jurisprudence that has always interested me."

Dave pulled up beside the police and rolled down his window. He smiled.

Two of the cops took a step back from the car. The third was shining his flashlight in Dave's face. He didn't try to engage in small talk. He said, "Could I please see your licence?" He peered at the licence and then looked at Dave and said, "Where are your glasses?"

Without waiting for an answer, he handed Dave a little machine and said, "Blow."

Dave is not sure who was more surprised to find there was no alcohol in his bloodstream. Dave had, after all, drunk six cups of eggnog.

Dave and the cop were both squinting at the machine when Sam joined the conversation from the back. "Can I blow, too?" he asked.

Dave said, "Maybe that's not a good idea."

But the cop, who was friendlier now, said, "It's okay. I don't mind."

Dave said, "Oh, well."

Sam blew into the little machine.

The cop pointed at it and said, "See, son, if you had been drinking, the arrow would be . . ." His voice trailed off. He squinted at his machine and took a step backward. He looked at Dave, who shrugged and smiled. He opened the back door of Dave's car and looked closely at Sam, with the streaks of dried blood across his face, and said, "Is that blood, son?"

Sam said, "Our family motto is 'There are sewers aplenty yet to dig.' "

The cop frowned and said, "Son, I want you to get out of the car."

Sam slid over to the far side of the backseat and said, "Come and get me, copper."

Then he threw up.

Dave folded his head into his arms and rested it on the steering wheel.

The Schellenberger baby started to cry.

So did Dave.

Bernie Schellenberger called a taxi from the police station.

By the time Dave had explained everything and got back to the party, the Andersons' house was dark and locked up. Sam was asleep in the backseat. He didn't stir when they got him home, and Dave carried him upstairs.

Just like the old days, thought Dave.

Morley was waiting in the living room. The whole house was dark except for the coloured lights glowing on the Christmas tree.

"I love it like this," she said. She was sitting with her legs up on the sofa, an empty cognac glass beside her.

Dave sat at the other end of the couch so their feet met in the middle. They compared stories.

"It took five minutes for the police to get Sam out of the car," said Dave. "They wouldn't let me help. When they got him out, he had blood all over him, and he didn't have a winter coat, and he was missing a shoe, and he was drunk."

Morley told Dave what he had missed at the Andersons'. "It was like homecoming at a frat house," she said. "Pia Cherbenofsky got herself into the Christmas tree, and no one saw her until Ted Anderson began to light the candles for the carol sing. Pia was hidden in the branches halfway up the tree, and she started blowing the candles out as fast as Ted could light them.

"At one point," said Morley, "there were ten adults trying to coax her down with candy."

Then she told him about the McCormick baby.

"He was missing for half an hour," she said. "He finally turned up asleep in a laundry hamper with the youngest Anderson boy squatting beside him."

Bobby Anderson had wrapped himself in an large green terry-cloth towel.

"I'm the three wise men," burped Bobby. "That's the baby Jesus."

Sam was never able to tell Dave the name of the girl he had his arms around in the basement. No one seemed to know who she was.

"She was in a red dress," said Dave.

"When I left," said Morley, "there was a girl in a red dress standing at the top of the spiral staircase, singing 'Don't Cry for Me Argentina.' "

Dave got up and poured himself another drink. "What did Polly say?" he asked.

"Last I saw of Polly Anderson," said Morley, "she was in the hallway protecting her bonsai collection."

Morley stood up and hunched over. "She looked like a football player ready to make a tackle. She was screaming: 'Stand back. Stand back. Don't come a step closer.' "

"Who was attacking the bonsai?" asked Dave.

"Her eldest son," said Morley. "He was trying to shoot the origami birds out of the trees with a Nerf gun."

The only child who wasn't sick, singing, or passed out was their daughter, Stephanie.

"I told her I was proud of her," said Morley.

The truth of that dawned on Dave later, when they were upstairs and Dave was in the bathroom brushing his teeth. He walked into the bedroom, holding his toothbrush at his side.

"Stephanie was the only kid drinking from the adult bowl," he said.

"Oh," said Morley. "Oh."

"Merry Christmas," said Dave.

The Jockstrap

Of all the gifts that Morley received last Christmas, nothing showed more thoughfulness and understanding, nothing made her laugh out loud with quite the same surprise and secret pleasure, nothing changed her life, like the present Dave and Sam gave her together.

From your boys, read the card.

"What's this?" Morley asked, holding up the box, shaking it.

"Don't tell her," said Dave.

"Guess," said Sam.

"I don't know what this could be," said Morley.

"Open it," said Sam.

And so she did.

She wouldn't have guessed what it was in a thousand years. Morley hadn't known such a thing existed.

A battery-operated heated seat cushion.

"For watching your hockey games," she said to Sam. "It's perfect."

And it *was* perfect.

Morley hated watching Sam play hockey. Hated it.

Well, that's not exactly true. What she hated was the arena. Or, more to the point, the arena benches. Slabs of concrete so cold a woman could freeze to death. Or worse.

"I love this," she said. "Who has batteries?"

She sat on it during supper.

"I *do* love this," she said. "You have to try this. This is won-derful."

She took it to bed and put it down by her feet. "I love my cushion," she said.

She took it to work. "This is my new friend," she said. "Everyone should have one of these."

Over the next few weeks, Morley found many uses for her cushion. Hugging it while she watched the news on televi-sion. Propping it beside her while she read. Sitting on it in the car until the heater warmed the seats. The cushion became a thing. It followed her around the house like a child's favourite toy, lying on the stairs, on the couch, on a chair in the kitchen. It felt good having it around, reassuring and comfortable. Warm.

"Sort of like a husband," she told her friend Ruth. "Only quieter."

Nice, but not what you would call life-changing. It wasn't until hockey began again in January that the cushion changed Morley's life.

Halfway through the first game, she turned to Dave and smiled. "Did I mention how much I love my cushion?"

It was the cushion that turned her into a hockey fan.

"Not a real fan," she explained earnestly. But she was at the arena every Saturday. The game was still a mystery, but it wasn't still mysterious. Or cold. Morley didn't miss another game all year.

A big change from last year, when it wasn't just the game that Morley had found overwhelming—it was everything. Even the equipment had threatened to defeat her. She had started off ambitiously enough, assembling the paraphernalia for her son's first year of hockey with confidence.

On the Wednesday night before his first game, she laid it

out on the kitchen table. The blue pants looked too large for her son. One of the thigh pads was missing, but she thought she could cut one out of cardboard. She looked at her list and ticked off "pants." The skates, she figured, would hold up another year. She ticked off "skates." Then she ticked off "elbow pads." She had bought them from the lady across the street. The shin guards came from a church sale. The kids had worn them on their shoulders for two years now for dress-up. Sally said she thought she had a helmet that would fit Sam and had promised to bring it to the rink. Morley ticked off "shin guards" and put a question mark beside "helmet." She stuffed everything into two plastic bags, propped them by the door, and went upstairs.

————

This is a father's job, she thought as they drove to the rink the next morning. Brian had phoned in sick, and Dave had gone to open the store. Sam was alone in the backseat holding his stick. They weren't talking. They'd had a fight after breakfast because Sam wanted to get dressed at home. The only thing he had said in the last thirty minutes was that they were going to be late. The second time he said it, Morley told him to *get in the car.* Now she was regretting yelling. Why did they have to fight before his first game of hockey? Was that what he would remember?

In the dressing room, Sam slumped on the bench, and Morley stared at the two bags. For the first time in her life, she had no idea how to dress her son. She didn't know where to begin. The man beside her was lacing his boy into a set of shoulder pads. She didn't have shoulder pads. The list had said they were optional.

"We don't have those," Sam said accusingly.

"We don't have to," Morley said. "You don't have to have them."

She started with the pants.

Then she was stumped.

"Do the shin pads," said the man beside her. "Then put the socks over."

Sam was the last kid on the ice.

On Thursday after school, Sam said he needed a jockstrap.

"What for?" said Morley. She was frying sausages for dinner and reading a gardening magazine.

"Everyone has one. I have to."

"*Who* has one?" she said.

"Paul. He wore it to school. It's a penis protector."

Morley phoned Paul's mother after supper.

———

Friday morning Morley drove to Canadian Tire. When she got there, she sat in the parking lot. She wasn't sure what to ask for. She knew "penis protector" couldn't be right, but she wasn't sure about "jockstrap." She didn't know if it was a word you could use in a Canadian Tire store. It might be a little-boy word. Like "fart." She certainly wasn't about to say "penis" to a man she didn't know.

She drove home and phoned Dave.

"Sam needs a jockstrap for hockey," she said. "That's your job."

"Okay," he said without enthusiasm.

———

Saturday, Morley took Stephanie to get her hair cut. Dave took Sam to hockey.

"How was the jock?" Morley asked at supper.

"It didn't fit," said Sam, pointing at his father as if he were a witness in a murder trial. "He didn't get the holder."

Morley opened her son's equipment bag on Wednesday night and fished out the jockstrap. It looked just like the masks painters wear on their faces when they're sanding dry wall. It was a size medium.

She phoned Paul's mother again.

"That's just the cup," Maggie explained. "There's a holder it slips into. Like a garter belt."

How could Dave watch all the hockey he watched and not get the holder? The way he hollered during hockey games, you would think he had at least a rudimentary knowledge of the equipment. Morley felt resentment well up in her as she thought of the Saturday nights she had struggled to get the kids into bed while Dave sank onto the couch in front of a hockey game. If he hadn't *learned* anything, what was the point?

———

Morley went back to Canadian Tire on Thursday night. As she passed through the automatic doors, she realized she still didn't know what the holder was called. She had looked over the equipment list again before she left home. "Jockstrap" definitely wasn't on it. She had a tick beside everything on the list except "shoulder pads." She had double-checked. Shoulder pads *were* optional.

———

There were four aisles of hockey equipment. She spotted the holder on her second pass. They came in three sizes: medium, large, and extra large. All things considered, Morley was surprised to see how small the extra-large one was. The package came with a cup identical to the one Dave had bought plus the elastic belt he had neglected. Morley was holding a medium in her hand when she saw the salesman coming. This was what she'd been hoping to avoid.

"For your husband?" he asked.

"My son," said Morley.

"How old is he?"

Thank God, thought Morley. She had thought he was going to ask how big it was.

"He's seven," she said.

"This is too big," said the young man, taking the package from her. "You'll need extra-extra small . . . We're out. Try maybe Sears."

She was smiling when she got back to the car. ATHLETIC SUPPORT, it had said in big white letters on the red package. It was on her list after all. She had ticked it off. Morley thought *she* was the athletic support.

––––––

She got the jock at the Bay. "An extra-extra-small athletic support for a seven-year-old boy. He is playing hockey," she said nonchalantly. "It's his second year." She wasn't sure why she added the lie.

––––––

Sam put it on as soon as she got home. He put it on over his pants. Then, before she could stop him, he ran across the street to show Allen. Why not? thought Morley. She watched them from the window, Sam standing proudly on the front lawn. He looks like a ballet dancer, she thought. Then Allen kicking Sam between the legs. Her son laughing. "Again!" he shouted. He wore the jockstrap to bed that night. And to school the next day, under his jeans. Morley was going to say no, and then she thought, Why not? For a week she kept finding it all over the house—on the stairs, on the couch in the TV room, slung over his chair in the kitchen. She felt no compulsion to put it away. She was as pleased with it as he was.